FRACTURED

TRIPLE CANOPY
BOOK 8

RILEY EDWARDS

Fractured
Triple Canopy 8

Cover design: Lori Jackson Designs

Written by: Riley Edwards

Published by: Riley Edwards/Rebels Romance

Edited by: Rebecca Hodgkins

Proofreader: Julie Deaton & Kendall Barnett

Book Name: Fractured

Paperback ISBN: 978-1-951567-46-0

First edition: April 25, 2023

To my family - my team – my tribe.
This is for you.

CONTENTS

1

ECHO

"Thanks for picking me up," Griff said from the passenger seat.

"Anytime. Besides, I'm headed to your house anyway."

"Did Phoenix tell you that my mom said I could keep Dasher?"

"Good news, bud."

Like there was ever a doubt Wren would tell her boy he couldn't have one of the horses he helped rescue.

"Yeah. Sucks that Simon and King can't stay but Chels has her hands full with Rebel and Trigger and running "the bar" even with me going over there to help."

The kid used air quotes around "the bar" and I couldn't hold back my laughter. I hadn't been there, but the way Phoenix told the story Wren about had a heart attack when she got to Matt's house to pick up Griff and he was wearing one of Matt's Balls Deep shirts instead of his school shirt while painting the side of the barn. Griff hadn't noticed what the t-shirt said until his mom yelled at Phoenix for letting him wear it. The kid was fourteen—he knew what that meant so now when he called it the bar he used air quotes.

"Yeah, Chelsea's pretty busy."

I wasn't even out of the school parking lot yet when Griff asked, "May I ask you something?"

I really wanted to say fuck no. But this was Griff, and the kid was my nephew even if his mom and my brother hadn't made it official.

Born from years of practice, I kept my body loose and my tone even when I answered, "Sure, whatcha got?"

"Did Phoenix tell you that Conor set money aside for college for me?"

Shit.

"Yeah. He told me."

"Do you think I should take it?"

And there it was, the question I was afraid he'd ask. At first, Wren was completely against accepting any money from her ex. But since then, she'd softened to the idea. Phoenix didn't care one way or another. If Wren didn't take the money, Phoenix would back her and the same went if she took the money.

"What do you think you should do?"

"I don't want anything from him."

Yep, I figured that would be his answer. Just like my brother, the boy was holding on to anger instead of ridding himself of the burden.

"Education's important. It's also expensive. You're coming up on high school and in a few years, you'll have to start thinking about what you want to do after you graduate. That money might be a big help."

Griff fell silent and I waited until I stopped at a red light to glance over at him. "What're you thinking about?"

"You'll think it's stupid."

"Bud, I will never think anything you're thinking about or asking about is stupid."

"I think the guy's family who Conor killed should have it. He had kids. I think they need it."

Likely Conor's estate had paid restitution to the family. The money set aside for Griffin's college was probably in an account that couldn't be seized.

"Griff, that's far from stupid. That's kind and generous. Have you talked to your mom and Phoenix about it?"

"No. I wanted to ask you first."

I'd officially become a guardian at twenty-one. But long before that, I was already raising my siblings. That was damn near half my life being a parent. But Shiloh, Phoenix, and River stopped needing me in any real way a long time ago. I never thought I'd miss arguing about homework and cleaning the house, but it was far better than living alone in a spotless house. Griff had Phoenix, but it felt good to have the kid around, feeling needed again.

"Talk to your mom about it, tell her what you're thinking, then maybe wait awhile until you make a decision."

"Yeah. Okay. That sounds good."

My phone rang and one glance at the dash display made my jaw clench.

"Who's Jaclyn?" Griff inquired.

The woman who I fell in love with over a weekend then lost because I was a jackass.

"No one."

"Then why are you grinding your teeth?"

So, maybe I was wrong. Living in a quiet, clean house with no kids around was the way to go. I was too fucking old to be interrogated by a teenager. Been there, done that.

I ignored Griff's question and the call and made my turn onto Phoenix's street.

"You grunt just like Phoenix," he noted.

"No, Phoenix grunts like me."

Griff shifted in his seat and stared at me.

"Is there a difference?"

"Yes. I'm older. So Phoenix is copying me with the grunting."

"Okay," Griff muttered and went back to looking out the window.

My phone stopped ringing and my jaw relaxed.

I pulled into the driveway and killed the engine. But instead of hopping out of the car like he normally did when I brought him home, he sat there. I knew the kid's brain was working overtime. I figured he was about to call me out on Jackie when he veered way off track and asked, "You raised Phoenix, right?"

Not knowing where the conversation was leading, I warily answered, "I did."

Griff's face broke out into a wide shit-eating grin.

"So does that mean I should call you Uncle Echo or Grandpa Echo?"

I grunted.

The little shit's smile turned smug.

"No, I got it," he continued. "Uncle Grandpa."

"You call me grandpa I'm kickin' your ass."

The kid smiled and I winced. Damn, I was out of practice. It had been a long time since I'd parented teenagers. Not that I was parenting Griffin, my brother was.

Was an uncle allowed to tell his nephew he was going to kick his ass?

Probably not.

Before I could rectify my fuck-up my phone rang again. Work.

A welcomed distraction.

Wasn't it always?

"Gotta take this," I told Griff. "I'll be in in a minute."

"Sure, Gramps," he muttered, hightailing his ass out of the car.

Christ. That kid was going to give Phoenix a run for his money.

It was on that happy thought I answered, "Long time. Everything good?"

"Wish I was calling to shoot the shit."

I didn't miss the frustration in the DEA agent's tone.

"What's up?"

"Remember Jimmy Lone?"

Sour hit my gut.

Every cop and fed in a hundred-mile radius remembered Jimmy Lone and his crew he called the Lonesomes. They'd moved a shit ton of contraband. If it was illegal, Jimmy had been moving it. Everything from narcotics to guns to cigarettes. The asshole thought he was clever, but even the smartest criminals fucked up and got caught.

It had taken multi-agency cooperation and a new task force being formed but Jimmy Lone was locked up and had been for a good long while.

"He's not a man you forget," I reminded Tucker.

"Well, someone on the parole board forgot what a piece of shit he is, because they granted his parole. Word's spreading fast he's getting out."

I didn't bother asking how it was possible he was getting out five years early. The unfortunate truth was criminals knew how to work the system. A few years of being on their best behavior, playing the part of the model prisoner could get them a lot of years shaved off their sentence. It was a small price to pay for their freedom.

"His crew?"

"Coming out of the woodwork like cockroaches."

Fuck. I was afraid of that.

"And you? Where are you in this?" I asked.

"Coming your way."

Thank fuck.

Tucker Mitchell was a damn good agent.

"Though, I might have a problem," he continued.

I caught sight of Phoenix coming out of the house. I held my hand up, gesturing for him to give me a minute. My brother stopped a few feet away from my car, a look of concern mixed with impatience evident.

"What's the problem?"

"Matthew Kessler."

"Matt?" I asked while keeping my gaze on my brother.

"The Zanetti case," Tucker reminded me.

Matt Kessler came from money, the kind of generational wealth that meant he could retire, buy yachts and private jets, have no issue sending his children to Ivy league school, and still be able to set those children up to never have to work. However, that wasn't Matt's style. He worked for Triple Canopy. Before that he served in the Navy. He didn't buy yachts and private jets or flaunt his wealth. Though he did buy a bar, but that proved to be a sound business investment.

Matt's father however was a greedy fuck who got in bed with the mob. Unfortunately, Vern wasn't smart enough to understand that his money didn't mean jackshit to men like Zanetti. Once he had you by the balls you couldn't buy your way out. Vern just got deeper and deeper until Matt's mother caught on and turned her husband in to the feds. That had led to Vern's arrest. Matt's sister Alessandra attempted to save the lifestyle she'd been accustomed to—which was to say, expensive everything—by marrying Zanetti and having Matt's woman Chelsea kidnapped and held for ransom.

Tucker had been undercover and had played a part in holding Chelsea hostage. But from what I'd heard, he'd also protected her when bullets tore through the mansion where she was being held.

"As far as I know, there's no bad blood," I told him. "Unless I'm missing something."

"Good to know, but I still think a sit down is in order. I'm gonna reach out to Jason, see if he can arrange that. I'd like for you to be there; it'll also give us an opportunity to fill them in on Jimmy and his crew."

Jason Walker was former DEA. He was also the son of Jasper Walker, one of the founders of Triple Canopy. Jason had taken over the day-to-day operations of TC along with his cousins, Nick Clark, Carter Lenox, and Quinn Walker Lancaster. Hadley Walker had recently joined the team leaving Liberty Hayes, Ethan Lenox, and Jackson Clark as the only holdouts in the family. Though rumor had it

Liberty wasn't re-enlisting in the Army and would soon join her cousins. Adalynn Walker Durum worked at TC but not for the company. She was a physical therapist and used the gym on premises and back office to run her practice. Meaning that Triple Canopy was a family, something I understood and appreciated. Jasper, Lenox, Clark, and Levi had built a legacy. Again, something I understood since I'd been running from mine for the last thirty years trying to build a better one for my siblings. A legacy they could be proud of and share with the families they make. Not the fucked-up one our parents had left to us.

"Let me know and I'll be there."

Phoenix shifted and crossed his arms, a sure sign his impatience was turning into annoyance. He was the kid who couldn't wait to open his presents Christmas morning. He'd wake up at the butt crack of dawn, then bang around until everyone was awake and downstairs. He did this knowing there were only going to be one or two cheap, shitty presents waiting for him. One of the many ways I'd failed my brothers and sister—Christmases and birthdays were absolute shit. I couldn't afford to buy presents, not when I was trying to put food on the table and keep the house from going into foreclosure and the lights on. Even before our father was arrested, money had been tight.

I should've made the kid wait, taught him patience and self-control.

Another failure.

"Will do. I'm wrapping up a case in California. It might be a week, two max, before I get out there."

"You ever think about taking some down time between cases?" I joked.

8

"Only every other day." He sighed. "It'd be nice not to have to live and breathe filth for months on end."

I ignored Phoenix's frown and asked, "How long have you been under?"

"Too fucking long. Sex club in Cali being used as a front to traffic girls and drugs. The operation was shut down months ago but we still had some loose ends to tie up and leads to follow. We're close to finding the supplier and making arrests. I'll be out after that."

One of the many reasons I'd never taken an undercover assignment even though I'd been asked by my unit as well as by the DEA. Time. You never knew how long you'd be under and I couldn't be out of contact with Shiloh, River, and Phoenix for extended periods of time.

"When you get out here, we'll go to the golf course. I'll kick your ass then buy you a beer to soothe the pain of your loss."

"You're on." He chuckled. "Though, just to remind you, you suck at golf just as badly as I do."

He wasn't wrong.

"Stay safe, Tucker, and call when you're in town."

"Will do."

I disconnected and folded out of my car.

The moment I closed the door Phoenix was on the move.

"What's wrong?"

What Phoenix lacked in patience he made up for with awareness.

I wasn't sure if that was a skill he'd learned living in a house with a volatile, drunken, piece of shit father or something he was simply born with. Seeing as River and Shiloh had the same ability to walk into a room and feel the mood, thus adjust accordingly I'd say it was something he learned.

"Other than your boy thinking it's funny to call me Uncle Grandpa, nothing," I returned.

His deep scowl turned into a wide smile at the mention of his boy. It was about fucking time Phoenix had something good in his life.

"I see you think that's funny," I noted, not caring at all the joke was at my expense.

My brother smiling and happy after decades of pain—that was everything to me.

Five minutes later I learned I should've asked Phoenix why he'd been so eager to come outside and get me. I should've asked why his smile had turned nervous when we got to his front door.

But I didn't. I'd been riding the high of seeing my youngest brother free of the weight that had been tethered around his neck like an invisible noose since birth.

So, I didn't see the ambush coming.

2

ECHO

I GLANCED AROUND THE ROOM AGAIN TO MAKE SURE I wasn't imagining the scene playing out before me. But when River yanked me into a hug and with bone-jarring force pounded my back, I knew him being in Georgia wasn't a hallucination.

"Brother," River rumbled. "Good to see you."

The sound of my brother's voice pulled me from my stupor but did nothing to quell my irritation.

"You, too," I returned, then as we broke apart asked, "What's with the surprise?"

"Last minute decision to come out for Logan and Lauren's wedding."

No doubt that was the excuse, but River had never been able to successfully lie to me.

"Happy to see you, River, but don't bullshit me."

My brother's lips twitched before he called his fiancée Letty over. She broke away from Wren, Phoenix, and Griff making her way over with a radiant smile that was not for me but for my brother. As soon as she was close she tucked herself under River's arm.

Another brother smiling and happy, free from the ties of his shit childhood.

"Okay, River, spill," Shiloh demanded. "You made us wait a year until Echo came in."

My baby sister, ever the drama queen. Though, that was no longer my cross to bear, it was her fiancé Luke's. A man who'd taken on her demons and bested them, something I'd tried and failed to do for her. As far as my brothers and I were concerned, Luke Marcou was a fucking saint. He'd survived her Killer Frost freeze out, came out the other side, and made her stupidly happy.

A very welcomed addition to the family. Same with Letty; she'd healed deep-seated trauma River had been holding onto.

All was right in my family.

But with River and Letty's unannounced visit something felt off.

"We wanted to tell you in person," River started. "I'm gonna be a dad."

My chest tightened, my heart thudded in my chest, my soul burned with gratitude.

"I'm gonna be an aunt," Shiloh breathed her excitement.

"Brother." One word but no less emotion from Phoenix.

River's eyes bore into mine. There was nothing but pride shining. No anguish. No sorrow. No rejection.

Fucking hell, he did it.

River would be the first to break the cycle.

The thought was so heavy my gaze went to the floor.

"Echo?"

"Don't have the words needed to tell you how happy I am for you," I choked out.

"Then why do you look like I just kicked you in the gut?"

I lifted my eyes, first settling on Letty. "Congratulations, sweetheart."

"Thank you," she said softly.

A tone I had never heard the outspoken woman use. Like my sister, Letty was full of sass and drama. Always smiling, always quick with a comeback or a joke. She fit. Not only with River but with the family.

I transferred my stare to my little brother. The boy I'd raised who'd grown into a teenager who had helped shoulder the burden of raising a family at an age when he should've been carefree and having fun. From a teenager to a man who was strong and trustworthy. Who worked hard, who put his life on the line for the greater good. A man who other men should aspire to be like.

I cleared the emotion that clogged my throat and told him, "You're gonna be an excellent father."

"Damn right," he beamed. "Learned from the best."

I blinked at his bizarre statement. The only thing Lester Kent had been the best at was being a drunk. He didn't even excel at being a criminal if growing up poor the way we did was anything to go by.

"Say again?"

River's face transformed from happy, soon-to-be-dad to furious in a nanosecond.

"You're shitting me," he spat. "Right, Echo, you're fuckin' shitting me?"

"Riv—"

"You know, Griff came bouncing in, and once his shock of meeting the good-looking Kent brother wore off he told us what he said to you in the car. To him, it was a joke— Uncle *Grandpa*. But after we all finished laughing our asses off it hit me—that's the truth. You're more than my brother. More than my best friend. You're the man who raised me. Raised all of us. You taught me everything I know. You're not my brother, not my dad, you're my *everything*, Echo. You held us together. You made us who we are."

Fuck.

Before I could formulate a response, he went on, "Remember what you said to me before I left for Idaho?"

Again the words were lodged in my throat so even if I remembered—which I didn't—I wouldn't have been able to answer. Apparently, River didn't need a response.

"You told me Sunny was getting married soon. I was leaving to go find Letty and you said I wouldn't be far behind her. Then you said, Phoenix would find a woman."

I had no idea where River was going with this, I just knew I didn't like it.

"That's what you said when I asked you when you were gonna start working toward your happy." River swept his free hand around the room. "Look around, you did it. We're there. You gave us this, Echo. This is what *you* created. Now, brother, I'm asking you again, when are you gonna start living for *you*? When are you gonna find *your* happy?"

Someone had a big fucking mouth.

My gaze sliced to Phoenix. His mask of indifference was firmly in place. No help. I found Shiloh burrowing into Luke with her lips pinched and her eyes averted.

"Sunny," I growled.

Luke's arm already around her shoulder curled tighter.

Hell no, he is not protecting her from this.

"Shiloh?" I snapped.

"Take a breath, Echo," Luke warned.

My eyes narrowed on him, all my earlier thoughts about the man immediately retracted.

"Someone had to do something," she blurted out, giving herself away.

"Yeah, and what something did someone have to do?"

She pushed away from Luke and moved around River. At the same time, Phoenix broke away from Wren.

Then standing before me was the Kent brigade—each of them pissed.

"Phoenix and I talked," Sunny continued, throwing Phoenix under the bus. "But I called River. Phoenix wanted to wait until after the wedding but I didn't want to take the chance. It's been months, Echo. Months and months and months and you've done nothing."

She was talking about Jaclyn Haines who would be in town for her brother's wedding imminently if she wasn't already.

"There's nothing to—"

"I saw you," Sunny cut me off. "I saw you with her."

Jesus fuck, I hoped like hell my baby sister wasn't saying what I thought she was.

"Ew." Sunny's face screwed up into disgust. "I didn't see *that*," she clarified. "I saw you with her right before she left. I saw you holding her. I saw the pain when you said goodbye."

Okay, it's time to stop this shit once and for all.

Sunny wasn't the only woman I knew who'd been nosing in my personal business. Thankfully the men—even Logan, Jackie's brother—had the good sense to mind their business.

"You have my heart, Sunny, but mind your fuck—"

"This is my business," she interrupted me.

I made sure my tone left no room for negotiation when I stated, "It's not."

"So, your happiness isn't our business?" Phoenix joined.

"My personal life isn't," I clarified. "And if it was, now would not be the time to talk about it when we have something to celebrate."

"Nope." River shook his head. "My wife and I—"

"Your *wife*?" Sunny asked.

My sister's inclination of rudely interrupting was at an all-time high today.

River cleared his throat and glanced back at Letty.

"Yeah, the second part of our good news. We slipped off to Vegas and got married. We'll do a big party after Rhode and Brooklyn get married."

"More like *snuck* off to Vegas," Sunny unhappily muttered.

Brooklyn was Letty's best friend. Last I'd heard, River was getting impatient with the wedding planning taking so long. Couple that with Letty being pregnant and it wasn't a surprise he'd run off to Vegas to marry his girl.

River ignored Sunny's remark in favor of continuing to piss me off.

"So we're there. I'm married with a baby on the way. Shiloh's planning a wedding. Phoenix is settled and happy." River paused and in an uncharacteristic show of drama, looked around the room. "Where's your happy?"

What the fuck?

"I'll marry Luke right now, today," Sunny announced. "One less excuse for you."

I heard Luke grumble under his breath. Likely not in disagreement; he'd wanted to get married months ago. Shiloh had been the one waiting for all of her friends to get married before she set a date so she didn't "steal anyone's thunder" as she called it.

"My mom and Phoenix can get married today, too," Griffin blurted.

My gaze went to my brother just in time to catch his reaction to his boy's proclamation. The only thing that had been stopping him from asking Wren to marry him was Griff. He'd wanted to give the boy time to settle into their relationship before another big change.

Unfortunately, I wasn't in the right headspace to fully appreciate my brother's smile.

I was furious.

Also unfortunate—I was fucking pissed when we should've been celebrating River and Letty.

More than that, I was done.

"River, Letty, beyond happy for you both." I calmed my tone just enough for them to know I was sincere. "As for the rest of this shit, I'm done. Straight up, my personal life is not anyone's business. *Period.*"

With that I turned and walked out the door.

It wasn't until I was at home that I checked my phone.

Two more missed calls from Jaclyn and a text.

I know you said we were over. But I need to talk to you. It's important.

Fuck my life.

3

JACLYN

"Would you please stop?"

I didn't spare my sister Jill a glance as I continued to pace around the living room of our Vrbo. Any other time I would've already made myself a cocktail and would've been lounging by the small pool enjoying the lush greenery of the backyard.

But today wasn't any time or any other day. It was the first time I'd been back to Georgia since Echo had ended our very brief...

Relationship? No, it wasn't that but it also wasn't a one-night stand unless one-night stands span months. A booty call? Maybe that was what we'd shared. I couldn't even say we had a friends with benefits situation because we weren't friends, not in any real sense. I only knew what Echo wanted me to know. I only saw what he wanted me to see. Throughout our short-lived affair...yes, that was what we'd had—an affair, I was only allowed the bare minimum. There had of course been fleeting moments of realness when Echo forgot to close down and hide from me. As rare as those times had been they were what had kept me going back for more. I'd craved those flashes of the man beneath the façade—the unfiltered, the raw, the authentic Echo.

Lived for them.

Then he'd taken them away—all the moments, even the ones where he kept himself closed off. One phone call had changed everything. One slip-up on my part had Echo retreating like a scared little boy. The absurdity of that thought wasn't lost on me. A six-foot-five beast of a man being compared to a boy. But there was no other way to describe his behavior.

And the excuse he gave?

Our thirteen—well, twelve years now—age difference.

It was as insulting as it was lame.

"Jackie!" my sister snapped. "Seriously, you have to stop."

This time I looked up to see my sister frowning.

"I still can't believe you chopped off all your hair," I noted.

That was a slight exaggeration but she'd taken her mid-back length up to a cute, stylish bob. There were many upsides to having an identical twin; one of those pluses was knowing exactly what I'd look like in a new hairstyle. Side note: I'd look adorable with short hair. However, I preferred long hair. It was easier to throw it up into a ponytail and go about my day. Short hair meant blow dryers and flat irons and styling. All things I didn't have the patience to master, so long hair it was for me.

"That's why you're pacing like a crazy person?"

Jill's irritation was multi-layered. She knew why I was pacing, however she didn't have the specifics. She knew I'd hooked up with Echo after our brother Logan's friend Quinn's wedding. After all, Jill was my best friend, I told her most everything. It was the *most* part that had been bugging her because she knew there was more to me and Echo but I'd refused to confirm. Further from that, she knew I was nervous to see him but again she didn't know exactly why.

"Nope. I'm pacing because I'm excited to see Lucy and Dotty," I semi-lied.

Jill's eyes rolled to the ceiling and to further exhibit her annoyance she tipped her head back and shook it.

"You're a shit liar," she reminded me and righted her head. "The real question is why you're bothering to bullshit me when you know I know you're lying."

That was easy—because I was on pins and needles and didn't want to discuss why.

"I am excited to see Lucy and Dotty."

That was the truth. I hadn't seen my older sister and her wife in months. Such was the sad reality when family lived in different states. And another big change was happening soon. Ian my stepdad—correction, the only real father figure we'd ever had outside of my brother Logan— had retired and my parents were in the process of moving to Georgia.

Finally my mom was leaving Bad Axe, Michigan.
Finally.

Like Logan, I hated Bad Axe. Not because I had any personal recollections of my father and what he'd done to Logan and my mother. It was simply that everyone knew. I hated that, after all this time, people still gave me, Jill, and my mother weird looks. The thing was, none of the looks were accusatory or in disapproval, they were side glances of pity. I didn't need or want pity but more to the point—my mother was a survivor, not a woman who needed to endure people gawking at her or worse, looking at her like a battered woman. My mom was a strong, resilient, resourceful woman who taught our family what it looked like to overcome. That wasn't to say my big brother hadn't stepped up to help, he did.

If my mother was the quiet example of strength, Logan was the ferocious example of protection and responsibility.

Logan left Bad Axe as soon as he could. Lucy had never said one way or another how she felt but she also jumped at the chance to move to Alabama when her wife was offered a job there. Jill didn't care about the looks or the whispers about how she lived her life and gave zero fucks what anyone else thought. I, on the other hand, cared what people thought. So, I was not so happily following my mom and Ian to Georgia. Something that had excited me a few months ago, but now not so much.

"Jaclyn!" Jill snapped her fingers in front of my face. "What in the world is wrong with you?"

Echo Kent was what—or more specifically *who*—was wrong with me.

But I wasn't going to admit that out loud.

I rocked back and asked, "What's wrong with *you*?"

"Nothing's wrong with me. You're the one who's wearing a hole in the rug, checking your phone every five seconds."

I was taken aback by her harsh tone.

"The floors are hardwood," I noted.

Jill threw her hands up in exasperation.

"You know what I mean. Now, spill, Jackie. Are you really this nervous to see Echo?"

Yes!

Thankfully my phone rang. Unfortunately the butterflies chose that moment to kick up the flutters that meant my sister watched me place a hand on my stomach to quiet them down.

"I have to take this," I told her without looking at my phone.

Bedroom, where Jill could eavesdrop, or backyard where the neighbors could possibly hear?

Backyard.

I opened the door and stepped out into the Georgia humidity. I wasn't fond of air so thick it clung to you but I was less fond of Michigan winters so the tradeoff was worth it. Or it would be, come January when I wasn't out shoveling snow.

By the time I made it to a lounger I was questioning my sanity. I'd tied myself in knots waiting for Echo to call me back. I'd reached out to him not for my benefit but for his. Now I felt like I was going to puke.

Big-girl panties...pull them up, Jaclyn, and talk to Echo. You know, the man who crushed you.

I jabbed the green icon on my phone and slowly brought it up to my ear.

"Hey," I greeted.

Was that my voice? I sounded like a frog.

"I'm calling you back," Echo said matter-of-factly.

"Yeah. Thanks. I...um..."

Holy Hannah, what is wrong with me?

"You what?"

Just say it.

"I don't know if I should be telling you this," I started. "But I thought you'd want to know so you weren't blindsided. Shiloh called me."

I heard a frustrated growl. Despite the Georgia heat, chills raced up my arm. Echo had a great gravelly voice when he was...

Nope.

Not thinking about sex with Echo.

"Why'd my sister call you?"

One could say, I adored Shiloh. I'd only met her a few times. The first time I was in Georgia, the rest of my visits had been kept a secret not only from Echo's siblings, but from my brother.

I had some remorse about this. I loved my brother and missed him, but Echo and I agreed it was best if no one knew I was visiting him. It wasn't a hardship to stay hidden in Echo's house. We'd found good use of our stolen weekends together.

"She called to ask when I was coming in for the wedding. I told her I was already here, then she invited me to Phoenix and Wren's. She sounded..." I trailed off, not knowing how to explain.

"Conniving," he supplied.

"I wouldn't go that far. But, yeah, like she had something up her sleeve. And I knew I was right when she told me that River and his girlfriend Letty were there."

"Wife," he weirdly said.

"I'm sorry?"

"River's *wife*, Letty," he explained. "That was his big announcement. That and he and Letty are having a baby."

Relief washed over me. I'd been wrong.

"Okay, so I was wrong. Sorry to bother you."

There was a stretch of silence so I nervously filled it.

"Congratulations. I mean, congratulations to them. That's exciting."

God, I sounded like a fool. I needed to end this call.

"What were you wrong about?"

Gah.

"Shiloh was asking a lot of questions, like if I'd talked to you, and if we'd made plans to go to the wedding together. Then she was asking about my move and when I'd be here permanently. Stuff like that. Now, I love your sister but she's never been nosy like that so I got worried that maybe she thought there was something...you know...going on between us. And with your brother and his girlfriend, I mean wife..."

Sweet baby Jesus, what the hell was my problem? It was like I'd forgotten how to string a sentence together.

"You weren't wrong," he grumbled. "I walked into a Kent ambush."

Damn.

"I'm sorry, Echo. I called as soon as I hung up with Shiloh to tell you."

There was more silence. This time I didn't attempt to fill it with my broken thoughts. I'd tried to save him from being blindsided but I'd been too late. Though, if he'd answered my call he would've known that Shiloh had been planning something.

"You'd break my sister's confidence to warn me she'd planned some sort of fucked-up intervention."

Was that a question or was he telling me that was what I'd done?

"Well, it's not like she told me not to tell you we'd talked. And just so you know, if she'd asked me to keep our conversation a secret but I thought you were walking into something uncomfortable I'd struggle with what to do. I keep my word, Echo, you know that. But I also don't like those I care about getting smacked in the face."

As soon as the words left my mouth, I regretted them. This conversation had all the beginnings of the one that had ended our brief affair. Me admitting I cared about him and suggesting we meet up in Atlanta the next time we got together so we could go out and not be locked in his house while I was visiting.

That had led to him ending things.

Now we were done and had been for a few months.

"Right," he muttered.

Something dawned on me.

"An intervention?"

When he didn't answer right away, I tried to retract my question. "Never mind. That's none of my business. Anyway, that was all I wanted to tell you. I should let you go."

He surprised me by saying, "They're all happy and have moved on. Sunny set that up because she wanted backup when she confronted me about why I haven't moved on."

Ouch.

That hurt. Though, Shiloh didn't know that we'd been together, so logically I knew she couldn't have been asking why he hadn't moved on from me. But still, the thought made my stomach roil. Another reason I was nervous about my move—seeing Echo with other women. He was friends with my brother. I had become friends with my brother's friends. I'd make my own friends once I got settled but until that happened, if I wanted social interaction, it would be with Logan's very soon-to-be-wife and she was close to Shiloh and the rest of the women who worked at Triple Canopy.

This was going to be a nightmare.

I'd have to avoid all of them.

My heart couldn't take seeing Echo with someone else.

"I'm sorry, Echo. That had to have been uncomfortable."

"Uncomfortable," he hissed. "No, Jaclyn, it wasn't uncomfortable; it was bullshit."

Oh, boy, he sounded pissed.

"It's not bullshit when your family loves you and wants what's best for you," I braved telling him. "It's no different than me and my sisters wanting Logan to move on from our past. You know he was basically my dad growing up. He was the one who helped my mom. He allowed us to be kids and grow up untouched by my father. All we ever wanted—"

"It's not the same and you know it," he cut me off. "Logan protected you and your sisters. I didn't protect mine from shit. All of them lived it right alongside me."

"Echo—"

"I didn't protect mine, Jaclyn," he interrupted again.

My gaze on the pool unfocused when I heard agony overshadowing the anger.

Damn, I should've kept my mouth shut. Not that I

knew how he felt about his childhood or him raising his siblings beyond the pride I saw when he looked at Shiloh and Phoenix. But it didn't take someone with my brother's observation skills to know that Echo had a God complex.

"Okay," I said softly, not knowing what else to say. "But I think they'd disagree with you."

"Jac—"

This time I interrupted. "You have your opinion and I have mine. I don't know everything that went on with your family, however, I did grow up with a big brother who took the place of my father. I know what that means to me, I know what he sacrificed, I know he felt deeply responsible for what happened to my family. I also know your brothers and sister feel the same gratitude I feel for my brother. So, let's leave this here."

He met my suggestion with a frustrated grunt.

"Is that all you called for—to warn me my nosy sister was poking around my business?"

There were a lot of other things I wanted to say and ask. But none of those things would be welcomed.

"Yeah."

"Great," he clipped. "Appreciate the heads up. Have a good day."

With that he hung up, leaving me staring at the still water in the pool. I dropped my phone in my lap and fought back tears of frustration.

I had yet to get my emotions under control when I felt something cold press on my forearm. I glanced over and saw what I assumed was a margarita on ice. And since it was my sister who was shoving the drink my way, I knew my assumption was correct.

I took the glass, mumbled my thanks, and went back to staring at the pool.

"Mom called. They're on their way back here with Lucy and Dotty."

Great. I had a half hour to pull myself together before I'd be under the watchful eye of three women who, like my twin, knew me too well. Then there was Ian, who was arguably more astute than the rest. He'd picked up on my heartbreak before my mom and Jill had. Not that he'd called me out directly but he had found a quiet moment to tell me that when I was ready to tell him what happened, he was there to listen.

"Awesome. I can't wait." I feigned as much excitement as I could muster.

Jill took the lounger next to me and settled with a deep sigh before she said, "Just tell me one thing. Do I need to hate Echo?"

I knew if I said yes, my sister would loathe him until her last breath. No questions asked, no details needed. She would have my back no matter what.

"He didn't do anything wrong," I returned.

That was the problem; he hadn't promised me anything. He hadn't led me on. He hadn't offered a relationship. I knew what I was getting into before I found myself in Echo's bed. He'd been clear. I'd accepted the risk. It wasn't his fault I couldn't separate sex from emotion. It wasn't his fault I'd missed him during the times when we'd been apart. And it wasn't his fault I'd stupidly told him.

"Your idea of wrong and mine are probably two different things," she unhappily mumbled.

She was correct, but only because she loved me and didn't like seeing me mope around.

I had to do better.

"I'm serious, Jillian." I interjected as much conviction as I could when I went on, "Echo did nothing wrong."

"He's just like Logan."

Jill was correct again.

"Yep."

"You should talk to Laurie."

At my sister's odd suggestion, I turned to look at her.

"About what?"

"How she broke through Logan's thick skull."

That was a conversation I was never going to have. There were multiple reasons for this. The first and most important was I'd heard her threat to shock him using some sort of collar. As his little sister I had no desire to know if my big brother was into kinky sex that included being zapped. The second reason—only one tiny step down was that Echo was a lot like Logan but I was not like Lauren. I didn't have her strength. Echo would chew me up and spit me out. Hell, my heart was already fractured. A few more months and he would've shattered it.

I didn't remind Jill about the shock collar, saving her from the visions of our brother and his fiancée getting their kink on. I'm a great sister that way.

"I'm not interested in breaking through," I lied. "Echo and Logan might be similar in a lot of ways but they're not the same. Logan just needed the right woman to come along and show him what true love looked like. He needed to find a woman who was strong enough to stand by him when he came to the realization he's not the monster that

Dad was. Lauren taught him to trust himself. Echo is... I don't know what he is. But he made himself crystal clear who and what his priorities were and those do not extend to him."

"What does that mean? His priorities don't extend to him."

I took a sip of my margarita and nearly choked.

"Tequila much?" I sputtered.

"You looked like you needed a heavy pour."

I took my time taking another sip, this time ready for the tequila with a splash of margarita mix and hoping that Jill would forget she'd asked a question.

"Priorities," she prompted when I lowered my drink.

"I can't explain it, Jill. It's a gut feeling. He's just more concerned with Shiloh, River, and Phoenix. Their happiness means more to him than his own."

"So, Logan with me, you, Lucy, and Mom."

I glanced around the backyard while I contemplated chugging my mostly tequila margarita.

"You should've been a journalist," I noted.

"That's random." She laughed. "Stop evading."

"Or a terrorist."

"You mean an interrogator," she wrongly corrected.

"Nope. A terrorist."

"Don't let Logan hear you joke about terrorists."

My sister sighed and took a drink of her margarita. No doubt hers wasn't poured like mine.

"Fine." She gave in. "When do you want to look for apartments? I'm only here until Sunday."

"I might just jump from Vrbo to Vrbo. Try the area out for a while."

I was only half joking. Especially if I could find short term rentals with kickass deck furniture and a pool like this one had.

"Why doesn't that surprise me?" I couldn't help smiling at my sister's disgruntled question. We were the same in some ways and the complete opposite in others. Jillian planned her life to the nth degree. I was happy to float through life on a whim. She had a ten-year plan. I had a tomorrow plan.

Speaking of...

"I have a job interview tomorrow."

"Well, at least there's that," she returned haughtily. "You'll blow through your savings fast jumping from rental to rental."

Savings? Like a savings account? Yeah, she had one of those. I didn't.

In an effort to save myself a lecture about fiscal responsibility I didn't remind her of my spending habits.

"Hurry up and down that. Lucy will be here soon and if she sees you looking like you did when I came out here, you're gonna wish you were at the hands of a terrorist."

Jill wasn't wrong. Lucy never let anything go. She was the big sister who would shave off your eyebrow and threaten to shave off the other, which was a hollow threat since you had to do that anyway to pencil them both in so they matched—true story, she'd shaved off Jill's when we were kids. Mom was none too pleased. However, growing up in a family where there had been physical violence, none of us had ever threatened to hit or kill or kick or any of the other silly things siblings threaten. Instead, we pranked each other, though the results of those pranks could be

unpleasant. Like Jillian walking around eyebrowless for two months. I quite liked my eyebrows and paid a fortune to have them threaded and did not want Lucy to come near mine. One of the reasons I didn't have money in a savings account. All of that to say, Jill was right. I needed to down my drink and pour another before my big sister saw me mopey.

"Thank you for being the best little sister ever." I didn't have to look at Jill to know she was rolling her eyes as I lifted my hand to the side, presenting my glass. "May our penises always be harder than our lives."

"Please tell me you're not practicing your toast for Logan's wedding," she chided.

"Of course not. That one is for us. I have a better one for the wedding." I clanked my glass against her glass. "Cheers."

My drink was half gone when she told me, "You know we don't have penises so that doesn't work."

I shrugged and slurped the rest of the liquid around the ice.

"Not *our* penises, but the penises we—"

"Please don't finish that," Logan rumbled from the door.

Jill jumped out of her lounger and rushed to our brother. I stayed where I was, not only because I'd just downed at least three shots of tequila but also because even after all this time Logan had been with Lauren, I was still taken aback at the happiness that shone from him.

4

JACLYN

WHEN IAN ORDERED FOOD, HE DID NOT SKIMP. WE'D all eaten and there was still enough food scattered over the ginormous island in the kitchen for another ten people.

"I love Jill's new cut," Dotty gushed when she joined me in the kitchen. "Now I don't have to wait for one of you to talk to know who I'm talking to."

I bumped my sister-in-law with my hip and reminded her, "That hasn't been the case for years."

Her eyes tipped up as did her lips. Dotty was the only person I knew who made me feel tall. She was a dainty, petite woman with a big, feisty attitude. I didn't know if that was something she'd come by naturally or if it was because she was barely five-foot. Whichever reason, I loved her to pieces and I doubly adored her personality. She brought Lucy out of her too-serious-all-the-time shell and made my sister laugh.

"No, I just got better at hiding how I didn't know who the hell I was looking at," she returned.

I knew she was teasing but I played along. "How sure are you that Jill got the haircut and not Jaclyn?"

"Sure enough to ask you if you've talked to Echo."

Well, damn.

"Jill's got a big mouth," I complained.

"It wasn't Jill, it was Logan."

Dotty's lips pinched like she was trying to hold back either a smile or a laugh.

"Girl, your face," she sputtered, losing her control. "It's somewhere between furious and shocked."

"Logan doesn't gossip." I told her something she very well knew since she'd known my brother a long time.

"He does now. I heard him telling Ian he was gonna talk to you."

Shit.

Logan was worse than Lucy.

"Will you please tell Ian to tell Logan I'm perfectly fine and there's nothing to talk about?"

"Sure. After that I can tell Lucy to tell Jill to tell you that you're nuts."

Okay, she was right, that request was a little nutty.

"Why won't everyone leave this Echo thing alone?"

"So there *is* a thing with Echo?"

Instead of answering that I busied myself putting the lids back on the takeout. Dotty allowed me four containers before she leaned in close and whispered, "You know all you Haines women are stubborn as fuck."

I didn't know why she was whispering. It wasn't a secret, and she was married to the most stubborn out of all of us.

"To answer your question, your sisters, mom, and Ian

36

won't leave it alone because you were all jazzed up about moving to Georgia and now you're lukewarm about it. Which makes them worry that something did happen with this Echo guy. But I think it's something else for Logan."

I was still excited to move to Hollow Point. I just wasn't excited for the Echo run-ins I was sure to have.

"Something else for Logan?"

Dotty looked around the kitchen, then out the big window in front of the sink out to the backyard. Once she ascertained we were still alone she lowered her voice and said, "I heard Logan telling Ian he'd never seen Echo happy except for the few months after Quinn's wedding. I think Logan wants to figure out what happened because he thinks you're the reason Echo was happy but doesn't know for sure."

Another reason I loved Dotty; she was a gossip—until you told her a secret then she was a vault.

"I wasn't the reason," I denied.

"I think you're either lying on purpose or lying to yourself."

She called me out.

I wasn't lying.

"He's been happy because River has Letty, Shiloh has Luke, and Phoenix has Wren. They're his world. If they're happy, he's happy. Now can we please drop this, grab a bottle of tequila, and rejoin the party in the backyard?"

I thought she mumbled 'you're gonna need it' but it was so muffled I wasn't sure. I also wasn't going to ask since she snatched the bottle off the counter and started for the back door.

I also didn't ask if we were drinking straight out of the

bottle since that was exactly what I'd planned to do if I was going to be interrogated by my siblings.

I was classy like that, what could I say?

I KNEW I shouldn't have had that last shot.

I wasn't drunk, but I was a tiny bit past buzzed, on my way to feeling tipsy.

Not good when I was sitting at the patio table across from Logan, Lauren, Lucy, and Dotty. Jill had been sitting next to me but she'd excused herself to go to sleep. Now it felt like I was in the hotseat, about to get grilled.

"Logan, Lauren, Lucy," I singsonged. "That's a lot of L's."

"Great, she's ready." Lucy laughed.

"*She's* not ready," I corrected. "Tell me about Alabama."

"It's hot," Dotty answered. "Speaking of hot, Jill told me that this Echo guy was hot."

"Smooth, Dot." Logan smirked.

"Well, you people are taking too long and the suspense is killing me. Spill, Jaclyn."

I pinched the material of my tee and shook it. I really wished I'd remembered to grab a paper towel; the boob sweat was out of control in Georgia.

"I'm not talking about my sex—"

"Nope," my brother growled. "You are absolutely not talking about that."

Check. Mate.

"I wanna hear—"

"No, you don't," my brother interrupted his fiancée. "You don't want to hear anything about Echo, *ever*."

Someone's growly.

I gave my sister an eek face. Her smile in return was... serene. We'd all waited a long time to see Logan happy, see a good woman at his side who gave him a reason to behave like an overbearing fool but would put him in his place when necessary.

Like now...

"Do I need to get out the shock collar?" Lauren hotly threatened. "I think it's still in my purse."

Logan lifted his hands in defense.

"Nope," I parroted my brother. "None of us need to know why you carry a collar in your purse or about your kinks."

Logan groaned. Lucy and Dotty laughed. But Lauren gave me big eyes.

"I'm all for a little spice and kink in the bedroom but your brother would never—"

Simultaneously Lucy, Dotty, and I brought our hands to our ears.

"Too far," Lucy squeaked.

Dotty lowered her hands and smiled at Lauren.

"I don't know why I'm covering my ears; he's not my brother, and I've got questions."

Sweet Jesus, Dotty was serious. She'd have no issue prying for details.

Fortunately—or very, extremely *un*fortunately—my phone rang.

The fortunate part was the conversation about my brother's sex life halted.

The very, extremely unfortunate part was that my phone was on the table screen-up for all the world to see the name displayed. Also very extremely unluckily, Echo's name might as well have been flashing in neon.

Everyone saw.

Including Logan, who was staring at my phone with narrowed eyes.

"*Bzz, bzz,*" Lauren buzzed from beside my brother.

His eyes widened again and he asked, "Aren't you going to answer that?"

Hell. To. The. No.

"It's probably a butt dial."

"I heard the man's six-foot-five. I bet he's got a great—"

"Dot." Lucy laughed. "You're not helping."

My phone kept ringing.

"I'm sorry, I didn't know I was supposed to be helping with something," Dotty returned.

My brother's gaze lifted to mine. I hated that three days before his wedding his eyes were sparking with contemplation and concern.

"Answer it," he quietly told me.

"No, Logan."

"Answer it," he repeated.

"We're enjoying a rare Haines family sit-down minus the Beauty Sleep Queen."

Logan dipped his chin and stared at me with a pointed look.

"Jaclyn. Fix this."

40

My back shot straight. My happy tipsy effects from the tequila were no longer humming through me.

Fix it?

What the hell?

"That's a mighty big assumption that I was the one who broke it."

"I have no doubt he's the one responsible for whatever went wrong. But I know it's you who's gonna have to fix it."

My phone was still ringing but getting closer to going to voicemail. The flashing green slider taunting me to answer.

I wanted to flip my brother the bird just to remind him that I was no longer ten and didn't have to follow his orders. Instead, I snatched my phone off the table and answered as I was pushing myself away from the table. If I was going to talk to Echo it would not be in front of my family.

"Hello?"

"Have you checked your email?" Echo's grunted question annoyed the hell out of me.

I dodged the lounge chairs on my way around the pool and snapped back, "Has anyone ever told you your phone etiquette is shit?"

"Phone etiquette?"

I stopped near the back fence and lowered my voice so I wouldn't disturb the neighbors.

"Yes, Echo, you know, ring, ring, *hello?* Or, hi, Jackie this is Echo—"

"Are we really doing this?" he cut me off.

"Yes, we really are. You're rude—"

"Christ."

"And that's another thing—interrupting someone while they're speaking is rude, too."

I heard him draw in a deep breath, something he did a lot when he was fighting for patience. Normally I heard that inhale when one of his siblings called and was trying his last nerve. And I'd heard it once before directed at me right before he'd ended things.

"Have you checked your email, Jaclyn?" he asked in a much more polite tone.

"Not in a few hours, why?"

"Lauren made some changes to the lineup," he told me.

Oh, shit. I had a feeling I knew where this was going.

I was a bridesmaid. Echo was a groomsman. However, I was supposed to walk down the aisle with Drake. I didn't know who Drake's wife, Liberty, was walking with and I didn't know who Echo's partner was. Moreover, it never occurred to me to ask.

Now I had a sinking feeling in my gut Lauren was making last minute changes to push me and Echo together.

"Wanna guess who you're walking with?" he rapped out.

"Damn," I whispered.

I glanced over my shoulder. Lauren, Lucy, and Dotty were deep in conversation but Logan was staring at me.

"You didn't know?"

Echo's question pissed me off in a big way.

"Wait. You thought I asked her to rearrange her wedding party after months of her planning so I could walk down the aisle with you?" I sneered. "I'm not sure if that's you being arrogant thinking I'd *want* to walk with you or if you think I'm so fucking desperate I'd put my sister-in-law through that kind of hassle, again so I could walk down the aisle with you. If that's your ego talking, hate to tell you, big guy, but you've got an overinflated opinion of yourself. And if you think I'm that desperate you can fuck right off."

"Jaclyn—"

"Jaclyn nothing, Echo. Seriously, you're a dick."

"Thought it was rude to interrupt people," he noted.

I felt a growl of frustration bubble up in my chest. Before I had a chance to tell Echo he wasn't only a dick but an arrogant prick he went on. "If you didn't know about the changes, I made an incorrect assumption."

Well, fuck me sideways. Now he'd apologized so calling him names was off the table. I was hotheaded, but not bitchy or unreasonable. I didn't badger someone after they admitted they were wrong just to prove some sort of stupid point that in the long run only made me look like an asshole for not letting it go.

"Thanks for that. If that was all you were calling for, I'm busy."

"Listen..." he trailed off.

I gave him ample time to finish his thought. When he didn't, instead of prompting him, I moved to end the conversation.

"I have to go, Echo. Have a good night."

I gave him a moment to answer me. When he didn't, I disconnected the call.

"What was that about?" Logan asked from behind me.

Sneaky bastard could always sneak up on me and my sisters so I knew this particular skill wasn't learned in the Navy. Though I was sure it had helped him when he'd been a SEAL.

"Lauren changed the attendant order," I grumbled. "And Echo thought I had something to do with it."

"Lauren didn't change it, I did."

At Logan's admission I turned to face my brother.

"What? Why would you change it?"

"Because I believe in you," he started. "I believe you're the only person who can wring the miracle of making Echo Kent open his eyes."

Hearing my brother tell me he believed in me was an incredible feeling but seeing the veracity behind that statement shine in his eyes was otherworldly. Growing up the way we did, Logan risking his life to protect me, my sisters, and my mother, all I ever wanted to do was make him proud. That didn't mean I wasn't a pain in his ass, I was his sister, but Lucy, Jill, and I all were very aware he'd literally taken a knife to his stomach to stop our father from turning his temper on us.

So, actually hearing my big brother tell me he believed in me wasn't incredible—it was everything.

It meant *everything*.

But with this? He was wrong.

"Logan, I know you don't want to hear this, but Echo made himself clear. Whatever we could've been is done. He's done. The reasons he gave were stupid excuses, but as stupid as I think they were, I have to respect them."

"So you're just going to give up?"

Give up? Was he crazy? I wasn't a stalker, or a nutty ex-girlfriend. I didn't chase men.

"He gave *me* up, brother. Don't you want better for me?"

Without hesitation Logan leaned close and lowered his head so we were eye-to-eye.

"I want you to have the best. The absolute best of

everything. If I didn't think Echo was worth your time, I'd be happy as fuck he quietly ended whatever the two of you had going on and saved me the trouble of kickin' his ass. But I know he's worth your time. I know he's a man with just as much loyalty and integrity as the rest of the men who will stand next to me when I marry Ren."

Logan paused and the lightness that had been in his eyes fled. Back was the old Logan who had been my fiercest protector. "Ren and I saw you in his car. We were driving back from dinner and we stopped next to the two of you at a red light. I was going to call you but Ren stopped me."

Oh, shit. He knew I'd been in Georgia and didn't call him. It had to have been one of the times Echo had picked me up from the airport because once I was at his house, I didn't leave exactly for that reason. Hollow Point wasn't a small town but it was a small enough city we'd be easily caught.

"You know what I saw?" Logan continued.

I had no idea what he saw so I shook my head.

"Echo smiling. Then you said something and he laughed. Fuck me, Echo Kent smiling like he was carefree and happy. Never had I ever seen that before. The man is friendly once you get to know him. He laughs and jokes with the rest of us. But never is he carefree. That man carries more burdens than I can begin to imagine. You did that for him. And fuck but I love knowing he sees in you what I know you have—the power to lift his burdens. The problem is, he sees it, he recognizes it, but he doesn't understand it. He doesn't think he deserves it. In all his success leading his family out of darkness all he sees is failure."

The conviction in Logan's tone made me think he was

speaking from experience. We all knew and understood why my brother didn't believe that real, true love existed, up until he met Lauren. But never in my wildest thoughts did it occur to me that Logan would think he failed in any way. He'd successfully kept us all safe.

"Is that what you saw?" I whispered.

"Fuck yeah, Jackie. I did everything I could to protect you, Jill, and Lucy but I failed Mom."

My brother's admission felt like my heart was being torn from my chest. I hated—no, *loathed*—that he thought that.

"Three days before your wedding isn't the time to talk about this," I began. "But, Logan, you didn't fail any of us. We owe you our lives and all of us know it. Most especially Mom."

"Yeah, I can reconcile that now. But before I met Lauren, no. I was happy to live in my perceived failures. That's what I'm telling you, Jaclyn—Echo is where I was. Living vicariously through Shiloh, River, and Phoenix's successes but not able to see his own. His only happiness comes from them being happy. I know that road; I lived it until I met Lauren. And the only way I could keep her was if I did what I'd never had the strength to do before. Self-reflection is a sonofabitch. Self-forgiveness is harder. Echo needs a reason to do the work so he can move on."

"And you think I'm enough for Echo—"

"No, Jaclyn, not enough. You're everything. Everything he needs to open his eyes and do the hard work so he can keep you."

I swallowed down the lump in my throat and asked, "What if I'm not enough?"

46

"Again, we would not be having this conversation if I didn't believe that Echo was good enough for you."

I noticed Logan hadn't answered my question so I tried a different route.

"And you gleaned all of this from seeing us together in the car one time?"

"No, I know I'm right about this because while the two of you were carrying on in secret Echo was a different man. After it ended I watched him retreat. I know what a man in love looks like. But more—I know the look of a man who fucked over the woman who was meant to be his. I watched Carter pine over Delaney for years. I didn't understand it then. But looking back, all the signs were there. Echo knows what he lost."

I wasn't so sure my brother was right. But I also knew he'd never steer me wrong.

In order to end the conversation and rejoin our family I told him, "I'll think about it, Logan. And it scares me to admit this to my overprotective big brother but when he ended things it hurt me. I'm not sure I'm ready for more pain and rejection."

Just as I thought—a scary look passed over his features before he pulled me into a hug.

"No matter what you decide, I got your back," he murmured into my hair. "All I want is for you to be happy."

That, I was sure about.

That was my big brother, always looking out for the rest of us. Always there to push us forward, hold our hands, wrap us up in a hug, encourage us, and pick us up when we fell. There was no better man than my brother.

"I love you, Logan."

My brother gave me a squeeze that stole my breath.

I was no closer to figuring out what I should do about Echo, but he'd have to wait. Tonight was about celebrating Logan and Lauren. Or more to the point, it was about celebrating the woman who had given my brother the peace and love he deserved.

5

ECHO

"Brother, you look like you're ready to commit a felonious act," River mumbled beside me.

That was a strong possibility at this point. I'd suffered through Jaclyn on my arm as we walked down the aisle. I'd suffered through watching her aim her beautiful smile at her brother the whole walk to the front of the church. I'd suffered through watching her wipe away tears when her brother and Lauren had exchanged vows, and more suffering walking her out of the church.

From start to finish it had been torture to have her so close yet not be able to breathe her in, not kiss her, or hold her closer than what would be considered appropriate for acquaintances. Which was what we were supposed to be. Two people who barely knew each other—except I knew every goddamn inch of her body.

And now she was in some jackass's arms slow dancing to some sappy love song.

"You know Jase would never move in on Logan's sister," River continued, only further pissing me off.

Right, Logan's sister.

That was why Jase wouldn't make a move, not because he knew if he attempted anything of the sort, *I'd* break his fucking neck.

I ignored my brother's sigh in favor of keeping an eye on the couple on the dance floor.

"You know you can end the torment and go ask her to dance."

That made me look over at River.

"Why in the hell would I do that?"

Instead of answering me, he gave me a disappointed shake of his head. I took this nonverbal answer as an opportunity to change the subject.

"Were you able to talk Sunny out of her crazy plan?"

"I'm sorry, was that a real question?"

If anyone could talk sense into Sunny it was River. My sister was stubborn being that she also liked to buck authority. And since I was the authority figure when she was growing up, as an adult she still liked to push back when I tried to talk her out of something. Phoenix was like a bull in a China shop and had zero finesse when it came to our sister. River was my only hope, he was level headed and diplomatic. Out of the three of us he could normally make her see reason.

"Did you even try?" I asked.

"Sure."

Fucking shit. He hadn't or if he did it was half-assed at best.

"River—"

"I didn't try very hard because I don't see a problem with her and Luke getting married."

That wasn't the issue.

"You know that's not the problem," I growled.

"I'll rephrase. I see no problem with her and Luke getting married tomorrow."

Again, that wasn't the issue. Hell, I was shocked it had taken them this long to get hitched. The problem was the reason why she was rushing when she'd wanted to wait. Not to mention she roped Phoenix into her craziness.

"And Phoenix and Wren?"

I glanced around Logan and Lauren's wedding reception, keeping my gaze purposefully away from the dance floor when my eyes landed on Dee Haines smiling at her daughters Lucy and Jill. Which was a miracle in and of itself after the trauma the Haines family had endured. The mere thought of what would've happened to Jaclyn had Logan not been able to keep her and her sisters safe sent a wave of anger over me.

"You were there, Echo." My brother's voice pulled me from my violent thoughts. "Wren is all about a double wedding. Phoenix was only waiting until he could have a talk with Griff. You also know they went out, had their talk, and Griff was more than happy to walk his mom down the aisle as long as he's walking her to Phoenix. It's all good."

"You keep saying that, River, but you put this notion in their heads that I've put my life on hold until they're married. That's bullshit. A few signatures and some vows don't change anything."

"You're forgetting name changes, too," River joked. "We're losing a Kent but gaining three more if you count my son."

My gaze sliced back to River.

"You're having a boy?"

"You're the first to know," he told me. "We found out right before we came."

Christ, my brother was having a son.

I wished he was having a girl so he'd know my pain. Maybe next time.

"Couldn't be happier for you, Riv."

"We talked about it and we want you to be his godfather."

Jesus fuck. I felt some sort of strange moisture coat my eyes.

"Be my honor." Was all I could choke out.

"No more bitching about the wedding. Tomorrow you're walking our sister to Luke. She wants this and if she needs this excuse to jump the line and get married before her friends, you're gonna give this to her. And so what if Phoenix and Wren are rushing to give this to Sunny? It's still not wrong. They want to get married; it doesn't matter to them if that is literally tomorrow or in a year from now."

It fucking sucked when my brother was right.

"Sunny's getting married tomorrow," I murmured.

"Luke's a good man," he rumbled the truth. "He'll take care of her."

That was never in question. Luke would give up his life to protect my sister.

I pushed all thoughts of my baby sister getting hitched aside, hoping the knot in my chest would loosen, and circled back to River's son.

"You got a name picked out for your boy?" I asked.

"No, but it'll be something normal like John or Tom or Frank. None of that hippy shit Mom had going on."

I didn't know what River was bitching about. At least he didn't have the name Echo.

"She could've called you Babbling Brook," I pointed out.

I stood frozen when my brother busted out laughing. It had been a long time in the making to get to a place where we could laugh about the mother who'd abandoned us. It was Shiloh we had to thank for that. Her facing the demon that none of us had the strength to seek out. In some ways Shiloh was the strongest of us. She always had been but it wasn't until she found Luke that she came to recognize it.

Now she wielded that knowledge and called a family meeting behind my back, planned shotgun weddings, and meddled in my personal life.

I'D WAITED until Jaclyn had broken away from her family and left the small ballroom before I set my drink on the bar and followed her. I was nearly out the door when I caught Phoenix watching me with a smile. The bastard even had the audacity to wink at me.

Nosy asshole.

I walked through the foyer of the turn-of-the-century manor house turned boutique hotel, down a small hallway, and leaned against the wall opposite of the women's restroom and waited for Jaclyn.

It was pure luck that when Matt had rented out all the rooms for the bridal party I'd been assigned the only room on the bottom floor. That meant I wouldn't have to drag Jaclyn too far before we had privacy.

The bathroom door opened, Jaclyn stepped out, then stumbled to a halt. She raised her hand and placed it over her heart.

"Jesus, Echo, you scared the shit out of me. The men's—"

I reached out and grabbed her hand. With one sharp tug she was out of the doorway.

"What are you doing?"

I didn't bother answering. She'd find out soon enough what I was doing.

"Echo!"

I stopped in front of my door, fished the key out of my pocket, and inserted it into the lock.

"What are you doing?"

I thought it was pretty fucking obvious what I was doing so again I didn't bother answering. I opened the door, pulled her through, slammed it behind her, and spun her around until her back was pressed against the wood.

"Having fun?" I growled.

She blinked up at me, her hazel eyes flashing with uncertainty. Her natural beauty was hidden beneath the makeup she didn't need and didn't normally wear. Her hair was pulled up in a complicated twist I wanted to rip out so I could run my fingers through her silky strands.

"What?"

"The little game you're playing. You having fun?"

I was well aware I sounded like a jealous idiot. I also didn't give a fuck. Not after the shit she'd pulled for the last three hours.

"Game?"

She didn't bother hiding her smirk, which was good because the game she was playing just got switched up.

My palms went to the door, bracketing her in. I bent down and brushed my lips over the shell of her ear.

"Panties off, Jaclyn."

My lips trailed down as her head tilted to the side to give me access to her neck. My mouth hadn't made it to her shoulder when I felt her shimmying out of her panties.

"Now pull up your dress," I demanded and scraped my teeth along her shoulder blade.

"Echo—"

"Dress up, Jaclyn. Around your waist. Then I want you to pull me free."

I waited until she was pulling the hem of her dress up her thighs—not that the fucking dress had far to go—before I continued to skim over her neck with only my lips. I paused to take in her perfume, a scent that I missed more than I wanted to admit when it had faded from the pillow she used when she'd stayed with me.

Floral with a hit of cedar.

A complicated mixture that never failed to drive me insane.

Jaclyn undid the button of my dress pants, then the zipper. When her fingers circled my already hard cock, I groaned my appreciation against her throat.

Two, long, slow strokes later, my hand covered hers, taking the slow glides to rough. My mouth moved back up to her ear, still not giving her what I knew she wanted.

"No more games, Jaclyn."

"Mmm," she hummed and craned her neck wordlessly

asking me for more. "I don't know, seems silly to stop when I'm winning."

"Are you?" I asked and lifted my head.

I watched as her teeth swiped her bottom lip.

"Feels like I am."

Jaclyn tightened her grip around my shaft.

Silly woman.

"I'm the one getting a hand job, baby," I reminded her and kept our hands moving.

Her pretty eyes flashed fire.

"Right." She smiled then it turned wicked. "And in less than two minutes you'll be buried inside me."

I had to lock my legs to prevent myself from hoisting her up and slamming her down on my cock, proving her right.

"Bad girls don't get fucked," I tsked. "Knees, Jaclyn."

Her smile turned smug as she lowered herself to the floor, our hands still jerking me off.

"Hand between your legs." I waited until her hand disappeared before I issued my next order. "Open your mouth, I want your tongue."

As soon as her mouth opened, I leaned forward and smeared the bead of come over her tongue.

"You still enjoying your game?"

So many emotions flitted through those gorgeous eyes before she settled on wanton and nodded. I watched as the tip of her tongue traced the head of my cock. When she tried to suck me into her mouth I pulled back.

"You want my cock in your mouth?" I asked even though I knew the answer.

Another sharp nod.

The need to thrust into her mouth was growing by the second. The desire to reclaim what was mine, remind her of all the ways I could own her, was so intense it was almost necessary.

But I had a point to prove.

A point that seemed pretty fucking stupid now that her cheeks were flushed, her eyes were hooded, and she was rocking her hips finger-fucking herself on her knees in front of me.

I jerked my dick harder and asked another needless question.

"You like watching me jack off, baby?"

A groan escaped her open mouth. She liked watching me almost as much as I liked watching her. There was nothing shy about Jaclyn Haines. Not in the bedroom, not outside of it; the woman was confident, bold, beautiful, intelligent, and had a great sense of humor.

A combination that scared the shit out of me.

Just because she looked closer than I was I leaned into my hand, resting on the door and jerked my cock faster. I didn't need to dip into the memories of how good her mouth felt wrapped around my cock. How fucking tight her cunt was, how wild she got when she rode me or how good she tasted when I ate her. The sight of her on her knees, pretty face tipped up, eyes locked with mine, mouth open and ready for my come was enough to set me off.

"Swallow me," I grunted as pleasure rushed through me.

Jaclyn groaned when the first jet of my come hit her tongue. By the time I flooded her mouth her eyes were closed and she was panting out her release.

The sight was so fucking hot I couldn't take my eyes off her as her orgasm ripped through her. Long moments passed before she slowly opened her eyes and she swallowed the mouthful I'd given her.

Christ, she was perfect.

And that scared me the most.

I had yet to come back to myself when she stood, shimmied her dress down, and gave me a shove. Meaning in my stupor, I stumbled back even though I had more than eight inches on her and a hundred pounds.

Her hand went to the door, she craned her neck and smiled.

"See you around, Echo."

Then she was out the door.

I stared at the space she'd vacated wondering what the fuck had just happened.

It wasn't until I was tucking my dick back in my slacks that I saw her black lace panties on the floor.

Seems silly to stop when I'm winning.

It was debatable who had won seeing as she went back to the party with the taste of me fresh on her tongue, but there was no denying I'd been played.

6

ECHO

I shouldn't have been surprised my sister could pull off planning a wedding in three days, yet looking around the ballroom—the same room Logan and Lauren's reception had been in last night, now reset for Sunny and Phoenix's reception—I was surprised it had all come together so quickly.

"There you are." A distinctly exasperated female voice came from behind me.

Letty.

I turned to greet my sister-in-law but before I had a chance to say anything she went on, "Phoenix is dressed but he'd like a word with you before you go to the bridal suite." Letty paused to take me in. "You know, sometimes I'm in fear for my vagina."

My body jerked, my neck twitched, and I asked, "I'm sorry, what?"

"My vagina." She repeated the one word in her previous statement that I never wanted to hear her say again. "I'm not tall so I'm hoping my contribution to the giant I'm growing makes him more manageable. I might be able to push a Phoenix out. Well, not a full-grown Phoenix but a baby giant Phoenix. River's pushing it. But if this kid takes after you, I fear for my vagina."

One thing was certain, when Letty was around there was never a shortage of laughs. However, I wasn't feeling in the mood to laugh and it had nothing to do with Jackie playing me last night then keeping her distance for the rest of the reception. I'd woken up with a churning in my gut. The feeling of loss heavy on my chest. Neither of which I could shake.

"Hate to tell you this, sweetheart, but Phoenix was nine pounds when he was born."

"Nine pounds," she gasped. "How big was River?"

"A little over eight and Sunny was a few ounces shy of nine."

"And you?"

"Big enough to make you ask for a C-section," I told her.

Letty's eyes went wide.

"I see I didn't think this through," she grumbled. "My vagina's not up for Kent-sized babies."

And I was done talking about my brother's wife's vagina.

"You get this is a weird conversation, right?"

Letty stared at me with honest to God confusion.

"What's weird is you Kent boys are the next-sized-up humans. One day your wife will face the daunting task of birthing your child…"

Letty might've said more, however my thoughts drifted to Jaclyn growing our child. My mind skipped over the pregnancy straight to the kind of mother she'd be. Jaclyn would never abandon our children; she'd love and protect them the way her mother had. She'd literally kill anyone who attempted to harm them. She'd be a fierce mama bear. She'd teach them how to love and how to be loved.

"Echo?" Letty called, snapping me back to the conversation.

Fuck.

Her voice was mellow when she asked, "You okay?"

Hell no. I was far from okay.

"Absolutely," I lied.

My sister-in-law took a moment to assess my lie then wisely dropped it.

"Come on, Phoenix is waiting and you only have thirty minutes until the excitement starts."

By excitement she meant me walking my sister down the aisle.

I found nothing exciting about giving my baby sister up even if I was giving her to the only man other than my brothers, I trusted with her.

"Echo, you're wanted on the dance floor," the DJ announced.

My irritation spiked as my eyes sliced to the dance floor to see Sunny in her pretty dress dragging a chair behind her.

What the fuck?

"That's you, brother." River chuckled beside me. "Now

aren't you glad I eloped and didn't make you go through this father of the groom shit?"

Father of the groom?

Christ, my family was killing me today.

"I don't dance," I grumbled.

"Looks like you do today."

With a shove, River propelled me toward the dance floor, my gaze never leaving my sister who was no longer a Kent. She was now Luke's wife—a Marcou.

When I made it to Sunny I tipped my eyes down and asked, "What are you doing?"

Instead of answering me she lifted her hand and demanded, "Help me up."

I took her hand and watched her pull up her floor-length gown and step up onto the chair.

In that moment memories of my baby sister as a child climbing onto chairs, onto the coffee table, or the couch, or any surface really that would make her taller so she'd be eye-to-eye with one of her brothers flooded my brain. I was more than a foot taller than my sister, had been since I was in my teens, and I'd heard her incessant bitching about how unfair it was that she was the shortest Kent ever since she was little and it had never stopped.

"I know you don't dance," she said and gave my hand a tug. "So we're not going to dance but you're going to stand here with me and listen."

Listen to what?

I'd said all that I'd needed to say to Sunny before I'd walked her down the aisle and I'd had the decency to do it in the privacy of her room. You know, since it was a *private moment* between brother and sister.

Before I could ask her why the hell we were standing in the middle of the dance floor talking, the music started, and by that I meant the words to a song I knew—because everyone on the globe knew the damn song—filled the reception room.

For all the times you stood by me...

Though it wasn't Celine Dion's iconic voice singing; it was a cover sung by a much younger woman.

"Listen to the words, brother," Sunny whispered. "Each and every one of them is true."

Fuck, my sweet sister.

I stepped closer to the chair and wrapped my arms around her. The moment I did, her head rested on my shoulder.

And there we stood. Me uncomfortable but no less moved by Sunny's love.

When the song ended, she lifted her head but didn't let me go. The strumming of a guitar started as River and Phoenix joined our huddle. River hooked his arm around Sunny and placed his hand on my right shoulder. Phoenix's hand went to my left, and his other arm went around Sunny, completing the circle.

At the first words of the new song my muscles tensed. By the second line, my chest burned. By the third, my head bowed and my eyes closed to fight back the emotion. And by the time the chorus hit I was breathing heavy.

Brother, let me be your shelter...

None of us moved. There was no swaying, no words exchanged. Not that any were needed when Tyler Braden was singing his rendition of a really great fucking song.

I felt River's hand tighten on my shoulder when Tyler

sang about not being made for rivalry and how he couldn't face the world alone. A second later Phoenix's hand did the same as the lyrics revealed the best line of the song.

I know that in my weakness I am strong...

And neither released their grasps until the final chords played.

"You are our shelter, our fortress, the light that will always bring us home," Phoenix croaked, his voice cracking as he spoke.

"Brother." My voice was equally emotional, making it impossible to go on.

"Thank you for always bringing us home," Sunny added.

My gaze lifted, shifted around our circle, pausing on each of my siblings but landing on Sunny.

Thankfully Sunny jumped off the chair before I had to say anything that would bare just how moved I was.

"It's time to cut the cake," she announced. "If my husband smashes it in my face I fully expect one or all of you to go all big brother on him."

"Nope." River chuckled. "An hour ago Echo gave you to that poor sap; he's all on his own."

"This isn't the 1930s, River; he didn't actually give me to Luke."

"Yeah, Sunny he did," Phoenix joined. "I watched him walk you to Luke and put your hand in his."

"You're an idiot," Sunny returned.

Nothing like curbing an emotional breakdown than Sunny ending an argument with Phoenix by calling him an idiot.

64

Children, teenagers, or adults—some things never change.

Thank fuck.

"THAT DOESN'T LOOK GOOD," Phoenix said as he stopped by the table where I was sitting.

Since my eyes had been glued to the situation he was in reference to for the last ten minutes I didn't have to ask what he was talking about.

He also wasn't wrong.

Sunny and Jaclyn were talking. Or more to the point, Sunny was conspiring and Jaclyn was soaking it up.

"You need to break that shit up before they hatch their plan that will likely involve inflicting maximum pain." Phoenix's pause was purely theatrical. "That pain being inflicted upon you."

My brother the drama king. Though he wasn't wrong about that, either.

I shoved my chair away from the table just as Jaclyn ended the conversation. I watched her cross the space, weaving around the partygoers, skirting by the tables until she slipped out of the reception room.

Perfect.

"Be back." I dismissed my brother, uncaring it was his wedding day and I probably should have stayed at his reception.

When I found Jaclyn she was standing in front of my hotel door. No, she wasn't standing there; she had her shoulder leaned against the door, arms crossed over her chest, eyes aimed down the hall with an impatient stare.

She knew I'd follow her.

Though that wasn't a surprise, seeing as I hadn't hidden. I'd been watching her all night. And as I stalked toward her, I didn't hide how I was taking her in. From her red heels to her short black dress that showed off every curve, to her cleavage. The woman was fucking gorgeous in a pair of ratty ass sweats and tee with no makeup and her hair pulled up. But in a dress, heels, whatever shit she put on her eyelids to make the green in her hazel eyes stand out, all that thick brown hair tumbling down her back in soft curls, it would be a miracle if I got her into the room before I fucked her.

And she knew it.

She knew what she did to me. She knew every time she'd strutted her pert ass past me at the reception, I was fighting the urge to drag her out of the room. Which meant she'd gone out of her way to parade herself in that dress in front of me.

"Took you long enough." She smiled.

It's going to take less time than she thinks.

Jaclyn straightened and moved to the side. I fished my key out of my pocket and wasted no time unlocking the door. I pushed it open. She caught the door and walked in. I closed the door behind me just as Jaclyn started. "We need to—"

She got no more out.

"Dress off. Leave the shoes."

Her eyes narrowed on me, no doubt to tell me off about not letting her finish.

"Or you can leave," I finished.

Those narrowed eyes watched as I took off my suit jacket and tossed in on the dresser. They continued to watch as I unbuttoned my shirt, leaving it hanging open, slipped off my shoes, worked my belt and the button of my pants.

Her reaching for the hem of her dress wasn't the first indication she was going to follow my orders. It wasn't the shiver as she pulled the silky material over her head, baring her naked body to my grateful eyes. It wasn't even the way her irritation had morphed to hunger.

It was the smirk playing on her lips.

The challenge she issued with her eyes.

Fuck, she was stunning.

"Bed, Jaclyn. Knees bent, legs open, heels on the mattress."

She added an extra sway to her hips as she followed my directions. As if her challenge wasn't enticing enough. As if I needed any more incentive to shrug my shirt off and let my pants fall to the floor.

With rabid fascination I watched her climb onto the bed and pull her legs up.

"Wider, Jaclyn, I want to see your pussy."

Her head came off the bed. Some of the challenge in her stare waned as the fullness of what she'd started set in. She knew better than to test my control; she knew when it came to her, I had none. Never did. Not when I knew I should've stayed away. Not when I knew starting a relationship with her was a bad idea. Not when I fucked her the first time, the last, or any of the times in between.

"Wider," I repeated when she didn't move.

By the time I was at the edge of the bed her legs were wide, her pussy open to me, so I took advantage, bringing my hand up, using a finger to trace her slit.

"Been watching you in that dress all night."

"I know."

"I know you know," I needlessly confirmed and pushed two fingers inside her pussy. "Been thinking about doing this all-fucking night."

I leaned over her, trailing my tongue up her stomach, over the swell of her tit, around her nipple, then paused to issue another order. "Move, baby. Fuck yourself on my fingers."

Without hesitation her hips rocked. I smiled against her peaked nipple before I drew it between my lips and swirled my tongue. The harder she fucked herself the harder I sucked until her pussy fluttered around my fingers and she moaned her orgasm.

Fucking perfect.

I lost her nipple in my mouth when my knee went on the bed. My cock replaced my fingers, and in one smooth drive my cock was enveloped with her tight, wet heat.

"Echo," she groaned.

"You like my cock, baby?"

"Yes."

"Yeah, you do. Wrap me up."

Her legs went around my waist, the points of her heels dug into my back, her nails scored down my spine adding to the pain, fueling my need to fuck her hard. I drove my cock deep, pulling another breathy moan from her. Desire shot through me and I unleashed all of the pent-up hunger, the undeniable craving I couldn't satisfy. Months of missing her, denying us both of what we wanted powered my thrusts. Her hands tore at my back, her heels scraped, her breath was coming out in quick pants.

I'd stupidly given this up.

All the beauty I'd thrown away—the feel of her soft body wrapped around mine, the way her pussy clutched and pulsed around my cock, the way she sweetly moaned my name, the closeness, the intimacy of being inside the woman I couldn't get enough of.

All of that gone.

And now she was holding back, giving me her body, playing a game but keeping herself locked away from me.

"Echo."

Yeah, I missed the fuck out of that, too. My name a breathy sigh while her cunt fluttered with her climax.

I shifted so I could watch her go under, get swept away in the pleasure I created, and she didn't disappoint. Her eyes hooded, her mouth opened in a silent scream, and her head tipped back.

"*So.*" I drove in hard. "*Fucking,*" I groaned. "*Beautiful,*" I finished and planted myself deep, spilling the evidence of my pleasure into her.

I buried my face in her neck for no other reason than to breathe her in. Take in the sweet smell of perfume I missed on my sheets. A moment later the spell was broken when Jaclyn patted my shoulder. I rolled some of my weight off her and glanced down.

The second I saw her face I braced.

"Jaclyn," I warned.

"Off, honey."

For some insane reason instead of pinning her to the

bed until I could talk some sense into her, I rolled. As soon as I did, she threw her legs over the side of the bed and was up.

"Jaclyn—"

"I have to get back to the party," she said conversationally.

I watched as she picked up her dress, pulled it over her head, smoothed it down, and without bothering to fix her wild sex hair, she strutted her ass to the door.

And just like last night she gave me a smile before she left.

With a groan of frustration, I rolled to my back and stared at the ceiling.

That was the last time she was pulling that shit.

No, scratch that—that was the last time she was walking away from me, period.

7

JACLYN

"Yes, Mom, I'll stop by after work."

"Jaclyn? Did you walk away from your phone again?" I barely heard my mother ask.

Damn.

I walked back into the bedroom, spotted my phone on the bed where I'd left it, and tried again while buttoning my jeans.

"Yeah, sorry, I forgot you weren't in my ear and went to the bathroom to start my hair."

"In your ear?"

I didn't have time for this conversation, I needed to get to work. So I forwent explaining how I didn't have in my AirPods in favor of the original topic.

"I'll go by your house after work and check the appliance delivery."

"The bedroom furniture, too."

"Yes, Mom."

I took a sip of my green tea, swallowed the liquid, and

for the fifth day in a row I wondered why the hell I'd thought it was a good idea to give up coffee.

New state, new job, new healthier me—that was this year's motto. I'd even joined a gym, though I'd only been three times in the two weeks I'd been back in Hollow Point. I was thinking the gym was going to be a wash, but my coffee addiction needed to be curbed. Actually, it wasn't the coffee per se; it was the five tablespoons of sugar I added to said coffee that I needed to cut out.

"I don't understand why you don't just stay in the house. We're not there for a few more weeks."

I set my mug on top of the paperback I had on the nightstand—sacrilege, I know, but better my book than the nightstand that didn't belong to me.

"I told you, I'm watching the townhouse next door while the owner's on vacation."

The owner of the Vrbo I was renting was a sweet old lady. After her husband passed, she sold the house she'd lived in for fifty-two years and purchased both sides of a duplex. One she lived in, one she rented out, unless one of her children was in town, then they stayed in what she called her guest house. I thought the woman was a genius. Not only did she live next door to the rental so she could keep an eye on the people who stayed there but the property maintenance was included in the HOA fees or so she'd told me over tea one morning.

"Yes, I remember. I just think it's a waste of money, you renting somewhere when we have an empty house you can stay in."

Empty was the operative word. No couch, no TV, no

dishes, and since I didn't have any of those things anymore a fully furnished Vrbo worked for me.

"I like it here and Miss Louise is only charging me half price for the week she's going to be gone since I'm watching her place. Plus, I'm looking for an apartment."

That last part was semi-true. I was looking, I just wasn't finding anything.

"Listen, Mom, I have to finish my hair and get to work. I'll call you later."

"Okay. I love you, sweetie."

"Love you, Mom."

I disconnected, leaving my phone on the bed, and no sooner did I step foot into the bathroom there was a knock on my front door.

Damn!

I grabbed a hair tie off the counter and resigned myself to going to work with wet hair. One of the many perks of working with animals was they didn't give a shit what you looked like. I'd started working for an equine vet Chelsea hooked me up with before she left on her three-week destination wedding-slash-honeymoon extravaganza so I mostly worked outside, which meant makeup was not an option.

I made it to the front door, checked the peephole, and my stomach clenched.

Damn, *damn*, damn.

I knew this day would come. I was just hoping it wouldn't be for another few weeks, or maybe another month, or next year would've been even better.

I opened the door and smiled.

Shiloh Kent was not smiling, nor did she return mine

when she pushed herself into the house asking, "What gives?"

I now knew that Echo had passed down his lack of a proper greeting to his sister.

"Good morning, Shiloh," I chirped. "I'd offer you coffee but unfortunately, I've given up the nectar of the gods so I only have tea. And really, I don't have time to offer you a mug seeing as I have to walk out the door in five minutes or I'll be late for work."

"*Morning*, Jackie," she returned then went right back to why she was there. "I thought we had a plan."

We didn't have a plan; we had a loose plot. One that was hatched after I'd had a few drinks and was feeling uppity since I'd outplayed Echo two times in as many days. But since then, I'd gone back to Michigan, sold all my stuff, packed what I was keeping into my car, and moved to Georgia. And in that time, I'd thought better of plotting or putting any plan into action that had to do with Echo.

"I can't do it," I told her.

"What do you mean you can't do it?"

"Shiloh, I'm gonna get hurt."

The annoyance marring her beautiful face disappeared.

Hell, just looking at her hurt.

The Kent siblings all looked alike with only slight variations. Shiloh with her blue eyes, blonde hair, and similar features proved that boy or girl, the Kent genes were dominant, and furthermore, that those genes produced beauty.

"Jackie—"

I didn't let her finish. I knew she'd be able to talk me

back into a scheme that would leave me bloody and broken if it didn't work.

"I'm in love with your brother. He's made it clear he doesn't feel the same. I thought I could go through with it but when it turns bad I not only lose him again, I could lose you, too. And what if Logan gets pissed and he and Echo lose their friendship? Then there's Phoenix and Wren—"

Shiloh put her hand up halting my explanation.

"I get it. But what if it doesn't go bad? What if you break through?"

If the impossible happened then I'd have everything I ever dreamed of.

But the risk was too scary.

"That's a lot of what-ifs."

"It's *two* what-ifs," she returned. "Just two. He's been in a mood since you left. Not his normal brooding one either. He's been a total grouch. Do you know why?" Shiloh didn't let me answer before she told me why. "Because you left without returning his calls or texts. And since you've been back you haven't called or texted *and* you've been avoiding him, which means you've been avoiding *all* of us. So you tell me, Jackie, does that sound like a man who doesn't feel the same? If he didn't care he wouldn't have reached out. If he wasn't struggling with his feelings, he'd go about his life happy he didn't have to run into you when we all get together. But that's not what's happening. He looks for you. He waits to see if you're gonna show and when you don't, he gets pissed. I know my brother. I know when he needs a kick in the ass and I know when that kick needs to come from one of us and when it needs to come from the woman he's fallen in love with."

Since Shiloh hadn't walked that far into the house she didn't have far to go when she made her way to the door. As if the lashing she'd given me wasn't enough she turned to finish me off.

"I know it's gonna be hard. I know all the reasons why he is the way he is. I know why he thinks he doesn't deserve you. But he's wrong. The same way your brother protected you, my brother protected me. I know you get it. I know you understand the sacrifices he made for me. The same way you only wanted the best for Logan, I only want the best for my brother. And when Logan found that in Lauren it stitched up the last of the leftover childhood wounds you carried. I understand you're afraid of getting hurt but what I'm telling you is, he's worth it. So, you're up, Jackie."

With that, she left.

I was not bloody and broken—only Echo could eviscerate me like that.

But she did leave me gutted, so I was winded when I grabbed my backpack and purse and headed out the door to work.

By the time I pulled up to Dr. Maddy Robinson's equine center I was no longer starving for oxygen but I was thinking.

I didn't need Shiloh to tell me that Echo was worth it, I knew he was. I didn't need her to tell me that our brothers had protected us and given up most of their childhoods to raise us. It wasn't a surprise she knew about the wounds I'd carried into adulthood and the guilt I felt. Nope, the parallels weren't lost on me. What I couldn't stop thinking about was the implication that Echo was in love with me.

Suddenly the what-ifs flipped to, what if she was right?

What if I lost my chance with Echo because I was too scared to take a chance?

Before I lost my nerve, I grabbed my phone out of my purse, opened up the text app, and scrolled to Echo's thread.

Seven unanswered messages.

I hadn't seen or spoken to him in three weeks.

I took a breath, tapped out a message, closed the app, and tossed my phone back in my purse.

Then I got out of my car and went to work.

"GOOD MORNING, CHIPMUNK," Preston Robinson greeted as soon as I walked into the barn.

"You caught me with a mouthful of sunflower seeds *one* time." I laughed at my boss's husband's tease.

"Girl, I didn't know a person could shove so many seeds in their cheek."

I glanced around the barn noting all of the stall doors were open.

"Already turned 'em out," Preston answered my unspoken question. "Maddy's out checking the water troughs are full."

The Robinsons had a beautiful setup—a hundred acres outside of city limits. They'd built their equine center at the front of their property and their house was more than a quarter mile back hidden behind a stand of trees. Not only was Maddy a vet, she was also a champion barrel racer. Preston had never been into rodeo but that didn't mean he wasn't a cowboy hailing straight from

Texas. As he explained, his roots were cattle ranching and with that came being on the back of a horse since he was a toddler. He left the cattle to his brother back in Texas and went into equine breeding. That was how he'd met Maddy. They were a match made in heaven. I couldn't say I'd never seen two people so well suited for each other but only because Ian had come into my life and I'd witnessed firsthand my mother falling in love with her perfect fit. I'd also had the pleasure of meeting Jasper and Emily, Lenox and Lily, Clark and Reagan, Levi and Blake. Those four couples were proof soulmates existed. But if Ian hadn't come into my life and I'd never met the Clarks, McCoys, Walkers, or Lenoxes, Maddy and Preston would've been my number one pick for the perfect couple.

It was strange how much your life could change in a few years. I'd gone from siding with my brother thinking that love wasn't real to seeing it in action. It made me question if Logan and I were wrong when my mom finally met a man who adored and cherished her, making me believe that with the right person love was real. Then Logan fell on his ass in love with Lauren and that sealed the deal for me.

Now I was a believer.

And being a believer, I'd put myself out there for the first time and gotten burned.

Thankfully the burn had been contained but that didn't mean I wasn't all fired up to see what would happen if Echo had another go at me.

It was on that thought, I pawed through my purse for my phone.

Two unread texts.

I ignored the one from my sister Jill asking me if I'd found an apartment and went to Echo's.

My house 8.

I blinked at the words a few times before I reread the text I'd sent him thinking perhaps a word or two or five had autocorrected into something I didn't mean to send.

I thought we could use a timeout after the weddings. Move went well, thank you for asking.

Nope, no autocorrect. All the words were as I meant to send.

Okay, so maybe he sent me a text meant for someone else.

Think that was meant for someone else. Have a good day.

I added a laughing emoji, thought better of it, deleted it, and added a smiley one before I hit send.

His response was immediate.

My house 8 Jaclyn.

Before I could tell him I absolutely wouldn't be at his house at eight Maddy came into the barn.

"Hey, morning, Jackie."

I shoved my phone into my back pocket and turned to face my boss.

"Morning."

I watched her look me over and smile.

"Love your new boots."

She would love my new cowboy boots; she'd suggested them after I'd worn sneakers for the two weeks I'd been working with her.

Note: sneakers and horse shit do not mix.

"You scuffed the bottoms, right?" Preston asked.

79

Scuffed the bottoms?

"Um, I don't know what you mean."

I heard Maddy belt out a laugh and watched Preston smile.

"Those damn things have to be slick as snot."

Well, now that he mentioned it, I did almost bust my ass when I was walking to my car. But on the dirt, they seemed fine.

"What do you mean scuff 'em?"

Preston took a tattered piece of sandpaper Maddy held out and showed it to me.

"Sit down, city girl."

I shuffled back to a hay bale and plopped down.

"Just to say, I didn't grow up in the city. It was more of a small town," I corrected.

"Same thing." He chuckled.

It wasn't but I didn't get the chance to debate this before Preston knelt in front of me, grabbed my right ankle, lifted my boot, and started scuffing the sole with the sandpaper. When he was finished, he did the left.

"Now you won't fall and break your ass."

"Wouldn't want to break my ass," I mumbled. Then louder, I thanked him.

Preston winked before he stood up and strode away.

For a man nearing seventy he still had it going on with that wink.

"Stop flirting with Jackie," Maddy teased. "You ready? We have a long day."

I was totally ready. One of the best parts about working with Dr. Maddy—and there were a lot of good parts—but the absolute best was she genuinely, wholeheartedly loved the animals she worked with and it showed. She didn't rush through her appointments. She was thorough and kind. And since my only experience had been as a small-animal tech she was teaching me everything I needed to know about working with large animals.

"Ready."

It would turn out Maddy wasn't exaggerating; we had a long day, busy day. So busy I never got to respond to Echo. Therefore, when I got home at six I had just enough time to take a shower and throw in a load of wash before I was out the door on my way to his house.

I did this thinking it would be rude to stand him up or cancel at the last minute.

It was an excuse, a lame one at that. But I was holding onto it instead of admitting to myself I was going to execute the plan that Shiloh had come up with.

Fingers crossed Echo Kent didn't chew me up and spit me out.

8

ECHO

I WAS PULLING THE CHICKEN PARM OUT OF THE OVEN, listening to my brother tell me his plans for the weekend for the third time when the knock came. Jaclyn was early, just like I knew she would be.

The woman was a stickler about being punctual. I knew this not because I'd ever been late picking her up from the airport but because I'd heard her comment about how her sister Jill was always late and how rude it was. To which her mother had piped in and added how Jaclyn was the only one out of her kids who was always five minutes early to everything.

She wasn't five minutes early, she was ten.

"Come in!" I shouted.

"Who's there?" Phoenix asked over the speaker.

Fuck.

"Maybe you don't remember so I'll remind you. I never forgot to pick you up from school or feed you or make sure you brushed your teeth before bed or argue with you about taking a shower."

83

"I know you didn't," Phoenix said quickly if not irritated.

"Right, so I don't know why you think I'd forget to pick Griff up from school."

I watched Jaclyn toss her purse on my couch on her way through the living room. I watched as she stumbled to a halt when she noticed the framed pictures on what used to be a blank wall. And finally I watched as her lips hitched up into a grin.

It wasn't like my house was devoid of family pictures. I had plenty but they were all in small frames on the shelves on either side of my TV. The new additions were Shiloh's doing. A large family portrait taken at her and Phoenix's wedding. Shiloh was to my right, her husband Luke next to her. Phoenix on my left, his wife Wren next to him, Griff next to his mother, River and his wife Letty rounded out the family.

Everyone smiling.

My brothers and sisters with their spouses.

It was fucking perfect.

Surrounding the large frame were smaller ones. Me and my brothers. Me and Shiloh. Me and Griff. The women all together. Griff and Phoenix. And of course, Shiloh and Luke and Phoenix and Wren's official wedding portraits.

"I know you won't forget him," Phoenix spat. "But I'm allowed to be nervous leaving the state and not taking Griff."

I fought back the laughter threatening to bubble up, remembering Phoenix was a new dad even if Griff was a teenager.

"Brother, you're going to Charleston for the weekend. It's two and half hours away. I got Griff. How about you focus on taking your wife on her honeymoon and trust I got your boy."

I heard Phoenix sigh but I was still watching Jaclyn, and since my brother was on speaker phone, she'd also heard the sigh, if her shoulders shaking with silent laughter was anything to go by.

"I don't know how you did it," Phoenix grumbled.

That made the snake in my gut coil.

"We were poor, brother. I never went on vacation," I joked.

"That's not what I meant and you know it."

Fuck.

Not only was Phoenix hitting me with shit I didn't want to talk about but Jaclyn's gaze was now laser focused on me.

"You just do it," I told him honestly. "Listen, I've gotta go."

"Who's there?"

That was a hell to the no. I wasn't telling my brother Jaclyn was over.

"Go bug your wife and kid. I'll talk to you tomorrow."

I reached over and ended the call, turned back to Jaclyn, and soaked in the sight of her back in my house.

"I find it interesting that big, bad Phoenix Kent is the one nervous about leaving Griff and not Wren."

I didn't want to talk about my brother or my nephew or my sister-in-law. I wanted to talk about why I'd asked her over.

"You've been back two weeks," I unnecessarily told her.

"Is there a reason why you're ignoring your brother and Lauren?"

The woman didn't blink before she threw attitude.

"I'm sorry, Echo, I must've missed the memo where you were invited to comment on my personal, family matters."

Normally I loved her spark, the one that fired up when she was being sarcastic.

Not so much right now.

"Two invitations to Balls Deep, one to a cookout, and one for dinner before River and Letty left to go back to Idaho. The last one your sisters, mother, and Ian showed up to, but not you."

Again my reminder was gratuitous seeing as she knew the invites she'd turned down but I had a point to prove.

There was at least twenty feet separating us, Jaclyn still in my living room and me in my kitchen. I thought the separation was essential. Jaclyn within touching distance was a detriment to my sanity. Her closeness meant if I didn't latch onto my control, I would touch her and if nothing else the last two times we were in close proximity I had zero control when it came to her. So I could attempt to wrestle my desire and lock down my feelings but need always won.

A restaurant would've been a better choice for this conversation.

Or I should've called her—not that she'd answered one of the many times I'd tried.

So dinner at my house. Tempting fate was the avenue I decided.

But now that she was closing the distance between us, I

realized her in my house didn't leave me at a disadvantage —it meant I was well and truly fucked.

"Cut the shit," she said as she passed me on her way to the fridge. "The question you want to ask is why I'm ignoring you."

Jaclyn helped herself to an Angry Orchard, went straight to the drawer where the bottle opener was, popped the top, tossed the opener back in, and shut the drawer. Throughout all of that I kept silent, mainly because it hit me that other than family no one had ever helped themselves to anything in my house. No one other than Jaclyn had spent enough time in my kitchen to know where I kept anything. No one but Jaclyn had ever changed my sheets or washed a load of towels or cooked or cleaned my kitchen.

Just her.

Why months later the knowledge was dawning on me I had no clue. It wasn't like while it was happening I didn't see it, but I'd missed the enormity of it.

"You don't have to hide behind Logan," she continued. "Or make up excuses if you want to ask me something."

Hide behind Logan?

What the fuck?

"It wasn't me who invited you. It was him."

Jaclyn being Jaclyn had no problem calling me out.

"Right, but see, I know you're smart enough to suss out the situation and figure out I turned down those invitations from my brother because I didn't want to see you."

For the most part when she wasn't dodging me Jaclyn was direct and to the point—one of the many things I appreciated about her. Also, the reason I'd ended our relationship. She hadn't hidden the fact she'd slid from a causal sexual relationship to wanting more. It was the *more* I was incapable of giving her.

"You had no problem seeing me at the weddings."

It was Jaclyn who smirked.

"No, Echo, I had no problem fucking you at the weddings. That doesn't mean I wanted to hang out with you."

I took that blow even though I knew it was bullshit, leaned my ass against the edge of the counter, and tried something else.

"What were you and Sunny talking about at her reception?"

I saw her flinch before she recovered and remembered to blank her expression.

"We talked about a lot of things," she evaded.

"I bet you did. But I'm specifically asking about when the two of you were huddled by the bar. As you said, I'm smart enough to know when my sister's plotting."

Jaclyn's gaze went to the chicken parm cooling on the stovetop. With her eyes diverted she mumbled, "I didn't say you weren't smart enough to know—"

I knew where she was going with her correction so I cut her off.

"Are we really gonna stand here and play word games?"

Not taking her eyes off dinner she shrugged. What she didn't do was answer.

"This shit you're playing at isn't you."

That got me back her eyes.

"How would you know?" she snapped. "You don't know me."

The fuck I didn't.

"I know you, Jaclyn. And the shit you pulled a few weeks ago was just that—total bullshit. We were never about a quick, meaningless fuck. Yet, that's what you made it. You sucked me off and left, then the second night, you took your orgasm and walked out the door while my dick was still wet."

I saw her cringe, but even if I hadn't, I still would've known her next statement was more bullshit.

"Sorry, I didn't know I was supposed to stick around for cleanup. Or did you want to cuddle?"

She tried to pull off smug but failed miserably. I wasn't so stupid I didn't catch her game the first night. So the second night when she was waiting for me in front of my hotel door I was prepared for the fuck-and-run and that was exactly what she'd done. But unlike the first night, the second I'd purposely stayed in bed and watched her fine ass waltz out the door when we were done.

"So this is the new game?" I needlessly asked. "You pretending that this is who we are? Did you and my sister come up with this?"

That thought made my stomach churn. But it was a real possibility Sunny had suggested such a thing. She tended to blur the lines of boundaries when she was scheming.

Thankfully Jaclyn's face scrunched up in disgust.

"Um, no. Your sister absolutely didn't suggest I—"

I held my hand up, not wanting her to finish.

I took a moment to take her in. She looked like my Jaclyn, all long legs and curves. Hair pulled up like she usually wore it when she'd be relaxing at home. A pretty face that bordered on sweet and innocent when I knew she was anything but. Long lashes that needed no artificial help showcasing her beautiful eyes. Full lips that I knew from experience could gently glide and tease or be firm and demanding. All of her, top-to-toe stunning.

But the woman in front of me wasn't the woman I knew.

She was someone altogether different.

It was time to call her out and see how far she was willing to go.

"This is who we were to you?"

Her one-arm shrug told me more than she wanted to reveal.

"You can't even utter the lie, can you?" I taunted.

That earned me narrowed eyes.

"Yes, Echo, that's who we were."

"Say it then," I demanded.

Once again I lost her eyes when they scanned my kitchen looking for something other than me to focus on.

I knew she was stalling when she took a slug of her disgusting, apple-flavored beer. She further delayed when she set it on the counter and rubbed her hands together.

"Right," I muttered. "Dinner's ready. Grab the plates. I got the silverware."

Then she waited until my back was to her before she lied.

"That's all we were," she declared. "It was good so when I got my chance at the weddings for more, I took it."

I craned my neck and caught her staring at the floor.

"It wasn't good," I denied and went to correct her understatement. "It was fucking fantastic. But that's not what I want you to say and you know it. I want you to tell me that it was meaningless."

Jaclyn's gaze lifted to mine. She pushed her shoulders back and opened her mouth but no words came out.

"That's what I thought."

I went back to pulling out the cutlery when she mumbled, "You're a dick."

"Maybe, but I'm not an asshole who orders a woman to her knees to suck me off then expects her to wipe my come off her lips and motor. Yet, that's who you made me. I'm also not an asshole who fucks a woman then kicks her out of bed and out of my hotel room while my come drips down her thigh. Yet, you did that to me, too. So I gotta know, Jackie, you want the asshole who will bend you over my island, fuck you breathless, then send you on your way? Or do you want to stop this bullshit and maybe we can repair the damage we've created and move this to something friendly?"

It took a moment for her to answer and when she did, I had to strain to hear her.

"Why can't I have both?"

Why did hearing her ask that make me want to punch a wall when that was the very arrangement we'd had before I'd ended things, with the only variation being she didn't leave after we fucked? We were friends, nothing more. Which made me wonder—if she'd lived in the same state when we had our thing if I would've allowed her to spend the night or change my sheets or wash a load of towels or cook in my kitchen.

I knew the answer to that.

I was in way too deep with her.

It was a damn good thing she couldn't see my face screw up into a scowl when I asked, "That's what you want? An invite over to get off, then you roll off and out?"

"Not so unlike what we had before," she rightly noted. "But I agree we need to do some damage control and get to a place where I can go out with my friends instead of avoiding everyone because I'm too afraid to see you."

I tossed the forks on the counter and turned back around.

"*Afraid* to see me?"

"That's not...I didn't mean afraid like scared," she corrected. "I just meant I don't want to avoid going out so I won't run into you."

I didn't know what to make of that. What I did know was I didn't want to be the cause of her not seeing her friends.

"Let's eat, Jaclyn, then we'll finish talking."

With a nod she handed me a plate.

Again, it didn't escape my notice she knew her way around my kitchen.

And now I was fighting for a different kind of control—I'd managed to keep my hands to myself and my mouth off hers but I could barely shove aside how good it felt having her home. How right it felt having her back and how much I'd missed her.

9

JACLYN

I was going to throw up Echo's delicious chicken parm all over his spotless floor.

This was what I got for listening to Lauren and Shiloh —an upset stomach and frazzled nerves.

I thought I could pull off blasé and act all badass cool. As it turned out I couldn't act nonchalant, never mind badass. Hell, I couldn't even lie with a straight face, and if Echo had continued to push me I would've broken down and told him the truth, including the part where both nights after I left his room I had to go into the hotel bathroom for more than clean up.

The little tidbit about using no-string sex came from Lauren. Much to my chagrin she'd told me the story about how she and my brother first hooked up, including the part where she'd been royally fucked over by an ex (the same one who had later kidnapped and drugged her) and was not looking for more than a hookup, which worked for my brother. Approximately three minutes into this arrangement my brother decided he didn't like hearing Lauren agree with him that love didn't exist and so began their struggle. This was mostly my brother trying to convince Lauren to take a chance on him. She thought that same game would work with Echo. Turns out, Echo was smarter than my brother or I'd done the sex part wrong. So that was now scratched off the list.

Shiloh's plan to win Echo was somewhat easier though it would cause the most pain if I failed. Luke won her by not giving up. It sounded easy enough but I was already in love with Echo, so sticking around and not leaving him even when he pushed me away sounded worse than attempting a third go at meaningless sex. Maybe meaningless wasn't the right word, more like a wham-bam-thank-you-ma'am fuck. It had sucked rolling out of bed and pretending I didn't want to stay. But not giving up sounded hard, which was also pretty much the advice Logan had given me.

"You want another fake beer?" Echo asked as he pushed back from the table.

I looked up from my plate, prepared to hassle him for making fun of my Angry Orchard but my gripe died a fast death when I saw him smiling at me.

Damn, he had a great smile—when it was real and not the fake one he'd put on when I first met him. Of course I hadn't known it was fake until the second time I'd flown to Georgia to visit him and I was teasing him about how neat and organized his linen closet was. I mean, it was unnatural for a single man (not in the military undergoing inspection) to have every towel folded and lined up perfectly. And don't get me started on his sheets and how precisely the fitted sheet was folded.

"No thanks, I'm driving."

I thought I saw disappointment flash in his eyes but it could've been wishful thinking.

Throughout dinner he'd asked me about my job and my living situation but now that those two safe topics were exhausted, I was afraid he was going to circle back to our conversation in the kitchen. I wasn't ready to go back there, especially because I'd stupidly asked why I couldn't have sex and friendship. I knew the rejection was coming and I wasn't prepared. Not when according to Shiloh that was one of the hurdles he was going to throw at me that I'd have to ignore.

"So, Phoenix and Wren are going up to Charleston and you're on uncle duty?" I asked as Echo was returning to the table with a fresh beer for himself and a bottle of water for me.

He sat back down across from me, rested his forearms on the table and clasped his hands together. Not an unusual position for Echo, but the way he was staring at me like he'd suddenly turned into Officer Kent was strange.

"Yeah," he finally answered. "They're leaving Friday morning after they drop Griff off at school and they'll be gone until Sunday night."

Charleston sounded like a perfect weekend getaway so I wasn't sure why Echo looked like he was upset.

"Do you not want them to go?"

"No, I want them to go for more than a weekend."

Okay, now I was really confused.

"Maybe Wren couldn't get the time off work. She's essentially working two jobs now that she's helping with Women's Inc."

"Yeah, maybe."

Echo's grumbled answer was unconvincing.

This was unchartered territory and I didn't know if I was supposed to push and risk him shutting down—thus shutting me out—or leave it alone.

Thankfully I didn't have to make that decision when he weirdly asked, "When you were a kid did you ever go on vacations?"

As strange as his question was, I didn't have to think about my answer.

"Yeah. Every year Mom would take us up to Huron Beach. Sometimes it would be a weekend trip, other times we'd stay there a week. Though we didn't start staying longer until..." I paused when the truth slammed into me.

"Until when?"

"Until Logan was older."

That he was old enough to have a job and he could contribute to the household finances or, say, help pay for a weeklong vacation at the beach. Holy shit, why hadn't I put two and two together earlier? I knew Logan had helped pay for a lot of things, not because it was told to us girls but because I'd heard my mom and Logan talking. I knew Jill had heard, too. One day she'd be all hip on taking guitar lessons then suddenly she'd change her mind—and she changed her mind after my brother had asked to speak to my mom in private. She knew Logan had told my mom he'd pay for them.

Echo gave me a sad smile that told me I didn't need to explain. Being the oldest and the guardian of his siblings he sadly understood.

It was then I started to understand why Echo looked so

dejected.

"You want Phoenix to go on a *real* vacation?" I posed it as a question but I knew his answer.

I waited until Echo nodded before I continued, "Echo, you're forgetting a vacation isn't a place or a length of time; it's about the people you're with. It's about disconnecting from life and immersing yourself in the people you're with. That's a real vacation and it can be one day, two, a month. It doesn't matter."

"You're right," he quickly agreed.

Too quickly.

"Echo—"

"Are you done with that?" He gestured to my mostly empty plate.

Oh, boy, here we are again. Do I let this slide or take the leap into the scary waters and take a gamble, meaning he could crush me if he told me to mind my business?

"Please talk to me."

"I am talking to you."

I summoned up my courage, held his stormy blue eyes, and took a chance.

"You're doing what you always do, you ask me questions but tell me nothing. Our conversations are one sided. That's me giving and you closing down. That's not a friendship or even friendly. It's you not trusting me even though I've proven I trust you. And I have to say, Echo, it doesn't feel all that great."

With that I stood and reached across the table to grab his empty plate then placed mine on top of it and started for the kitchen.

"You cooked. I clean," I reminded him.

That was our deal when I came to visit him. A rule I had to make after the first weekend I spent with him where he allowed me to do nothing. I was all for being spoiled and taken care of but I was also taught at a very young age to help around the house. This wasn't because my mother was a single mom working full time to feed her family. It also wasn't because I had a brother who, as soon as he could, got a part-time job to help his mother, so housework became all hands on deck. The lesson was about teamwork and that was what family was about—everyone working together, making quick work of the chores so we could spend time together. Showing our mom we appreciated her by helping where we could. My sisters and I started doing Logan's laundry when he took a job so he knew we understood his sacrifice. Not that my big brother appreciated his little sisters going through his room to gather his clothes, but he let us do it because he knew it was the only thing we could do for him.

I was at the sink rinsing the dishes when Echo came in. And by that I meant he came in and leaned his hip against the counter, his proximity so close he was almost pressed up against my side.

"I never got to take them on a vacation, not even for a weekend," he told me. "Not even when River started working to help pay the bills. I was struggling to pay rent and save to move us out of that shithole my father called a house while at the same time struggling to stay in college and put money aside for River's education. There were no vacations. No escaping the nightmare our parents had created."

My heart painfully pounded in my chest. Not because

of what he'd gone through, the struggles he faced, but because he didn't see all the good he'd given his family. Logan was right, Echo saw his accomplishments as failures.

That pissed me off.

I angrily shoved the plates in the dishwasher, closed the door, and turned to face him.

"Did you move out of that shithole?"

It took a moment before he answered.

"Yeah, after my dad went down, it took another year of saving but we moved."

"And did you finish college?"

He didn't answer but I knew he had.

"What about River? Did you get him through college?"

Again, no answer but again I knew he had.

"And Phoenix and Shiloh?"

"River helped pay for Phoenix and we all pitched in for Sunny," he said like it was a mortal sin his siblings had helped with each other's education.

"That's what family does, Echo. That's what you taught them. Family sticks together. Family helps family. Family steps up. Yet you seem to think because you created men who are loyal, loving, and strong you somehow failed. Then there's Shiloh, and I have to say as a little sister who was loved so deeply by my big brother, knowing all he gave me I can tell you with absolute authority what you, River, and Phoenix gave her, the safety and love and guidance made her into the strong, loyal, loving woman she is. But you three gave her something else, something that little girls need more than anything, and you led that charge, Echo. You three showed her how she is to be loved. You three showed her by example to never accept anything but absolute, unwavering, unconditional love because that was what you gave her. So fuck vacations, Echo. So fucking what you didn't take them to Disneyland, you gave them everything that's important and it's time you open your eyes and *see* the men and woman you raised. It's time you open your eyes and *see* they are who they are because of you and you alone."

When I was done, Echo looked pissed.

Oh, well, so be it.

He could chew on that for a while and stew. In the meantime I wasn't sticking around to find out if he was going to rebuke my efforts.

With the last of my courage, I placed my hand on his chest, rolled up on my tiptoes, and kissed his cheek.

Before I rolled back down, I whispered, "You're the second-best man I know, Echo. And it breaks my heart you don't see the man I see."

I was back flat on my feet, but before I could step away one of Echo's hands went to the back of my neck and the other went to my hand, effectively trapping me close. He lowered his head and kissed me.

Not one of his hot and heavy, out-of-control kisses that always led to fabulous wild sex. This one was different. It started with a slow brush of his lips against mine. A gentle trace of my bottom lip before I opened and his tongue slid in and glided with mine. He didn't fist my hair like he normally did but his hand did gently move until he was cupping my cheek. I couldn't recall him ever kissing me so sweetly. It was tender and soft and leisurely. Not the kind of kiss you give the woman you're fucking but the kind you'd give a lover.

Echo broke the kiss. My eyes came open. I was still in a daze but I couldn't miss the emotion swirling in his gemstone eyes.

"You're right," he quietly admitted. "I don't see them as they are now. I see them dirty, unfed, and scared. That's what I see when I close my eyes at night. I dream of the filth, the fear of being evicted or the power being turned off. Or worse—them going to bed hungry."

That pounding in my chest came back ten-fold, the beat so powerful I was surprised my body wasn't rocking with it. His agony surrounded us, covered us with the pain of his past that was very much still present.

I didn't know what to say. Hell, I didn't know *if* there was anything to say.

So I settled on the only thing that came to mind.

"But not you," I whispered.

"Not me?"

"You dream of them. You remember them dirty, hungry, and scared but not you being the same."

The shutters slammed close.

Damn.

I went too far.

Rejection was a bitch.

I stepped away, which meant Echo's hands fell to his sides, but my hand went back to his chest and covered his heart.

"Thank you for trusting me."

With that, even though I hadn't finished cleaning the kitchen I moved to the living room, grabbed my purse, and was at the front door when Echo called my name.

I paused with my hand on the knob and looked back to

see him standing in the middle of the room with his gigantic arms crossed over his wide chest, thick, tree trunk legs planted shoulder width apart, scowling.

"No more avoiding me," he demanded.

Oh, boy, here we go.

"Right."

"I'm serious, Jaclyn, no more dodging my calls and texts."

He looked serious.

That also meant he was planning on calling and texting.

"Okay," I agreed.

His eyes sharpened and he rapped out, "Okay."

I ended the conversation with, "See you around, Echo."

He said nothing else as I walked out the door.

But I did see him standing in his front window watching me get into my car at the curb.

When I got home and settled for bed I unlocked my phone in preparation to mindlessly scroll silly IG reels when I saw a text from Echo.

Let me know when you're home.

I shot back a message.

You could use the word 'please'.

His response was immediate.

You're home.

Ugh.

I'd closed the app but opened it back up to tell him one last thing.

Thanks for dinner.

I hit send then remembered something else.

And thanks for stocking my 'fake' beer.

After I sent that one, I thought of one more thing.

Thanks for remembering chicken parm's my favorite.

I hit send, then immediately regretted sending it and was going to unsend when Echo's reply came through.

You done?

God, it was embarrassing how lame I was.

Yes. Night.

A few moments passed. Long enough for me to open IG and start scrolling when a text alert flashed at the top of my screen.

I went back to the thread.

I remember all your favorites.

A warm squishy feeling came over me. Which was something I'd never felt when it came to Echo. He'd made me feel a plethora of ways: hot, turned on, sexy, powerful, smart, beautiful. But never had he given me butterflies from being sweet.

Another text.

I remember how you taste.

Another.

How you feel.

Another.

The whimpers you make when you're taking my cock.

Another.

How beautiful you look first thing in the morning.

Another.

I remember that you like shit beer and you like teasing about it so you can give me shit back. And my chicken parm isn't your favorite, my homemade pizza is.

Okay, he was correct. His chicken parm was almost as good as his homemade pizza crust.

Haven't forgotten anything about you.

The warmth in my belly intensified and I snuggled down under my covers wishing I hadn't left his house in such a hurry and he was telling me all of this in person.

I tried to forget everything so I could move on and give you what you needed when you moved here.

Well, that last text erased all the warm and fuzzy feelings and sent worry up my spine.

But you're unforgettable, Jaclyn. Unforgettable in a way that means there's no getting you out from under my skin. If you want out, you're gonna have to put in the work.

He sent that and I reread it five times thinking his phone must've autocorrected and he'd edit the text any second.

But an edit didn't appear.

This did...

Sucks, baby, but I think you get I'm fucked up. You were smart to avoid me but part of me being fucked up is I'm not gonna let you. I tried to let you go once and I failed. Now it's up to you.

To that I had a replay.

Why do you think you're fucked up?

What Lester left in me is different than what he gave them.

Lester Kent, the cop-killing asshole. The man was lucky he was in prison or I was pretty sure Luke would've killed him for what he did to Shiloh. And joining Luke would be Letty, Wren, and me.

I didn't want to ask but I had to know.

What'd he leave you?

I held my breath while I waited for Echo's response, not

knowing that what was to come would leave me chilled to the bone.

Hollow.

One word.

Yet it said everything.

Echo Kent was empty.

Starving for the affection he'd been denied as a boy.

A man who had given everything, received that back from his siblings yet still felt hollow.

I stared at my phone, making a decision.

I'm not going anywhere. The harder you push me away the harder I'm fighting to stay.

We'll see.

Yeah, we would.

Bet.

We'll see.

You've met your match, Echo.

After that nothing.

I tossed my phone on the mattress, no longer interested in mindless scrolling.

I had a new plan to hatch because I knew for certain I would walk through hot coals if it meant giving Echo what he needed. I'd go through hell, mend my heart back together time and time again if it meant in the process I was stitching him up.

That night I dreamed of a dirty little boy going hungry to make sure his brothers and sister ate. I dreamed of a boy who was never a boy but instead was born to be a hero.

10

ECHO

Contrary to what I'd told Phoenix the other night, I was a little worried I'd forget to pick Griff up from school. I had two alarms set on my phone—a ten-minute warning and a get-your-ass-on-the-road alert. Yet I still couldn't stop checking my watch so I knew I was running five minutes late when I walked into Triple Canopy.

Jaclyn would give me shit about being rude.

Lauren, however, smiled at me from behind her desk and waved toward the hall.

"Hey, Echo. Jason and Tucker are waiting for you in the conference room."

"Thanks, Laurie."

The next smile she gave me scared the shit out of me. It reeked of plotting and conspiracy.

"You're bringing Griff over to Chelsea and Matt's later, right?"

Chelsea boarded Griff's rescue horse Dasher, so I was taking the kid there after school so he could do whatever one does with a horse. Phoenix told me to plan on an hour so I was planning on this excursion taking at least two.

"After school," I confirmed.

"Then you're staying for the party."

I wasn't sure if that was a question or not but I did know she'd stated it slowly like I was dense. Which apparently, I was since I'd forgotten all about the welcome home party I'd been invited to.

"I'll see if Griff's up to it," I told her noncommittally.

"Jackie's gonna be there," she announced, and there was the reason she was smiling.

I mentally added a trip to Starbucks to jack Griff up on caffeine and sugar so he'd be up for a late-night party.

Uncle of the year.

"Right. I'll check with Griff after I pick him up," I semi-repeated.

I watched Laurie's smile fade. I felt like an asshole but the women liked to gossip. If I gave her even the barest hint I was jonesing to see Jaclyn that shit would spread like wildfire. And I was jonesing like a junkie needing a fix. I hadn't seen her since she'd come over on Monday. With her working days and me having to pull double shifts all week I hadn't even had time to call her. The only form of communication had been a handful of texts.

When the phone on Laurie's desk rang, I took that as my leave.

"See ya tonight," she called out before she picked up the phone.

Indeed, she would. Not that I would've confirmed it.

I heard the laughter before I hit the door to the conference room and it continued after I ducked inside.

Tucker, Jason, and surprisingly Jasper were sitting around the table all smiling.

"What's funny?" I asked.

All eyes came to me but it was only Tucker who pushed back from the table.

"I was just telling Jason and Jasper about my last assignment up in Idaho."

Tucker stopped in front of me, his hand extended. As soon as I reached for it he yanked me into a one-armed hug.

"Good to see you," he continued.

"You, too."

We broke apart and I asked, "Idaho? I thought you said you were in Cali."

"Yeah, small world. Case took me up to Coeur d'Alene. I heard River moved out there. I didn't see him, but I did meet some people he knows."

Before I had a chance to ask who he'd met I heard Chelsea's shocked, "Tim?"

Tucker stiffened, shifted to the side to face the door, and at the same time Jason and Jasper both stood.

Matt was standing next to his new wife, assessing the room. That was Matt—quick to calculate and measure his surroundings, slow to react.

Surprisingly, it was Tucker not Jason who spoke up. "Actually, Chelsea, my name's Tucker Mitchell." When he was done with the introduction he went to Matt. "Thanks for taking the time to meet with me."

"No problem," Matt returned and extended his hand.

Tucker relaxed and took the offering. When the men broke apart Tucker went on. "I asked Jason and Echo to set this up so we could formally meet before my case starts."

"Wait, your name's not Tim, it's Tucker?" Chelsea asked.

"Why don't we sit before we start with the explanations," Jason offered. "Matt, Chels, welcome home and congratulations."

Jason made his way around the table and Jasper followed. Once hugs and more well wishes were exchanged Matt pulled back a chair for his wife.

Chelsea looked at the chair then at Matt. "What's happening?"

"My guess is Tucker's going to explain to you that he was undercover and using a fake name when you met him," Matt started. "Then he's gonna make sure there are no hard feelings that he held you hostage while I was planning a rescue mission. During that, there's gonna be a lot of talk about how it was his job to scare the fuck out of you and keep you locked in a room."

"Before I sit, I want to remind you that when the bullets started flying, Tim...I mean Tucker did actually save me. He took me and hid me and stood guard until you could get to me."

Matt's eyes glittered when he looked back at his wife.

"But he did scare the fuck out of you."

"Well... yeah...but it *was* his job, Matthew. We should be focusing on the part where he kept me safe. And he did, he *carried* me to safety."

Matt pulled the chair out farther, a nonverbal cue for Chelsea to sit. Once he had her situated Matt's gaze went around the room and landed on me.

"I take it you know Tucker."

"We met on a case we worked together," I confirmed.

"We became friends through that. Now he's a close friend and has been for years."

"What case are you working on now?" Matt inquired.

"Let's get the other shit out of the way first," Jason suggested.

"I'm sorry I frightened you." That was Tucker to Chelsea. "I hope you understand I was never going to hurt you. And that was true before I knew you had ties to Matt. Your presence was an unforeseen complication. Hostages were not Zanetti's style. Up until that point he'd been careful with containment. The DEA was working on a way to get you out of there when Matt and his team came in."

"Yeah, and what was your plan?" Matt seethed.

Unfazed Tucker shrugged.

"Not as effective as yours," he admitted. "And the body count would've been lower. But what I can guarantee is Chelsea would've been safe even if that meant I had to blow the operation."

"There's no need to apologize. I get it." Chelsea looked at Matt. "You do, too, right?"

"Right," Matt gritted out.

I understood Matt's plight. I would be right where he was if someone kidnapped Jaclyn and held her hostage. Undercover DEA agent or not there'd be hell to pay. Not that Tucker did the actual kidnapping part but he had played his part as captor.

"So, Tim's your undercover name?" Chelsea smiled.

"No, T. I. M. are my initials. An old nickname from when I was a kid."

"What's the I stand for?"

"Isaac," Tucker surprisingly answered.

"Tucker Isaac Mitchell." Chels put his name together.

"Chelsea, you good?" Jason asked.

"Um...yeah, why wouldn't I be?"

Matt leaned back in his chair and with a resigned sigh he suggested, "Baby, why don't you go visit with Lauren for a few minutes so I can wrap this up and we can go home."

It was amusing how Matt thought he was going to get off that easily.

"I will if you promise me you're gonna be reasonable."

"I'm always reasonable."

"*Right*," she drawled disbelievingly and pushed back from the table. "Tucker, it was nice seeing you again and meeting you officially. I think I said it that day but I was a little out of sorts so I don't remember, but just in case I didn't, thank you for keeping me safe. I was scared and when the lights went out, I didn't know what to do. I probably would've done the wrong thing and gotten myself hurt, or worse, killed. *You* didn't let that happen. You have my gratitude and Matt's, too."

With that successful reminder to her husband, she left the conference room.

As soon as the door clicked closed behind her Matt launched in, "What case?"

"Matt—" Jason started but didn't finish.

"She's right." Matt spat the words like they tasted foul. "And bottom line is my sister orchestrated that. My own family had my woman taken. I'm still pissed as shit. I can't forget what happened. I can't forget those hours not knowing where she was, not knowing if she was being hurt or if I'd lost her forever. I won't ever get over that." Matt paused to look at Tucker. "But the part you played in that, she's right, you did protect her the best you could without blowing your cover. I get it. Doesn't mean I like it. But I fucking get it. Now, I'm still on Island Time. I'd like to get home and sleep for another five hours before my house is full of people."

Shit. Griff.

I glanced at my watch. Seeing I still had time, I eyed the folder in front of Tucker.

"If this is going to be a problem for you, we'll take a pass," Jason said.

Triple Canopy bowing out would fucking suck. It wouldn't surprise me, but it would leave us scrambling for support.

"A pass?" Matt asked incredulously.

"If you're not comfortable working with Tucker, if seeing him is going to bring bad shit up for you, this dies here. Period," Jasper spoke up.

Now I understood why Jasper Walker was present when he was retired and only came in to consult when his expertise was necessary. From what I knew of the man his field of military tactics and knowledge was wide and varied. However, Jasper wasn't there to lend his skills to mission planning; he was there to make sure that Matt Kessler knew he was family, and as such Triple Canopy's loyalty was to him—not the mission. And there was no better man to remind Matt he was valued than Jasper.

"My opinion—"

"Matters," Jasper cut off Matt. "In this situation, your opinion is the only one that matters."

There was a lot of talk about the bond of the uniform— whether that be law enforcement, fire and rescue, military.

Brothers and sisters in arms. That talk was shrouded in truth. But that bond was limited to men and women who risk their lives together. At some point there was a disconnect the higher you went up the chain of command. The grunts on the street lived and breathed protection. The suits were about the politics behind their decisions. There was no loyalty to the men and women strapping on the vests. Except at Triple Canopy. The opposite was true with these men. The higher up you went in their chain, the more protection you find.

It was not only damn-right refreshing, it was the way it should be across all branches of first responders.

"Then my opinion is I'm a man who knows how to separate my personal life from my professional one."

"That's not how this works," Jasper returned.

Fuck. This could go on all day.

I checked my watch again. There was still time to go over the case but my time was dwindling.

Matt's gaze sliced to Tucker.

"You had her two days," Matt started. "She never said and I checked her over and saw no marks but I have to know—did you put your hands on my woman?"

"Yes."

The room went electric, sparking with an angry current emanating from Matt and bouncing off the walls until it filled the space.

"The last day, she wouldn't come down for dinner," Tucker explained. "I wanted her to eat then get her back to the safety of her room as quickly as possible. She landed a left hook to my face. I couldn't take the chance one of Zanetti's men would either hear her yelling at me or see she'd marked me. I only had so much control over his men, one of them catching her hitting me would've been catastrophic. I pinned her to the wall, hands over her head, and trapped her legs so she couldn't kick me. I can't say I was gentle; she was kicking the fuck out of me. But I can say I only used enough force to get her to stop."

"Christ," Matt bit out and scrubbed his hands over his face. "That all?"

"Other than me holding her arm while I escorted her to and from her room. Your woman was unpredictable. She might've been scared but she was going to risk her life to get free so you didn't get hurt."

That sounded like Chelsea.

Matt's gaze stayed steady on Tucker and I was thinking Chelsea wasn't the only one who was unpredictable. Matt's normally steady demeanor was nowhere to be seen.

It took a few moments before Matt nodded and looked back at Jasper.

"What's the case?"

I had to hand it to Matt; I wasn't sure if I could be the bigger man in a situation like this. Tucker was a close friend of mine. I knew he'd never put his hands on a woman in anger, and when he said he didn't use more force than needed to subdue Chelsea what he really meant was he was as gentle as he could be while at the same time protecting her. But Matt didn't know Tucker the way I did and he was still going to set aside his anger.

"Jimmy Lone," Jason announced. "With the help of local law enforcement, the DEA made an arrest that led to his drug trafficking conviction. He made parole and was released last week."

"That's the case where you two met?" Matt asked.

"Yeah, Tucker was undercover in Lone's organization. Obviously his cover's blown, so he's here to provide information and support. Word is Jimmy's crew, the Lonesomes, are ready to hit the streets."

"You didn't take out the whole crew?"

Tucker pushed the folder across the table to Matt.

"We had to cut the operation before we had what we needed on the crew," Tucker explained. "We were able to take down a few low-level street soldiers and one of his lieutenants but the rest of his crew has been laying low."

Matt opened the folder and asked, "If the boss was in prison why didn't they move on or better, take over his territory?"

"Because of her," I told Matt when he narrowed his eyes on a glossy eight-by-ten picture of an old woman who had fled back to her home country before we could arrest her. "Jimmy was running Honduran cocaine. That woman there is Herlinda Gomez of the Flores-Gomez drug family. They're not the biggest cartel but they still move thousands of kilos through Guatemala, through Mexico, and into the US. Jimmy wasn't the boss, she is."

"Is?" Matt pressed.

"Herlinda went back to Chinda where she's untouchable. She reorganized, taking Jimmy's crew and splitting them up to new markets. Now that he's out, she's sending them back to Georgia with new product."

"Fentanyl," Matt surmised.

"Fentanyl, cocaine, meth, pills, Herlinda is a one-stop shop for illicit narcotics."

Matt closed the file, sat back, and glanced around the table.

"What am I missing? Why would the head of a drug cartel be loyal to an American dipshit who wasn't smart enough not to get busted distributing her product? She has his crew, it sounds to me like she doesn't need Jimmy."

"Two reasons," Jason rejoined. "When she came and expanded her market to Georgia, Alabama, and Mississippi she needed muscle. That was Jimmy. During his time as her guard, he saved her life. So he was promoted. Years later a deal went bad, she called in Jimmy to handle that situation and unfortunately, he took a bullet for her then, too. That's twice he took the hit for her. She's loyal to him the way you are to Carter. That's to say unshakable. She'll give him whatever he wants."

Matt looked at me and I fought the need to check the time.

Thankfully I had nothing to add to the conversation so a dip of my chin was all that was needed for Matt to ask his next question.

"Why am I specifically here? Beyond needing to clear the air with Tucker, am I acting as his guard? I'm not ground planning, that's Carter and Brady. I'm the man behind the glass and close cover."

Now that that particular question had been asked it was time to excuse myself from the conversation.

Tucker pushed his chair back at the same time I did mine.

As sworn law enforcement officers we could not be privy to any further information.

I watched as Matt's eyes bounced back and forth

between me and Tucker and since I was watching I saw the moment realization hit.

"We'll see ourselves out," I told the room.

"Appreciate the time," Tucker added. "If you need anything else from me, Matt, Jason has my number. You call and I'm wherever you need me to be—that includes not being seen if that's what you need. We need TC's help on this, but Jasper's right, not if it's at the expense of your peace."

Matt started to say something but Tucker spoke over him. "I get it. Every man in this room gets it. Job or not, I put my hands on your woman. I purposely scared her. I had my reasons. I also know those reasons don't mean shit to you and they wouldn't to me if I was in your place. Wish I could tell you I was sorry or I regretted what I did but I don't because her being scared then means today she's at your side smiling and happy."

When Tucker was done with Matt he turned to Jason. "Good to catch up."

Then with a nod to Jasper I followed Tucker out.

We were almost out the front door of the building when Chelsea called out, "Tucker."

At the same time my ten-minute alarm chimed.

Fucking shit, fuck.

I pulled out my phone to silence the sound so I missed whatever silently passed between Tucker and Chels.

But I didn't miss Chelsea's demand posed as a question. "See you tonight, Echo?"

Fuck me.

"You will, darlin'."

I didn't bother looking back at the women. I didn't have

to, to know that both of them were smiling and at least one had her phone out to initiate the gossip tree.

"I think you should take lead," Tucker said as we walked across the parking lot.

"Give him time."

"It's not him."

I rocked to a halt and asked, "Chels?"

"All I can see when I look at her is the fear. I had that woman for two days and the whole time she was fucking terrified. I thought seeing her with Matt safe and smiling would erase what I did to her but it hit different. All it did was drive home that I terrorized an innocent woman."

Jesus fuck.

If only Matt could see this side of Tucker. Know this part of the DEA agent. Understand the depth of commitment to protect the innocent and the guilt this man felt. No way would he be able to harbor anger.

"Then I take lead until you're ready to step in," I offered. "But my suggestion is, don't avoid her or Matt. What you did to her saved her life. I get you don't know Chelsea all that well, but she is not some shrinking violet, the woman is as mouthy as she is badass. If you hadn't kept her in check, she would've said the wrong thing to the wrong person and they wouldn't've nicely pinned her to the wall, they would've violated her and hurt her in ways Matt couldn't have fixed. Think on that, Tucker. Two days of fear for a lifetime of happiness. Seems to me like a fair trade."

"Maybe," he grumbled then quickly changed topics. "When am I gonna meet your new woman?"

I felt the muscle in my cheek tic.

Fucking shit, one of my siblings had a big mouth.

"Sunny?" I guessed.

"Yeah. I ran into her at the six-ten when I stopped to see what Gordy was up to."

J.D. "Gordy" Gordon was on Sunny's SWAT team. Damn good man who watched out for my sister.

"He tell you he's thinking of leaving SWAT?" I asked, hoping my change of subject would stick.

"Yeah, said he was looking into retirement."

"Don't blame him, he's done twenty-two years."

"He's only a few years older than you, old man. You're coming up on your twenty."

I flipped my friend the bird and shoved his too-close-to-home comment out of my mind. I was coming up on forty, Jaclyn hadn't made it to thirty. An age gap I wasn't particularly comfortable with.

"So, this woman," Tucker circled back. "When am I going to meet her?"

"You're not."

"But there's a woman to meet?"

"There's..." I stopped myself short of saying no one. Jaclyn wasn't a no one, she was... everything, special, an obsession I couldn't shake, all of the above...

"A woman," Tucker finished. "But I'm not gonna meet her."

"Yeah."

"But Sunny has," he continued.

"It's complicated. She's the sister of one of Sunny's husband's teammates."

"That is complicated," he repeated my understatement.

"You have no idea," I grumbled then finished with, "I

have to run and pick up Phoenix's boy from school. We'll catch up next week."

"Echo doing what Echo does best," my friend weirdly declared.

"What?"

"You don't know what to do with yourself unless you're taking care of someone."

The truth of that observation churned in my gut. The years of struggling together as a family, then one by one River, Phoenix, and Sunny went out on their own leaving me with nothing but a hollowed out empty feeling that never fucking went away.

"Trust me, I got plenty to occupy my time," I lied with a smile.

"I do trust you. I just don't believe you." Tucker slapped me on the shoulder and finished with, "But that's for another time, you gotta pick up your nephew."

Thank fuck for Griff.

"We'll get together next week," I reiterated and pulled my key fob out of my pocket.

Tucker gave me a chin lift before he took off to his truck.

As soon as I beeped my locks my second alarm went off.

I silenced the notification and pulled my text thread with Jaclyn.

You going to Matt and Chelsea's tonight?

I hit send and started my car.

It wasn't until I stopped across the street from Griff's school that I read her reply.

Yeah. You?

Hell, yes, I was going to be there.

See you tonight.

She returned a heart and smiling face.

I ignored the weird feeling seeing those emojis made me feel and told myself it had nothing to do with her belonging to a whole different generation from me, and she'd sent them because that was what women did. They sent silly hearts and fruit and eggplants.

I waited for Griff hoping the line at Starbucks wasn't too long. Either that or praying the kid was like Phoenix and had a never-ending supply of energy.

11

JACLYN

"Damn, girl." Chelsea dragged out the damn for a full three seconds when she saw my black eye. "I don't see a hoof print accompanying that shiner. Head-butt?"

She stepped aside letting me pass before she closed the door behind me.

"Yep. I was passing out horse hugs before we left the Peterman Ranch and Rosco snapped his head around and nailed me."

"Been there, done that," she muttered.

I was sure she'd had plenty of black and blue marks from getting bucked off a bull or a bronco seeing as once upon a time not too long ago she was a rodeo star. I just wasn't sure I believed an accomplished horsewoman such as herself would be idiotic enough to get head-butted but it was nice of her not to point out my stupidity.

"Your brother and Lauren are running late," Chelsea continued. "But everyone else is already here."

She started to move away, probably to guide me to the

back patio, but before she could get too far I grabbed her hand.

"You're glowing," I noted.

"Nothing beats an island tan."

That might be true. I'd never spent three weeks in Hawaii or any tropical island so I wouldn't know, but she was correct—her tan was fabulous.

However, that was not what I was talking about.

"No, girl, you...are...*glowing.*"

I didn't know Chelsea all that well. I'd only met her a few times so I felt a little silly but there was something different about her. Very different.

"I'm happy," she said softly.

"You look it," I confirmed.

"Sometimes I look around and can't believe this is my life." She paused and swept her hand around her beautiful living room then went on to clarify, "Not this. We could be living in my old apartment or in a shack and I wouldn't care. It's everything else. It's Addy, Hadley, Laurie, Delaney, Quinn, Liberty, Shiloh, Sawyer, Wren, and now you. It's the family he's given me. After a lifetime of feeling unsafe and really freakin' lonely he's given me peace. So I look around and I'm grateful. But more than anything I'm just happy. So happy I didn't know it was possible to feel this happy."

I hated that Chelsea had been lonely. I knew bits and pieces of her story. Not much but enough to know her brothers were total assholes and the man who raised her was a terrible man.

"Happy for you, sister. And just so you know, you wear it well. Your happiness, that is."

"Thanks."

I dropped her hand and smiled.

"I hope part of this celebration comes with a show-and-tell portion of the evening. I'm dying to see the wedding pictures."

Chelsea's slow smile lit her face.

"It was perfect. Just me and Matt. His mom was there but when we exchanged vows it was just us on the beach at sunset. No pictures, no recording. The promises we made, the vows we took are just ours. But we do have like a thousand pictures of our trip and yes, we're totally sharing those."

That didn't sound perfect—it sounded sublime.

"I love that it was just the two of you."

"Me, too."

With that she jerked her head in the direction of the back of the house.

"Food and drinks are set out on the patio. Oh, and just so you know, Quinn and the twins are in a tiff so if you hear any snide comments ignore them. It's already been a half hour so we have approximately thirty more before they get over it and move on."

I absolutely adored Addy and Hadley and not just because they were identical twins like Jill and me so I could totally relate to their bond. They were just kickass women individually. And Quinn was a lot like my older sister Lucy. Bossy, outspoken, and funny.

"What's the tiff about?" I asked as we walked through the living room.

"Baby showers."

I didn't understand how anyone could argue over baby

showers but I didn't get a chance to ask before I heard a door slam.

"Matt really needs to fix that stupid screen door," Chelsea muttered.

A moment later Echo came into view. I hadn't recovered from taking in the stretch of his tee across his very wide, muscled chest when I heard, "What the fuck?"

The growl was enough to make me take a step back.

I also stopped staring at his chest and looked up to find him scowling—at me.

"What?" I asked.

His scowl deepened, but worse his eyes darkened to two ominous pools of stormy blue.

"Who the fuck did that to your face?"

"I'll just let you two talk." Chelsea laughed as she skirted Echo.

"Rosco!" I matched his tone and volume.

"Rosco who? And why the fuck didn't you call me?"

There was something perversely appealing about Echo's Caveman act. Not that I would admit that to him. But seeing him furious because I'd been injured was wildly attractive.

"Rosco the horse."

I tried and failed to keep my smile in check.

"You think this is funny?" he asked as he stalked to me.

"Kinda," I admitted.

When he got near his hand came up. His gentle cupping of my cheek was a stark contradiction to his irritation. Not that I ever thought he'd touch me in anger but his thumb was featherlight as it brushed the skin under my black eye.

"Did you ice it?"

"On my way over, I did."

He tipped my head back and asked, "This just happened?"

I pinched my lips and nodded, getting the distinct feeling I was about to experience the downside of being on the receiving end of overprotectiveness.

"Fuck, Jaclyn, did you go to the ER? You could have a concussion."

Yep, I was right.

"I don't have a concussion. I have a bruised face."

"Your eye shouldn't be—"

"I'm fine," I cut him off. "My face just collided with Rosco's cheek when he turned. If I needed to go to the ER I would've gone. And before I left, Dr. Maddy looked me over."

"A *vet* looked you over?"

I decided to find the incredulity in his tone amusing instead of offensive.

"Yes, a vet. After all, we're all just animals, Echo," I joked.

"This isn't funny."

"It is," I argued. "I head-butted a fifteen-hundred-pound horse and he sidestepped like I'd hurt him. Which I might've and I felt bad so I went in for another nuzzle, this time making sure I didn't spook him like an idiot. I think he accepted my apology but now I'm left with a black eye as a reminder not to startle a large animal. So not only is my eye black and blue but my ego's a little bruised, too."

I stopped my long-winded explanation when lines formed around Echo's eyes, signaling a smile was imminent. I was right, he did smile though it was more of a soft grin. That coupled with the tender way he cradled my cheek, I was so taken aback I could do no more than stare.

"I'm glad he accepted your apology, baby. How about we get some ice on your eye and a beer in your hand?"

Since I was so lost in the way Echo was holding me, I had no idea what he was talking about.

"Huh?"

"The horse," he explained.

"Oh, right."

His grin slid from soft to a sexy smirk.

"I've got Griff this weekend," he weirdly told me.

"Okay."

"Monday night I want you over."

That snapped me out of my fog. I'd spent a lot of time thinking over the last week about how to proceed. I'd thought over everything Shiloh, Lauren, and even Logan had told me. They all had their own unique spin on how I should approach winning over Echo. But Echo wasn't Logan and he wasn't Shiloh; there were similarities in their trauma but Echo's was different. He'd been open and honest about his. I loved my brother and Lauren and appreciated Shiloh's input but playing games with Echo wasn't going to get me what I wanted and give him what he needed.

That had to end.

"We did your place last time. Why don't you come over to mine and I'll cook?"

His big hand was still cupping my face but he slid it back around my neck and squeezed when he said, "Like you in my house, Jaclyn."

Well, then.

"Then I'll be at your house on Monday. But I get to cook."

"I'm grilling steaks."

Damn. I loved his steaks so it almost had me rethinking my protest.

"I'm cooking, Echo."

I watched the muscle in his jaw clench.

"Jaclyn—"

"I. Am. Cooking," I repeated.

That muscle in his jaw tightened.

The man didn't know how to let someone else take care of him.

That was going to change, too.

"Are we gonna stand here all night staring at each other seeing who can be more stubborn or are you gonna get me ice and a beer?"

Echo's answer was to dip his face, brush his lips over my mouth, cheek, then stop at my ear to whisper, "Missed you, Jaclyn."

After he gave me that my belly did a full-fledged somersault and the rest of my insides warmed.

When he straightened, his hand dropped and he went to get me some ice. I went out the back door to find my brother and sister-in-law.

I was barely two feet onto the back porch when my brother's "What the fuck happened to your face?" was nearly shouted.

I scanned the area for Griff, happy the teenager wasn't in earshot of Logan's outburst.

"You know, when you have kids you're going to have to learn to curb the F-bombs," I told him.

"Cut the shit, Jackie."

"The S-word, too," I taunted.

"Jaclyn," he growled.

My gaze went to Lauren. She was studying my brother, not like he had a screw loose but like a woman who loved her man even if he had a screw loose.

"I head-butted a horse," I announced.

"How do you head-butt a horse?" Hadley asked from her position at the head of the patio table.

"You startle it so it whips its head around and it collides with yours," I explained for the third and hopefully the last time.

"Do you need ice?" Addy asked.

Before I could answer, Echo walked out with a Ziploc bag full of ice, a kitchen towel, and Bud Light Lime.

"Sit, baby," he said on approach, gesturing with the bottle of beer to the only empty chair around the table. "It's this or Modelo."

Dark beer, yuck.

No sooner was my ass in the chair Echo was handing me the bag of ice now wrapped in the towel.

"Keep it on for as long as you can," he instructed.

"Bossy," I muttered but took the bag.

"Keep it up, Jaclyn, and I'll show you—"

"Nope," my brother grunted and stood. "I'm being cool about this but I will never be cool with *that*."

"Zap. *Zap*," Lauren hummed.

"Ren, sweetheart, you can threaten your shock collar all you want. You get I'm a man, I know where he's going with that and she's my baby sister. There's only so much I can take."

My gaze had been ping-ponging back and forth from Logan to Lauren but at the mention of the shock collar my eyes went to Quinn who was sitting next to Addy.

"It's emotionally damaging for a little sister to know her brother likes kinky bedroom games that include an electro-kink."

"What's an electro-kink?" she asked.

Since I'd made that up on the fly I shrugged.

"I guess it's when you like to be shocked during—"

"Jesus," Logan snapped and looked down at Lauren. "See what you started?"

Lauren was unfazed and smiled.

"It's not my fault you can't behave." She turned her smile my way and finished, "Your brother requires a firm hand and correction."

It was her wink that did me in. I busted out laughing and the others followed. That was, all of the women. Neither Echo nor Logan found Lauren's tease funny.

"I'm gonna go play football and rethink how happy I am my sister's moved to Georgia," Logan announced but didn't move. I should've been prepared for my brother's retaliation but I was too busy thinking how happy I was to live close to Logan again after all the years he'd been gone. So I wasn't paying attention to what his smile meant when he looked back down at his wife. "That earned you a spanking."

"Low blow, brother," I grouched.

I heard Echo chuckle. I transferred my glare from Logan to him and declared, "Just wait until I ask Shiloh—"

"Jaclyn," he cut me off on a growl that made me shiver.

"Or I could just spank you later and call it even."

"If you can manage to get me over your knee, have at it."

I ignored the rude noise my brother made and went on.

"Oh, Echo, honey, there's more than one way to—"

"I'm leaving," Logan declared and stalked around the table to the three steps that led off the raised patio to the yard.

"You done?" Echo asked.

"Done annoying my brother or teasing you?"

"You're done," he declared. "Put that ice on your face."

With that he followed Logan.

"Bossy," I called out to his back.

"Brace, Jaclyn. Monday night, I'm showing you bossy," he returned without looking back.

"You say that like I've never..."

My statement died when he looked over his shoulder.

His blue eyes locked with my hazel ones and my lips pinched shut to prevent the groan that was bubbling up from becoming audible.

"I see you're feeling me."

Oh, I was feeling him all right. He was ten feet away and I was feeling him all over my skin in the form of goose bumps.

I sat silently watching him walk in the direction of where Matt, Brice, Brady, Trey, and now Logan were all standing watching Griff and Chelsea on the other side of the fence with Griff's horse Dasher.

"So," Quinn started on an exaggerated sigh. "I take it that was your coming out announcement."

132

Shit.

"We...um..." I paused, not knowing how to continue.

"Have been doing the horizontal nasty dance since my wedding," Quinn supplied.

"Can't you just say sex?" Hadley asked.

"They're all in a tiff," Lauren told me then went on like they weren't there. "Quinn wants to throw Hadley and Addy separate baby showers since they're twins and they always get lumped together."

I could totally relate to that. Having a twin meant shared birthdays. I couldn't say it sucked because I adored my sister but still, everyone else had their own special day and it was always Jillian and Jaclyn.

"That's thoughtful."

"That's not the issue," Lauren explained. "Neither of them wants a baby shower. Quinn thinks it's because—"

Lauren quickly clamped her mouth closed.

"Because?" I inquired when she didn't finish.

"Because I'm still not pregnant," Quinn huffed.

Oh, shit.

Shit. Shit. Shit.

"That's not why," Hadley snapped defensively.

"Then why don't you want a baby shower, Hadley? You're having twins, you need two of everything."

Quinn had a point. Two of everything was going to be expensive and she needed a baby shower to help with the expense.

"Baby shower or not, you know the family's gonna spoil these babies."

Hadley had a good counterpoint.

"Then why don't you want a shower?"

"Because I want Adalyn to have something special all by herself. Not, me having a shower then the next week she gets one. Delaney got two celebrations—just her. When your time comes, you'll get one—just you. I want Addy to have one—just her."

Well, freaking hell, Hadley had a very good point.

Then Hadley stopped giving Quinn narrowed eyes and looked at me.

Oh, shit.

"I know you get it. You're a twin."

Nothing like being put on the spot.

"I totally get it. If I was in your position, I would feel the same way. But, Hadley, what you're forgetting is Addy feels the same. Jill would feel the same. And that's why Addy doesn't want a baby shower, so you have something special without her taking any of the excitement away from you."

Hadley glanced at her twin.

"Is that your reason, too?"

"Of course it is," Addy answered, looking affronted Hadley would ask.

Hadley's expression went from irritated to contemplative in a flash but there was something strange about the way she was holding onto the armrest of her chair.

"Are you alright?" I asked.

"We don't need to worry about a baby shower," Hadley gritted out.

Damn, she was going to be stubborn.

"I want you to have one," Addy argued.

"Too late."

"We can do it next weekend—"

"Too. Late," Hadley cut Quinn off.

"Why are my feet wet?" Addy asked with wide eyes.

Hadley didn't answer.

Quinn leaned to the side and looked under the table.

"Holy shit, what is it with you people and your water breaking at special events?" Quinn grumbled then straightened. "Someone go get Brady."

I tossed the ice that had never made it to my face onto the table and shoved back from the table.

"I'll call Delaney." I heard Lauren say as I jumped down the three steps onto the gravel walkway.

I was nearly out of breath when I made it to the men.

With absolutely no preamble or finesse I announced, "Hadley's water broke."

Apparently, Brady didn't need any more than that. He took off like a shot, followed by Brice.

"Never a dull moment with those Walker women." Matt laughed then yelled, "Chels, put Dasher away. Hadley's in labor."

"About damn time. I was wondering if she'd turned into an elephant!" Chelsea shouted back.

"Griff, Jaclyn, and I will stay behind and put all the food away," Echo offered.

"Shit, didn't think of that," Matt muttered. "Thanks."

The next five minutes was pure bedlam.

My brother gave me a hug, gave Echo a weird look that apparently Echo understood since he dipped his chin in response. Brady and Hadley were in his truck racing down Chelsea and Matt's long dirt lane to the hospital with Quinn and Brice, Addy and Trey, Logan and Lauren, Matt and Chelsea following behind them. Lauren had called

Delaney who said she'd make the rest of the calls needed to cancel the party and reroute everyone to the hospital.

So there was nothing for us to do but put away the hamburger patties, hot dogs, and sides. We left the beer, water, and sodas in the cooler and the buns out on the counter. That meant clean up took all of fifteen minutes with three people making short work of the chore.

"All the horses put away?" Echo asked Griff.

"Yeah."

"Olive Garden or Rusty's?" Echo went on.

"I vote Rusty's," Griff told him.

I hadn't spent much time around Griffin though in the times that I had I noted he seemed a lot older than fourteen. Not only was he tall, he'd also lost any little boy in the face. Soon he'd fill out and all traces of teenager would slip away long before he was actually out of his teenage years. But more than the kid's looks and the deepening of his voice, he acted older. There wasn't a trace of teenage exuberance or immaturity.

"Jaclyn?"

"Huh?"

"Olive Garden or Rusty's?" Echo repeated the options.

"You two go. I have stuff for dinner at home."

"Don't know why I bothered asking," Echo grumbled. But before I could be offended, he continued proving the other night when he told me he hadn't forgotten a single thing about me he was telling the truth. "You don't like chain restaurants. Rusty's it is."

That wasn't entirely true. I didn't like some chain restaurants but, on the whole, I preferred mom and pop joints.

Griffin looked between Echo and me and smiled huge.

"Why are you smiling like that?" Echo asked.

"No reason," Griff evaded.

Or more to the point lied. There was a reason he was smiling because when Echo asked about it that smile got bigger.

"Griff?"

"It's just that I've seen this before. Phoenix asks Mom what she wants for dinner. She says she doesn't care but she really does. Phoenix is smart enough to know she cares so he waits her out until she tells him. I've timed this. It can take anywhere from four minutes to sixteen to break and tell him. But it only took you like one minute to suss out what Jackie wanted because you only gave her two options."

That was oddly insightful for a fourteen-year-old.

"And you're smiling because I'm smarter than Phoenix and know better than to give a woman unlimited options?" Echo surmised.

"No, I'm smiling because it might've only taken you a minute to choose the restaurant but it's gonna take you more than sixteen to get Jackie to agree to go to dinner with you."

Well, I guess we could add astute to the list of Griff's qualities.

Echo mumbled something I didn't catch and I was pretty sure he mumbled on purpose because whatever it was wasn't safe for teenage ears.

"Are you sure you're not thirty-two?" I teased Griff.

Then the kid proved that even though he might not be a Kent by blood and hadn't spent his childhood around

Phoenix, the Kent DNA ran so strong it could be absorbed through skin.

"No, but if I was, I bet it wouldn't take me sixteen minutes to get you to agree to go out to dinner with me."

I lost sight of the tall, teenage, boy-man who was too smart for his own good when my hands went to my knees, my head dropped forward, and I laughed my ass off.

This kid.

"Griff," Echo said warningly.

"Well? Are we going to Rusty's or what? I'm starving."

I watched Echo's big hand come up, tag Griff around the back of the neck, and smile.

"Yeah, kid, we're going to Rusty's."

Echo might've been talking to Griff but he was staring at me.

I guess I was going out to dinner with Echo and Griff.

Echo double-checked the patio door was locked, then together as a trio we made our way through Matt and Chelsea's house.

It wasn't until I was in my car following Echo to Rusty's that it hit me...

Not only did it not take Echo sixteen minutes to convince me to go to dinner with him and Griff, it had taken him exactly zero minutes.

12

ECHO

"Did Phoenix tell you I talked to him about the money Conor left me?" Griff asked from the passenger seat.

A weird sense of nostalgia washed over me.

Thinking back it seemed like Sunny and Phoenix had always waited until we were driving in the car to tell me what was on their minds. Back then I thought it was because driving one of them somewhere was when they got one-on-one time with me, thus privacy. But Griff had me all to himself the whole weekend and had waited until I was driving him to school before he'd opened up. So, maybe there was just something about the car.

"Yeah, he did," I confirmed. "Have you made up your mind?"

Griff's father had left him a pretty hefty sum of money for him to use for college. Unfortunately, Griff's dad was a criminal, a murderer who was rotting in prison where he belonged, and the money he left Griff was tainted with the blood of the man he'd killed.

"Phoenix said if I wanted to give it to the family of the

man Conor killed he'd back my play and for me not to worry about college. He and my mom have that covered."

Of course that was what my brother would say. And if he said it he meant it—he'd bust his ass to make sure he had the money to send Griff to college.

"So why do you sound so uncertain?"

"You said college is a lot of money."

"It is."

There was a beat of silence before Griff quietly said, "I'm not his son. He—"

"You're his son," I cut him off.

"You know what I mean."

No, I didn't know what Griffin meant. Biology didn't make a father. Blood didn't make a son. DNA was nothing more than your genetic makeup.

"What I know is, my brother loves you. And that has nothing to do with him marrying your mother. The love he has for you, is yours and yours alone. You're his, which means you're ours. Kents take care of family and you and your mom are family."

"We're changing my last name," he told me, something I already knew.

"Yeah."

"He's my dad like Phoenix is your son."

It was far too early in the morning to be called gramps again. Not that there was ever a time during the day when I wanted to be called gramps but still, I answered.

"Yes, Phoenix is my son."

As soon as the words left my mouth the truth slammed into me. A truth I had always wrestled to the back of my mind not understanding why. I was barely older than

Griffin when I started taking care of my siblings. It was then when I realized if I didn't feed them no one would. If I didn't make sure their homework was done no one would. That went for cleaning the house and making sure they had clean clothes, too. When he was old enough, I enlisted River to help when he could but I never wanted him to feel the weight of the burden. Being a teenage father of three children I didn't create wasn't the burden—the fear I felt everyday was. The constant worry I was going to screw up and River, Phoenix, and Sunny were going to suffer for my failure was the weight. And I'd fucked up plenty.

"I don't want the money."

"Then don't take it."

Griff's school was coming into view and I was wondering if I should circle the block to give the kid more time before I dropped him off. It wouldn't be the first time I drove aimlessly so Phoenix or Sunny could finish a conversation.

"I know who Jaclyn is." Griff changed the subject.

I wasn't sure I liked the direction this new topic was headed.

"You know who she is?"

"She's the happy that River, Phoenix, and Sunny were talking about that day they surprised you."

They didn't surprise me, they ambushed me, and I was still pissed they'd pulled that shit. Luckily for them, with baby announcements, weddings, and honeymoons I had yet to find time to rip into them about the shit they pulled. Though I hadn't forgotten and that shit was going to be addressed.

Also unfortunate, Griff was right about Jaclyn and

since I wasn't going to lie to the kid I didn't respond. Not that he needed me to before he went on.

"I didn't get it when they were talking to you. But at dinner on Friday night, I got it. You're different when you're with her."

"Different?" I asked before I thought better of it.

"You look at her the way Phoenix looks at my mom."

That didn't explain how I was different.

"How does that make me different?"

I felt the kid's eyes on me so I glanced over at him. Save the masculine features, Griff looked like a carbon copy of his mother. Which meant he had Wren's blue eyes and right then they were sharp on me.

"You just are," he told me with a shrug.

Sometimes it was easy to forget Griff was only four-teen. It was also easy to forget that it wasn't too long ago Phoenix had rescued him from a burning building. And if that trauma wasn't enough Griff had been at Matt and Chelsea's when Phoenix had been shot.

"Everything going okay?" I asked.

"Yeah."

His 'yeah' was questioning so I explained, "With us going over to Matt's house."

"I go over there all the time."

I knew he did. Wren and Phoenix made it a point to take him over there as soon as Phoenix was up and mobile after taking several shots to the abdomen. They did this in an effort to help Griff process and heal from what had happened to everyone there. Matt, being overly generous and rich as fuck, wanted to sell the house regardless of the fact he'd bought it for Chelsea and move somewhere new to wipe that memory away. Phoenix wouldn't hear of it, neither would Wren.

But I respected the hell out of Matt for offering.

I pulled into the parking lot of Griff's school and I knew from experience not to pull up to the front door to let him out. Phoenix had stopped allowing curbside drop-off when he was around thirteen. I found a spot near the front and parked.

"Have a good day."

"Thanks for letting me stay with you."

"Anytime. You know that, right?"

Griff opened his door, grabbed his backpack, swung it over his shoulder, and leaned down to look into my car.

"I know you're new to this but I don't think grandparents are supposed to cook vegetables and they provide ice cream."

I lifted my hand to flip the kid off but remembered at the last minute where I was. Likely giving the bird to a fourteen-year-old—no matter he was a smartass—would be frowned upon.

So I gave him a salute and a tight smile.

"Go to school."

Griff slammed the door and while I waited for him to walk across the parking lot I grabbed my phone and sent my brother a text.

Your kid is safely at school.

His reply was immediate, like he was waiting for the update.

Thx. We're leaving in an hour.

I didn't bother responding and since it was too early to

call River in Idaho, I tossed my phone back in the cupholder and went to work.

FOR A MONDAY MORNING this one was particularly shitty.

It was coming up on four and I was nowhere near done. Jaclyn was supposed to be at my house at five and I wouldn't be there to let her in.

"Ready?"

I looked away from the whiteboard I was studying to Evan Sanders standing in the doorway. Our briefing room at the station was a far sight different from the conference room at TC. The room assigned to the Drug Task Force was composed of two repurposed interrogation rooms with the wall separating them torn out. There was no large table with comfortable leather chairs, we had a scarred interrogation table and folding metal chairs. However, our technology rivaled TC's and with direct contact with the DEA and FBI, our access to information was quicker than what Dylan Walsh could obtain legally. That wasn't to say that in a pinch, Dylan couldn't acquire intel that as an officer he wasn't officially privy to, nor was I outright told how he secured his data. I could guess and I'd be correct but out of respect, conversations about Dylan's methods were kept confidential.

"Yeah, give me a minute."

I pulled my phone out of my cargos and pulled up my text thread with Jaclyn.

I'm running late. I need to get you my key.

I stowed my phone and looked at Evan.

"Did Dick get you an address?"

"Does Dick ever do anything he says he's gonna do?" Evan asked by way of answer.

Dick was an informant we used. His name was Richard Burns but for some reason known only to him he hilariously went by Dick.

Dick Burns.

Further from that, it was fitting seeing as his right arm was marred with burn scars from wrist to elbow from a cooking accident. Meth, not food.

So while Richard was indeed a Dick, he was also burned.

His name fit.

"Where to first?" I started. "Track down Dick or the store?"

"The store. Dick will find me when he wants something. Until then I'm not wasting our time tracking the asshole down."

Thank fuck.

The last thing I wanted to do was spend my night hitting crack houses.

My phone vibrated. I pulled it out and gritted my teeth at the first seven words I could see from the preview. When I opened it, my jaw relaxed. She wasn't outright canceling.

We can meet at my house or we could do dinner tomorrow if that's better for you.

I tapped out my reply.

My house. What's your 20 so I can drop off my key?

20?? Is that poh-poh speak?

Her silly response made me smile.

Location.

No sooner did I hit send my phone rang.

"I'm walking out the door," I told her. "Text me your location so I can swing by."

"Hello to you, too, Echo. I'm doing great. How are you doing this fine, bright and sunny Monday morning?"

Her correction was amusing, however I didn't have time for another lesson about phone etiquette.

"Baby, I got Evan standing here waiting for me. We need to hit a convenience store, talk to the owner, pick up the feeds from the cameras he allowed us to install, and hit a suspected stash house for a knock and talk. And swing around to drop off my key to you. I'd like to do all of that before midnight, so maybe you can help me out and tell me where you are so I can get you my key, yeah?"

"You need to hit a stash house?" she whispered.

"Suspected stash house," I corrected her.

"What's a knock and talk?"

"How about I tell you what that is over dinner?"

I was keeping my gaze purposefully on the whiteboard and averted from Evan. Though I didn't need to look at my friend to know he was going to give me shit as soon as I hung up.

"Okay, well, I was calling to tell you I'm out in Meadows."

Fuck. That was forty-five minutes from Hollow Point. I definitely didn't have time to drive all the way out there.

"So if you're firm on dinner at your house you can drop your key at TC with my brother or you can go by Dr. Robinson's ranch and leave it with Preston."

Who the hell was Preston?

"Who's Preston?"

"Maddy's husband," she snapped, obviously hearing the jealousy in my tone. "Do you think I'd send you to drop off your key to my side piece?"

"Jaclyn," I warned.

"You're too easy, Echo Kent." She laughed.

I debated the benefits of going out to the Robinson ranch and meeting Preston. Jaclyn spent the majority of her time with his wife, and some of her day before she left on vet calls with the doctor's husband. It would be good to meet the people she spent time with. However, TC was closer and my desire to get done with work and get home to Jaclyn outweighed wanting to check out Preston Robinson.

"I'll drop my key off with your brother. Do you remember the alarm code?"

"If you haven't changed it then yes."

Outside of my siblings Jaclyn was the only person who had my alarm code. I gave it to her so she could unarm it in the morning to go out back and sit with her coffee when she got up before me. To my recollection that had happened once.

"Code's the same. I'm dropping my key off to your brother."

"Copy that, Officer Kent."

Damn, she was cute as fuck when she was trying to be sassy.

"See you tonight, baby."

"Wait." I heard her say when I pulled the phone away from my ear.

"Yeah?"

"Aren't you supposed to say over and out or message received or copy back?"

Yeah, she was fucking cute.

"Next time you wanna play cops and robbers I'll educate you on all the lingo."

I heard Evan bark out a laugh.

Fucking hell, I forgot he was in the room.

I wouldn't catch shit for that comment. No, that just earned me months of ribbing.

"Oh, spicy. Though I don't wanna be the bad guy. I wanna cuff—"

"Remember when I said Evan was waiting for me? What I meant was Even is standing next to me waiting. He's heard enough for a lifetime of shit talk. I'd prefer not to give him any more. Though I'll leave you with this— there is zero chance you're getting me in cuffs."

With that I quickly disconnected and waited for the razzing to commence.

When it didn't immediately start, I turned and faced my partner.

"She the reason you were happy for a few months?"

Christ. That was worse than shit talk.

"Yep."

"I take it you're back together."

That implied he knew we'd ended.

Which wasn't necessarily surprising. There was a reason Evan and I worked so well together. There was also a reason I trusted the man to have my back; he wasn't only observant he was attuned to the people around him. In all my years of law enforcement I'd never met anyone who could walk into a room, feel the vibe, read the occupants, and make a judgement call based on that alone and be correct. I trusted his gut reaction more than I trusted my own.

"Working on it," I mumbled.

"Work harder."

"Come again?"

"I said," he enunciated slowly, "work. Harder. Never met her but I don't need to, to know she makes you happy. Grab hold of that, Echo, and don't let go."

Happy.

Now there was a multilayered word that over my life I'd felt shades and degrees of but I wasn't sure I'd ever felt the fullness of it. Not the way Sunny, Phoenix, and River had. Before I'd met Jaclyn, I would've said their happiness was all I needed to get by. Now after having her then letting go and getting a taste of what life could be like with her back in it, I knew I needed more.

But it was the *more* that terrified me. To get more I had to give more. The only way to keep Jaclyn would be to bare my soul; she'd accept nothing less. I'd have to tell her the truth, the secret I'd kept for eighteen years, and all my other ones besides. She deserved to know I wasn't the man she thought she knew. I was an asshole who'd lied to my siblings and continued to lie to them to this day.

So, yeah, working harder scared the fuck out of me.

13

___

ECHO

I was happy to see Jamel had put up the No
Trespassing, No Loitering, No Criminal Activity signs in
front of his store like we'd asked.

Not that the signs would do anything to stop the
loitering or the dealing going on in front of his store but
they did mean when he called in a complaint we could
detain, question, and make arrests on a trespass charge. It
was nothing more than a summons, but it helped us sketch
in the missing pieces to a much larger picture.

"Forgot to ask," Evan started as he pulled around to the
back of the store. "Which one's her brother?"

We'd gone by TC, however Evan had stayed in the car
when I dropped my key off with Lauren since Logan was
out on the range.

"Logan Haines."

Evan whistled before he chuckled.

"Damn, brother."

He knew Logan. Not well, but he'd met him a few
times when the department had leased range time for train-

ing. But you didn't have to know Logan well to know the kind of man he was—a brother who'd go to war for his little sister. He'd been shockingly calm about me seeing Jaclyn which meant Lauren had talked him around. That or Luke had put in a good word for me. Whatever the case was, it still surprised me. Logan Haines was not a man to stand down.

Evan made the ninety-degree turn to the back of the Stop N Shop and there was Dick doing what Dick did best —buying dope.

Both Dick and the dealer turned in our direction as Evan slammed on the brakes, but it was only Dick who ran.

"I got Dick," I told Evan and jumped out of the car before he'd rolled to a complete stop.

By the time I made it to the chain-link fence, Dick was up and nearly over it. There were times when being six-foot-five had its advantages—this was one of those times. I easily reached up and caught his ankle, halting his progress.

"Yo, Dick, why you running, buddy?"

He halfheartedly struggled to get over the fence before he gave up and dropped down. It was a weird thing to think —or maybe it wasn't—but for the most part Dick wasn't a bad guy. He was a man who was caught up in his addiction doing stupid shit to get his next fix. That didn't mean he wasn't an asshole, it just meant he knew how to play the game—he knew when to stop struggling and start cooperating.

Not that he kept his word but he'd never tried to resist once he was nabbed.

"You missed your appointment with Sanders."

"I did?" he lied.

"You did," I told him and shoved my hand into the side pocket of my cargos, coming out with a black Nitrile glove.

"What'd you buy?"

"Come on, Kent," he whined.

"You know the drill. Spit."

I held my gloved hand out under his chin. I watched as he worked his tongue around the inside of his cheek before he spit the crack rock out into my hand. There were a number of places for an addict to hide their score until they got to a place to smoke it. The inside of the lip or under the tongue were the most common. There were other places of course, places that would require a trip to the station and pants around the ankles to check.

I eyed the small rock, knowing Dick was out of money thus this next conversation was going to go one of two ways —either he'd be a wealth of information knowing he'd get paid or he'd say anything hoping he could bullshit Evan and still get paid.

There was no bullshitting Evan.

Dick ultimately knew that.

"Who's your friend?" I asked and jerked my head toward the cuffed dealer I'd never seen before.

"Don't know. He's new."

It was a long shot but I still had to ask, "He tell you who he works for?"

Dick shrugged his thin, bony shoulders.

"Didn't ask."

And that was when my shitty Monday turned into a shittier Monday that now included paperwork.

"You know I gotta take you in," I told him.

"Come on, Kent. I didn't even make it out of the parking lot."

Like that made a difference.

I glanced over at Evan and saw his radio in his right hand. He was calling in for backup.

When Evan caught me watching he jerked his head to the car.

"It's your lucky day, Dick," I told him. "You get the cushy back seat."

Without any further direction Dick started for the car.

"If I give you the address to the warehouse, will you leave the cuffs off?"

"No. But I'll wait until patrol gets here to take in your new friend."

When we got to the car Dick patiently waited while I popped the trunk. He followed me to the rear of the car and again waited while I retrieved an evidence bag, dropped the rock of crack into the pouch, pulled the tape from the adhesive, sealed the bag, and secured it in the trunk and slammed it closed.

I didn't have to tell Dick to assume the position—his palms went to the trunk, he spread his legs, and waited for me to search him.

"Got anything on you I need to know about?"

"Knife in my right sock."

"Anything else?"

"Nope."

Another contradiction that was hard to wrap my head around; Dick was for the most part an honest criminal. Anytime he was picked up he cooperated, he wasn't overly argumentative, he'd hand his stash over, and he was the only person in all my years in narcotics who would answer that question honestly.

My father wasn't an honest criminal. He was argumentative with the cops to the point of aggressive. He not only resisted arrest; he fought the police. He'd hidden stolen property around the house, the worst places being in Phoenix and River's bedroom. He wasn't an addict doing stupid shit to catch his next fix, he was a lazy, drunk, abusive asshole who could've done something with his life but instead was a thief.

That was, until he became a murderer.

Lester Kent didn't kill Officer Smith in a struggle. He wasn't resisting arrest when it happened, he wasn't protecting his stolen goods, he wasn't attempting to buy drugs, or any of the reasons a criminal pulls a gun on a cop. Lester killed Smith out of spite, to teach me a lesson. A lesson I still bore the weight of. A lesson I would never forget.

"Kent?" Evan called, pulling me from miserable thoughts.

Thoughts that plagued me daily.

Thoughts that invaded my mind no matter how many times I tried to shove them aside.

The very thoughts that had kept me from being honest with my siblings.

The reason I'd given up Jaclyn.

And now the reason she might walk away from me when she learned the truth.

By the time I got home I was an hour later than I'd told Jaclyn I was going to be. Beyond that I was annoyed as fuck Dick had decided today was the day that he was going to try his hand at negotiating his compensation as he called it. Evan was having none of it which meant we'd spent more than thirty minutes sitting in silence in an interrogation room before Dick broke and started talking.

We now had the address to a warehouse that was being used to cut cocaine and make crack. Dick also informed us he'd heard the cocaine was coming from Honduras and that was why he was making a buy behind the Stop N Shop. This was also confirmation that Dick had gone from wannabe meth cooker, to full-blown tweaker, and had graduated to crack smoker. It was time to cut him loose; we'd get no further credible intel from him once his newest addiction fully took hold. Evan knew this and spent a good deal of time with Dick trying to convince him to try rehab. Dick was having none of it.

There was a reason Evan was a narcotics detective and it wasn't because he got a thrill getting drugs off the street. It went beyond that; it was his mission. A deep-seated need to do everything in his power to make sure that no one else had to go through what his family had. Evan was far from stupid; he knew it was an impossibility and he didn't give the first fuck. The man worked himself to the bone. He took the time to talk to every junkie we pulled in. He gave his free time to halfway houses, shelters, and other organizations besides. So, now I was later than I thought I was going to be because Evan had done everything he could to get Dick help before he broke the news that we could no longer use him as an informant.

Evan wasn't surprised but I didn't miss the disappointment on my friend's face. I'd seen the look time and time again. And I'd see it a hundred more times. That was Evan Sanders, a man who deeply cared to the detriment of his own sanity.

I was coming into my house through the laundry room when I caught sight of Jaclyn standing on the counter holding onto the upper cabinets for balance and looking like she was attempting to negotiate a way to get past the sink without falling. I took in her bare feet, her bare legs, the cutoff shorts she'd changed into after work, her faded black t-shirt that if I wasn't mistaken had a screen printing of a Crown Royal bottle that said *if the crown fits, drink it.* Her hair was up in a clip which was an indication she'd been cooking. When I was done with my perusal my gaze went to the floor and I no longer needed to ask her why the hell she was standing on the counter.

Shattered glass and large shards of what looked to be my dinner plates were scattered all over the floor.

"I'm so sorry. I was balancing the glasses on top of the plates when I turned and knocked into the island. Everything slipped out of my hands and well..." She paused to look down at the floor. "That happened."

I ignored her unnecessary apology and asked, "Are you cut?"

Jaclyn shook her head.

Glass crunched under my boots as I made my way to her and lifted my arms.

Without hesitation she let go of the cabinet, twisted, and fell forward. I didn't need to tell her to wrap her legs around me when I lowered her but I should've braced for the feel of her pressed against me. I should've remembered how damn good it felt to have her in my arms. I also should've kept my hands off her ass as I carried her out of the kitchen but I didn't do that either.

"How long have you been standing up there?"

"Just a few seconds."

Well, that was a relief.

"I was getting ready to shimmy to the other side to crawl off the breakfast bar."

"The breakfast bar?"

"Yes, Echo, you know the place where you tuck your stools under."

I knew what the breakfast bar was.

"Baby, you're barefoot and there's glass everywhere."

I watched up close as her lips twitched.

"Yes, *honey*, I know. That's why I was going to get down on the other side."

I didn't find anything funny about the possibility of her cutting her feet to shit.

"Or you could've stayed there and called me." I gave her the safer alternative.

Now I was watching her blink at me like I'd lost my mind.

One of her hands moved from my shoulder up to my neck. Her finger curled into the back of my neck and she smiled.

"I'm going to say this as gently as possible but there's no way in hell I'm ever going to call anyone to come rescue me off a counter."

"Jaclyn—"

"Echo, it was broken glass, not a field full of bouncing

Bettys." To punctuate her point she'd tightened her legs around my waist and dropped her face closer to mine and locked eyes.

Suddenly I was no longer thinking about the glass or walking in to find her standing on the counter. All I could think about was how fucking good it felt to have my hands on her ass while she was pressed close and how much better it would feel if there was nothing between us. I changed directions and headed to the hall.

"Is there something in the oven?"

"No."

"On the stove?"

"No."

Thank fuck.

14

JACLYN

THIRTY-EIGHT DAYS...

Yes, I was counting.

Thirty-eight long days. So when he set me on my feet next to the bed, I wasted no time unbuttoning my shorts and shimmying them down my legs. And since I was in such a hurry, I pulled my t-shirt off and was reaching around my back unclasping my bra when it dawned on me Echo hadn't moved.

"Echo—"

I got no more out before one of his hands hooked me around the back of my neck and the other went to my bra. He tugged my bra free and me closer. My bare chest hit his black t-shirt and his mouth descended, taking mine in a scorching hot kiss. Back was the Echo who took control, who dominated, who held me where he wanted me in order to deliver mind-blowing pleasure that was borderline hallucinatory.

He broke the kiss with a growled demand, "Bed."

Early on I learned the faster I complied with Echo's

commands the greater the reward. Or maybe it was simply the quicker I did as I was told the faster Echo got down to business.

Now was no different.

As soon as I sat on the mattress Echo grabbed the back of my thighs, lifting them until I lost my balance and fell back. I was divested of my undies, shoved farther onto the bed, and my legs were over Echo's shoulders. Proving I was indeed going to be rewarded he wasted no time taking what he wanted. He was not a man to slowly ease into sex. He didn't gently coax. He overwhelmed. His tongue speared, his bared teeth scraped my clit, his head shook between my legs, and he ate until my back arched off the bed and my thighs trembled.

"Baby," I panted.

I felt Echo shift lower, his broad shoulders keeping my legs parted when his left hand slid around and down to cup my ass. His right moved the opposite direction up and around, homing in on my clit. I fisted the comforter in preparation for the onslaught.

Without lifting his head his next rumbled command sent shivers up my spine.

"Watch. Me."

I opened my eyes and righted my head. Our eyes locked and I watched as Echo devoured me.

There was nothing sexier than Echo Kent between my legs. Watching him use my body to take his pleasure was a close second. Watching the muscles in his neck contract as he spilled into me a close third. But nothing topped the magnificence of his mouth on my pussy while his lust-drunk eyes held mine.

"Echo."

His name was a whispered groan. I fought to keep focus as my orgasm threatened to pull me under. I was there. Right there. So close my hips rocked against his face, my whimpers sounded desperate, my body heated, and I broke.

Sweet relief washed over me.

The sweetest torture as my neck arched and I lost sight of Echo but not the feel of his lips as he sucked my clit between his lips, prolonging the ecstasy he'd created.

"Watch. Me."

The haze of my orgasm lingered as I dragged my eyes back to him.

I felt more than saw him cleaning away my excitement. His tongue moved from clit to ass then back up again. When he was done, he pressed a kiss to my center then another on my belly before he stood.

He didn't have to tell me he wanted me to keep my legs open while he undressed. He didn't have to tell me he liked seeing my pussy red from his stubble and wet from my climax.

Yet he still did.

"Wider, baby."

I let my knees fall open wider, completely exposing myself to him but at the same time feeling completely empowered by the way his hungry gaze lingered as he undressed.

Echo pulled his shirt over his head and tossed it aside, his gaze going right back between my legs. I watched as he opened his pants and shoved them down his muscular thighs. His thick erection came into view but that wasn't what had me enthralled. It was the way his eyes danced over my pussy, my legs, my stomach, my breasts. Never stopping for more than a second like he wanted to see all of me all at once and couldn't choose a place to settle on.

So really I was quick to do his bidding not only because the physical pleasure turned me inside out but also because he made me feel beautiful. Sexy in a way I'd never felt before. His gaze emboldened me. His demands freed me from my thoughts. Echo's control meant my freedom to discover a side of myself I'd never felt comfortable exploring.

"I like your eyes on me," I whispered.

Those beautiful blue eyes snapped to mine. There was no way to miss the desire that swirled in their depths. But if I had his hand going to his erection and giving himself a long, slow stroke would've been a sure sign of how turned on he was.

That only served to bolster my confidence.

"I like when you tell me to watch you."

Another stroke.

"I like how sexy you make me feel."

Another stroke but this time he moved closer to the bed.

"I like how safe I am when I'm with you."

Echo's knee went to the bed. His left hand went to the inside of my thigh while his right was still stroking when he said, "You're always safe with me."

"I know."

"No, Jaclyn, you are always *safe* with me. Safe to be who you are. Safe to want what you want, say what's on your mind, feel how you feel."

That wasn't the case a few months ago so I decided to test the veracity of his statement.

"I missed you," I whispered.

Pain slashed across his handsome face before a growl emanated, filling the room with a feral sound that washed over my cooling body until it burned.

Echo's hand left my knee, journeyed up my thigh, skimmed my belly, ribs, the swell of my breast until he captured my nipple between his fingers and rolled. He leaned forward and his mouth traveled the same path only on the opposite side—thigh, belly, ribs, stopping briefly to press a kiss between my breasts before his tongue circled my pebbled nipple.

It was a toss-up which I liked more—the pinch and roll that skirted pain or the gentle lave of his tongue. What wasn't in question was I wanted more and I knew how to get it.

I let go of the comforter. One arm wrapped around his shoulder, the other went to the back of his head and my fingers combed through his short hair. My back arched in a nonverbal demand. Echo read my invitation and sucked my nipple deeper, tweaking the other until the line between pain and pleasure was so blurred, I was panting.

"More," I groaned.

He quickly switched sides, soothing the sting with his tongue, twisting and tugging the other.

Back and forth he went.

The harder he pinched one nipple the softer his tongue flicked the other until I was whimpering from the conflicting sensations.

I bucked my hips and added, "I need you."

Echo rolled, taking me with him. Due to the height difference, I lost his mouth—not that I was complaining when the loss meant I got something better.

Way better.

I felt the head of his cock position where I needed it to be and I slammed down with a groan.

Full.

Full of Echo's thick, long cock.

I had yet to adjust to the invasion when he ordered, "Lean back. Hands on my legs. I want to see all of you."

I did as I was told, arching my back, fingertips digging into his muscled thighs.

"Fuck me, Jaclyn."

His words were coarse but full of something I'd never heard before.

I tipped my head, took in his chiseled abs, his well-defined pectorals, the corded column of his throat, the stubble that shadowed his square jaw, his full lips, until my gaze landed on his.

I wasn't moving.

I couldn't.

I then saw something I'd seen before, something that had been there from the very beginning but I'd missed it. Not that I could've known. But there it was right in front of me.

Echo Kent hiding in plain sight.

How had I missed it when it was right there in the way he looked at me. It was there in every demand he'd made. It was there with every touch, every kiss, and I'd stupidly overlooked the obvious.

"I missed you," I repeated.

He slowly blinked.

"So, much, Echo. Every day I missed you."

His lids opened and there it was again—pain. But this time I saw the regret, too.

I saw it. I knew it was there but I needed more.

"Fuck me, baby."

When I didn't move, his hands went to my hips. I pressed my knees to his sides and stayed planted.

Full of Echo and totally exposed, I waited.

He was speaking with his eyes, telling me he felt the same. His fingers tightened. His big body trembled under me with unleashed need. His jaw clenched with under-standing.

From the start Echo had demanded my vulnerability. He craved it. He needed it. At every turn he wanted me open and bare to him.

Unprotected.

Defenseless.

Now it was my turn.

Echo knifed up, hooked me around the back of the neck, and yanked me forward, pausing when his mouth lingered a hair's breadth away from mine.

"You have no clue," he snarled. "I didn't miss you, Jaclyn. I was empty. I ached for you. I needed you. I agonized over pushing you away until I was sick with the thought. You're too fucking young for me. You've been through enough—too much. You don't need to get caught up in my shit, but fuck if I can let you go."

That was all I needed to hear.

I closed the scant distance and pressed my lips against

his to silence him. I needn't do anything else; Echo took it from there and took over.

The kiss was searing.

It was meant to be an apology—and a promise.

When he slowed the kiss, I wrapped my arms around his shoulders and commenced fucking him with the small amount of space he afforded me. Which wasn't much but I made it work. And if the noises Echo was grunting into my mouth were anything to go by, it was working for him in a big way. I wanted to see him, but more than that I wanted him to watch me.

I pitched forward pushing him back to the bed, leaned back, and assumed my earlier position fully open to his perusal.

"Fuck, baby."

His moan spurred me to fuck him harder.

"Faster, Jaclyn."

His hands skated up and down my thighs and I knew from the strain in his voice it was only a matter of time before he flipped me.

Knowing my time in control was coming to an end, I let go.

All thoughts fled. The only thing that remained was me bearing down on Echo's cock—how good he felt, how close I was and getting closer with each drive, the sounds he was making, and even though my eyes were unfocused I knew he was enjoying the show.

"Fuck but I love watching you bounce on my dick."

I thought the flip was coming but instead I felt his hand slide up between my legs. His thumb went to my clit and started to circle.

"I want you to come," he groaned. "Then after that you'll take me."

A few more seconds and he'd get what he wanted.

"I am taking you," I pushed out.

Echo's response was to circle harder.

"Come for me, Jackie."

I was close, so close I was losing my rhythm as my orgasm threatened to break. So close I was fighting the impending ecstasy, wanting to prolong the buildup of pleasure.

Close wasn't what Echo wanted.

And what Echo wanted, Echo found a way to get.

His thumb ceased circling, his hand shifted, then he pinched my clit and rolled it the same way he'd done to my nipples—ruthlessly until I had no choice but to follow his command.

I was lost in a tidal wave of euphoria. From the tips of my toes all the way to my scalp my skin heated. The fog had yet to lift when I was yanked off Echo's cock, tossed on my back, rolled to my belly, and ordered to my hands and knees.

The directive barely registered. Not that it mattered; Echo would put me where he wanted me, and sure enough with his help I was hauled to my knees. He slammed back inside of me with my orgasm still coursing through me. My pussy clenched around his length and once more I was swept away.

"Christ," Echo bit out.

The pads of his fingers pressed into my hips, using his grip as leverage to pull me back into his driving thrusts.

Now I understood what he meant when he said I was going to take him.

This was not his normal wild thrashing; this was total possession.

"Echo." His name came out in a two-syllable puff.

"Told you before. I'll say it again, I tried to give you up. I tried to let you go. I won't do it again, baby. You want out, you have to say it."

Was he crazy?

He slowed his brutal pace, softened the harsh rasp of his voice, and continued.

"Can't. Let. You. Go."

Each word was punctuated with a thrust.

Each word tortured.

"Not ever," he finished.

And that was finished in two ways.

He slammed in, planted his hips firmly against my ass, tightened his steel hold, and stilled. The only movement I felt was his big body vibrating and his cock twitching as he silently spilled into me.

I waited until I sensed his orgasm left him before I pulled forward off his cock, scrambled to face him, and came back up onto my knees. My hands cupped his jaw. I leaned forward until nothing but Echo's face filled my vision, meaning I had his full attention.

"I told you once but I'll say it again, I'm not going anywhere. I won't let you push me away this time. I'll pry until you break. I'll find a way to get in. And part of that is me not letting you get away with telling me things without saying them."

Echo tilted his head in confusion. "Telling you things without saying them?"

I sucked in a breath, knowing that a few months ago my explanation would've sent Echo running far and fast.

"It's all there," I started. "Everything you don't want to say, but you still tell me with the way you look at me. I won't always need the words but for now I do. So when I tell you I miss you and I know you missed me, too, I'm not settling for a look, Echo. I'll wait you out until you tell me with your words."

I couldn't see his lips though I knew they'd tipped up by the way the lines around his eyes formed.

When the silence stretched, I asked, "Can you give me that?"

"No."

I tried to hide my disappointment when I returned a whispered, "No?"

"No," he repeated and twisted until we were on the mattress side by side facing each other. "Me giving you that means making you wait for something you need. I missed you, baby. I should've told you that straight away. You should never have to work for my affection and it's totally fucked that's what I was making you do."

Holy shit.

Who was this man?

I wanted to pinch him or myself to make sure this moment was real.

I was pretty much speechless so it was a good thing Echo finally found his voice.

"Something else. The other night when you were over and we were exchanging barbs I was acting like a dick to prove a point but I was still a dick. As pissed as I was, you didn't deserve that. But the point I was trying to make remains. What we had was never meaningless. You weren't then and sure as hell aren't now an empty fuck. That night I told you I wanted to take us to a place where we could be friends, I hope you understand that's changed."

I thought I understood but I wasn't used to this open and honest Echo so I asked for clarification, "Changed how?"

"Baby."

That was all he said but his tone spoke volumes and what it said was I was dim.

"Is this your way of asking me to go steady?" I teased.

"No, Jaclyn, this is me telling you I'm done fucking around. I'm done with the bullshit. I'm done pushing you away when I should've been pulling you closer, holding on as tight as I could."

I laid there in silence staring into the most beautiful blue eyes I'd ever seen. Gazing at the man who had owned me from my first glimpse of him and every day since. A man who was deeply wounded by a past that had left him hollow. A man who wasn't going to make me work for what I needed even though I knew it would cost him to be the one exposed. A man who deserved to be happy but didn't think he did.

I took in all that was Echo Kent and knew two things—loving him was going to be painful but once I navigated through the landmines of trauma, he would make all the pain worth it.

"I'm done fucking around, too."

"Just so I'm clear, we're doing this, Jackie. No more

hiding from Logan, my brother and sister, our friends. We are doing this and we're out there."

I didn't ask what "this" was or what "out there" meant. I didn't need to. He was making us official and not making us hide who we were.

"Maybe I should talk to Logan first," I suggested.

"I'll have a talk with your brother, though at this point I think it's unnecessary. He knows. Everyone does."

Echo wasn't wrong.

"Logan saw us together. That is, he saw us together in your car one of the times I came to visit you."

Echo's hand came up to rest on my cheek.

"Should've never asked you to hide us, baby. That was fucked."

I already had a pile of issues to work Echo through; I didn't need something new added to the top of the already gargantuan mountain.

"It was the smart thing to do," I told him. "Logan can be...well, Logan. And we share friends so us keeping what was happening a secret made sense."

"No, Jaclyn. You are no man's secret."

Well, damn.

If I hadn't already fallen in love with Echo, that alone would've done it.

But I had fallen.

Now the question was, had Echo?

15

ECHO

It was after we'd gotten dressed, I'd cleaned up the shattered glass and Jaclyn had sorted dinner. I was grabbing Jaclyn a fake beer out of the fridge when she asked, "What's a knock and talk?"

Two things hit me at once. The first being, as much time as I'd spent with her, she knew very little about my job. The second being, I really liked her asking.

Which made a third thought slam into me—why, when we started seeing each other, had I closed down all personal questions, and since when was my job personal?

"It's an attempt for a consensual search," I told her and closed the refrigerator door.

"Like you knock on the door and ask if you can go in and search?"

"Yep."

I popped the top of her Angry Orchard and grabbed my Blue Moon off the counter on my way to the table.

"That doesn't sound very exciting," she noted.

She was correct, there was nothing exciting about knocking on the door of a suspected drug house and trying to get permission to enter without a warrant.

"It's not, but if we can get in and convince the occupant to allow us to look around, nine times out of ten it bears fruit."

Jaclyn's nose scrunched.

"Just to say, if you knocked on my door and asked to look inside and I was hiding drugs I'd tell you no."

"We don't ask if we can search, we ask if we can come in and talk. From there Evan looks—"

"Who's Evan?"

Jesus, had I been so locked down I'd never mentioned my partner?

"My partner."

Pain flashed before she took a sip of her beer to hide the hurt.

Yep, I was an asshole.

"Evan and I have been partners for about five years..." I started then spent the next half hour while we were eating telling her about my partner. After that I cleared the dishes, led her to the couch, and spent another thirty minutes telling her about my job.

By the time I was done she'd sprawled out on the couch with her elbow in the cushions, hand propping up her head, and her feet were in my lap. She was also staring at me listening intently to every word I said. I wasn't sure if this was because she was that interested or more likely if it was because it was dawning on her how big of a dick I'd been all those months not telling her a single thing about my work.

176

"You've never been undercover," she recalled from earlier in the conversation.

"Nope."

"Do you *want* to go undercover?"

Her question took me by surprise, therefore I was unprepared for the effort it took to keep my voice even when I answered, "No."

"Why are you lying to me?"

Fucking shit.

Before I could think better of it or the ramifications, I told her the truth.

"Because lying about it is easier than admitting I regret not having the chance to do it. Because I've buried the regret for so long it's like second nature. Because I'm afraid if I allow myself to think about it, regret will turn into resentment."

Jaclyn shifted to her back but when she started to pull her feet off my lap, before she could pull away, I captured her ankles, keeping some part of her anchored to me.

"You didn't go undercover when you first started with the task force because you didn't want to be away from River, Phoenix, and Shiloh," she rightly surmised. I nodded and she continued, "And now?"

"Now I've been on the job too long to go under locally."

Proving that she'd paid close attention to everything I'd told her she asked, "But you work with other agencies. You couldn't go undercover with one of them?"

Another lie was on the tip of my tongue. An excuse to get myself out of a conversation I didn't want to have. A bullshit reason I could make sound convincing so we could move on.

The lie was right there...

Yet I couldn't bring myself to utter it.

"I've had offers."

"Recently?"

Fuck.

"Yes."

"So I don't understand."

Neither did I.

Or more to the point I didn't know how to explain without making myself sound like a total pussy.

"There's no time guarantee with undercover work. I could get an assignment that from the outside looks like it'll be a quick job but when I get there and dig in, it could turn into months or even a year."

Jaclyn's head jerked and her feet twitched in my lap. The movement was slight and if I hadn't been looking directly at her I would've missed it. Her feet were a different story. I couldn't miss the way they'd moved or the way her calves had stiffened before she'd relaxed them.

"Oh," she whispered. "But they're all adults now, Echo."

"Yeah, baby, they are. That doesn't mean I want to chance being away from them for a fucking year."

And there was the crux of my issue. Even though my siblings were all adults, all married, River had even moved across the country and I still couldn't bring myself to consider the possibility of being out of contact with them for an extended period of time. The issue was mine. The regret was, too. Which made staving off the resentment all the more ridiculous. I had no one to blame but myself.

My parents might've been assholes but the bottom line was my actions had taken Officer Smith's life.

My naiveté and impatience had destroyed lives. Not just my siblings but Smith's family as well. I was responsible for a little girl growing up without a father. A wife losing her husband. A sister losing a brother. A mother burying her son.

Me.

I had set the events in motion.

"I totally get that. I wouldn't want to be away from Jill, Logan, or Lucy for a year. But saying that, I wouldn't begrudge them doing something they wanted to do even if it meant I wouldn't see them." She paused then hesitantly said, "Logan left to go to the Navy. There were times when he was gone for extended periods of time and none of us saw or talked to him. And I'm sure you know how much he hated going to Bad Axe so he rarely came to see us there. Families make sacrifices, Echo."

"No, Jaclyn. I make the sacrifices. *Me.* Not Sunny, Phoenix, or River."

My biting tone hung heavy between us. The tension-filled silence should've been a sign to keep my mouth shut. Unfortunately, the memories had me in a chokehold; that had to be the reason for my continued lunacy.

"Logan leaving for the Navy is a totally different situation. You and your sisters had your mom. He didn't abandon you."

"Abandon?" she murmured low.

Fucking, *fucking*, shit.

"There's a difference—"

"Abandon?" she cut me off to repeat. "Is that what you think you'd be doing if you did something for yourself, something you wanted? That you would be abandoning them?"

A lifetime of poison gathered in my gut, swirling together with the dormant anger I'd learned to ignore, forming a toxic concoction that threatened to overpower my control. As gently as I could manage, I shoved her feet off my lap and stood.

I needed to get the fuck away from the memories. From this conversation. From Jaclyn before I said something I couldn't take back.

"Echo—"

The concern in her tone only pissed me off more. I didn't deserve her worry. I didn't deserve anyone's, especially not my siblings'. Their misplaced desire for me to find happiness had led them to orchestrate an ambush, gone as far as executing two shotgun weddings to force my hand. And in doing so took away all of my excuses—they'd called me on my bullshit leaving me with nothing but the truth.

A truth that had eaten a hole straight through my soul.

A truth I'd give anything to forget.

"I took everything from them," I spat.

"You gave them—"

In that moment, fury took over. Hate and pain and decades' worth of guilt exploded all over my living room, uncaring that it was Jaclyn who was going to be wrecked in the flare-up.

"Jesus fuck, you have no idea what I gave them or didn't give them. What Logan did for you, your mother, and your sisters is a far fucking cry from what I did to my family. He saved you, I put mine through hell. Logan and I are not the fucking same. He ended your pain. I caused my family's pain."

Jaclyn jumped to her feet and bore down on me, coming to stop a foot away with her arms crossed over her chest.

"I don't believe you."

What the fuck?

Before I could respond she elaborated. "No, I don't understand you. How is it a man who has literally dedicated his life to ensuring his brothers and sister didn't go to bed dirty and hungry can stand here and say you caused their pain? What will it take for you to open your eyes and see what you gave them?"

"I know what I gave them."

"Yeah, Echo, you do? So what did you give them?"

Bile rose quick and fast, clogging my throat. The putrid truth close to the surface and demanding to be told.

"Nothing," I choked. "I gave them nothing."

"How can you say that? You raised them. You took care of—"

No, fuck no, I didn't want to hear any more of that shit.

"I took everything from them."

"How's that—"

"I killed Officer Smith!" I shouted.

Jaclyn's eyes widened in horror and she stumbled back until the back of her legs hit the edge of the recliner. I distantly heard her mutter something but I couldn't make out what she said through the roaring in my ears or the pounding of my heart.

With that I did what I'd been taught to do by everyone who was supposed to love me.

I fled.

16

JACLYN

I should've gone after Echo. No, I should've stopped him before he left. But I stood frozen in shock and watched as he stormed through his kitchen out to the garage. I stood frozen as I listened to the garage door go up. I didn't move a muscle when I heard his car start.

I did nothing.

Now Echo was out there somewhere and I was sitting on his couch no less freaked out than I was when he'd taken off. But now worry had set in. He'd been gone a long time—more than an hour—and there I sat doing nothing.

I killed Officer Smith.

Echo's words still lingered in the air.

Or maybe they dissipated but soaked into my skin.

I would never forget the echo of his angry voice. I'd feel his anguish as it poured out of him. I'd forever know his suffering because it now lived in me—that was how pain-filled those words were as he hurled them at me.

I killed Officer Smith.

With shaky hands I snatched my phone off the coffee table where I'd set it after my last unanswered call to Echo. I went to my recent calls and tapped my brother's name.

"Jackie?"

At the sound of Logan's groggy voice something snapped inside of me. Worry for Echo and the gratitude of having a brother who would answer no matter the time of night warred in my chest.

"I need you."

I heard the rustling of covers before he asked, "Where are you?"

"Echo's."

"Where's Echo?"

Logan's angry growl told me I had approximately two seconds to calm my overprotective brother down or they'd be hell to pay.

"I'm fine. No one's hurt—"

"I didn't ask that," he cut me off. "Where's Echo?"

I sucked in a breath and begged, "Please give me a minute to explain. I don't need you to come over here. I need you to help me understand something."

"Jaclyn, I'm not gonna ask again, where the fuck is Echo?"

"We had words and he left."

"What kind of words?"

I glanced around Echo's living room hating that I was going to have to tell Logan what Echo said but I needed help and Logan was the only person I trusted.

He was the only person I knew who would understand. Who would know what to do.

"The kind that led to him telling me that he killed Officer Smith, right before he stormed out of his house and took off."

My stomach clenched at the betrayal.

Was it betrayal if I was seeking help?

Damn, I hoped not.

"Come again?"

There was no chance in hell I was uttering those disgusting words ever again so I didn't repeat myself but I did offer more information.

"We were talking about why he never did undercover work. The conversation...deteriorated quickly from there. He said something about what you did for me, Jill, Lucy, and Mom then he went on to say he was nothing like you—that he caused his family's pain."

"He didn't kill Officer Smith," Logan told me.

I wasn't sure if I was hurt or offended that my brother thought it was necessary to tell me such a thing. What I did know was I was pissed and I didn't bother to hide it when I spat, "I know he didn't, Logan. What I need help with is figuring out why he'd tell me he did. Has he ever talked about it with you?"

"Jackie..." my brother trailed off.

I gave him a moment before I prompted, "Well? Has he?"

"No."

Well, damn. Maybe Logan couldn't help me, which meant for no reason at all, I'd just told him something I should've kept to myself.

"I'll let you get back—"

"How long ago did he leave?"

I glanced down at my phone. The numbers in the corner made me wince.

"Almost two hours."

My brother cursed under his breath before he heaved a sigh that told me he was getting ready to say something I wasn't going to like.

"Maybe you should go home. Give him some time."

He didn't abandon you.

That would be a hell to the no. I wasn't leaving. I didn't know all the details of the Kent family saga but I knew enough to know Echo's mom had left her children to their criminal father. I knew that Echo's dad had a problem with taking things that were not his, mostly cars he could dismantle and sell for parts. On top of that he was an alcoholic who didn't care for his children.

I didn't need a PhD to know Echo had deep-seated abandonment issues. The last thing I needed to do was leave.

"I'm not leaving."

"Jackie, he needs time to cool off."

"No, brother, what he needs is to understand I'm not going to leave every time he gets pissed at me. I admit I pushed too far too fast."

"Fuck," he clipped. "I'm coming over there."

Sweet baby Jesus, that would be a disaster.

"No way. I only called because I needed advice and you're the only person I trust with this. Please don't make me regret it."

I was treated to another litany of profanity and an even longer exhale.

"My advice?"

"Yeah."

"I cannot fucking believe I'm telling you this..." There was a brief pause. "Keep pushing him."

I settled back into the couch, pitched to the side, and fell to the cushions.

"You didn't see him, Logan," I muttered. "He looked like his whole world was crumbling around him. Like he was almost scared."

"Yeah, Jaclyn. Having to tear down all the lies you've told yourself, facing old shit you've spent a lifetime hiding from, fucking kills. But he has to do it. And he won't unless the reward is greater than the pain."

My heart clenched. For Echo and my brother. For the man who had given everything to protect me and the man who had sacrificed his happiness for his family.

They were different but the same.

Cut from the same piece of priceless cloth.

"Logan," I whispered.

"It's gonna get worse," he warned.

"Worse?"

"He's gonna lash out. He's gonna tell you all the reasons why he doesn't deserve you and he's gonna do it in a way that's brutal to shock you."

I hated that my brother knew this from personal experience.

"He said he was done pushing me away."

"I didn't say he was going to push you away, I said he's going to tell you all the shit he thinks he failed at. All the shit that's holding him back from being happy. All the shit that he thinks he did wrong. And he's going to do it in the most shocking of ways so you'll walk away. If he succeeds in that then he's right and he's the failure he's always known he was."

"Like telling me he killed Officer Smith," I mumbled.

"Yeah, Jackie, like that."

I closed my eyes to keep the tears that had welled in my eyes at bay. Tears I desperately wanted to shed for the men in my life. But I knew neither would want that. Especially my brother.

"I can't say I'm not worried about you," Logan told me softly. "I need you to promise me something."

"What's that?" I asked.

I'd learned the hard way to ask before making promises to my brother. If you gave him your word, he held you to it. Not that I broke promises normally, but Logan took a promise as a blood oath you fulfilled even if it meant you did that on your deathbed.

"You call me, day or night, if you need me. If it gets to be too much and you need me to step in, you call. If you need someone to talk to or you need advice, you call me."

I could do that. Hell, I needed my brother to have my back on this.

But...

"One condition," I returned.

"No conditions. I need this from you."

My brother had asked very little from me or my sisters. Sure he could be an overbearing, overprotective beast but he only behaved like a control freak because he loved us. However, this was something different and as much as I wanted to give Logan everything he needed I needed something in return.

"I need to be able to confide in you without the fear of you going off on a tear. He's going to hurt me. The same way I'm going to hurt him as I'm muddling my way through this. I can't tell you things if I'm afraid you're going to—"

"Kill him."

"Logan," I snapped.

"Mark this, little sister; any other man drove you to call me nearing on midnight sounding the way you sound, I'd hunt his ass down and make it clear he was to forget you exist. But this…I know what this is. I know the man Echo is. I know what he has buried. I know the pain he's in. But more than that I know that when you drag him to the other side, he will love you so completely I will rest easy knowing he will never let harm come to you."

I know the pain he's in.

Damn, my brother was breaking my heart.

"I promise to call you."

"Text me in the morning."

"Will do."

"Love you, Jack Nuts."

My eyes popped open for the sole purpose of rolling at my brother's stupid, childhood nickname for me.

"Love you, too, Lo—"

My brother rang off before I could return a razz.

I sat up clutching my phone to my chest and contemplated calling Echo again or maybe doing the dishes to occupy my time while I waited for Echo to return.

I decided against both and made my way to Echo's room.

I stripped out of my clothes, went to the drawer I knew Echo kept his shirts in, and pulled out a tee. I used his toothbrush to clean my teeth, forwent washing my face, and crawled into his bed.

I didn't know how long I laid there hugging his pillow, breathing in the slight smell of his shampoo, when I heard the kitchen door open. I didn't move a muscle while I waited for him to come into the room. I stayed perfectly still while I heard him undress. When I felt the mattress compress, I let go of the pillow and rolled so he'd have room to slide in.

I didn't get far before his arm hooked me around my waist and he pinned his chest to my back. Moments later his face was in my neck.

"I'm sorry." Two words laced with so much anguish they made my teeth clench.

That night I'd lost count how many times it felt like my soul had been torn from my body. But right then feeling Echo's heart pounding against my back, listening to his choppy breathing, I'd sell my soul to the devil if it meant I'd never hear Echo's voice sound like that again.

"You're home, that's—"

"I'm so *fucking* sorry."

I scooted back, lifted my arms to rest over his, and held on tight.

"Baby—"

"Shh, Echo, we'll talk tomorrow."

He shoved his face deeper into the side of my neck and on a tortured whisper he groaned, "Please don't leave me."

Yep, my soul left my body.

"Never."

I didn't know how long we lay there in silence. Echo

holding onto me like I was his lifeline, me anchoring him to me the best I could, but eventually I fell asleep.

When I woke up Echo was gone.

17

ECHO

"Is there a reason you're checking your phone every four minutes like a teenage girl?" Evan asked from beside me.

Yes, there was a reason. I'd had to roll out of bed at the butt ass crack of dawn to meet Evan. Something I'd forgotten to mention to Jaclyn last night, leaving her to wake up in an empty bed. And after the shit I'd pulled I was now regretting my decision to let her sleep. I'd left a note by the coffee pot telling her to call me when she got up.

That call hadn't come.

"I'm waiting for Jaclyn to call."

"It's five-fifty-eight," he noted the time.

I shrugged off my insane behavior and said, "She starts work at eight."

Evan's gaze went back out the windshield, mine followed, and we went back to staring at a suspected stash house one of the neighbors had reported.

So far that morning we hadn't seen any traffic. But

according to last night's watch there had been plenty. Foot, bicycle, vehicle, even a man riding an electric scooter had stopped at the house, gone inside, and left within five minutes. All of the indicators were there; another day or two of watching, taking license plates, and getting descriptions of the visitors we'd graduate to a knock and talk. If that didn't work we'd follow the cars and if warranted make a traffic stop. But for today it was sit and watch—my least favorite part of the job. It was boring as fuck but necessary.

"Something happen?" Evan eventually asked.

No, something hadn't happened, everything had.

I'd fucked up so royally I wasn't sure how or if I could repair the damage. I wasn't sure if Jaclyn waiting for me to return was a good sign or if she was being her normal considerate self and was waiting just to make sure I'd made it home after my hasty exit.

Who the fuck was I kidding? My exit hadn't been hasty —it had been a full-blown outburst complete with a heaping side of twat after I'd told Jaclyn I was going to stop pushing her away.

Christ, I was a dick.

"We had..."

Fuck, what did we have, an argument? A discussion during which I admitted my darkest secret in the most fucked up of ways? Not only that, I offered no further explanation.

"Had a what?"

I didn't answer, couldn't answer past the lump in my throat.

Jesus, had I really told her I'd killed Officer Smith? Just blurted that shit out then left her there knowing what a piece of shit I really was...yep, I had. And yet she was in my bed when I got back. Not only that, she'd allowed me to wrap my arms around her and soak in her warmth until she fell asleep.

"Echo?"

"A fight. Or an argument. I don't know what we had."

"You don't know?"

I kept my gaze trained on the house even though I could feel my partner's eyes studying me. There was no getting out of this conversation. Evan called me on my shit quicker than my brothers did. As close as I was with my siblings, I was closer with Evan. There were just some things that I couldn't talk to River or Phoenix about and Sunny was out of the question. In some ways Evan knew me better than anyone. He'd earned my trust. It was with that in mind I gave him a rundown of last night's unfortunate turn of events—save the part about Smith. No one knew that secret except for Jaclyn.

When I was done, my admission was met with silence. I didn't need Evan to tell me how badly I'd fucked up but I had expected something, even if it was him telling me what a dick I'd been.

"You know." His shockingly soft tone made me brace. "It's not a contest."

"Say again?"

"I know your story. I know Logan's, which means I know hers or at least part of it and it's not a competition—who had the most fucked-up childhood. Which brother did more for their family. Whose trauma is worse."

That had my anger spiking.

"What the fuck are you taking about?"

He didn't explain but he unfortunately went on, and since I was stuck in the car with him, I had no choice but to brace and take the impact of his words.

"Her brother protected her, you protected yours, so she more than most knows what you sacrificed, including your career. Hell, when River was approached with an undercover assignment you encouraged him to take it. But you? One comes up for you, you always pass. And she's right; they're adults, they don't need you in the same capacity as they once did. But that's not the problem, is it?"

Evan's last statement wasn't a question—he knew damn well he was right.

"You're still trying to make amends for a felony that's not yours."

My jaw clenched while I fought to keep the rest of my body from tensing up. Evan knew a lot about my past but he didn't know everything and he certainly didn't know what the fuck he was talking about when it came to making amends. I hadn't even made a dent in what I owed my family for my fuckup.

I caught movement in my peripheral and snapped my gaze back out the windshield.

I reached for my phone on a muttered, "Fuck."

"Is that Jimmy?" Evan asked.

I didn't look up from my phone while I scrolled to the number I needed.

"Sure is."

"Fuck," he echoed my concern.

Jimmy Lone rolling up to a stash house at six in the morning was not a good sign.

"You think the house is one of his crews or is shit about to hit the fan?"

Seeing as we had yet to get confirmation Jimmy was back in Hollow Point, I didn't have an answer.

Tucker picked up the phone with a groggy, "Hello."

I hated waking my friend up first thing in the morning only to pile shit on him before he had a chance to get out of bed but this couldn't be helped.

"I'm on surveillance," I began. "And Jimmy just rolled up onto the house we're watching on foot." I kept my eyes glued to the man in question and watched as he walked by the front pathway. "Looks like he's scoping the place out."

"What's your twenty?"

I quickly gave Tucker the location, tacking on more information. "This area is not known for drug activity."

I heard the rustling of papers in the background, a few muttered curses, and finally, "That address isn't on the list of known locations."

He meant known locations the DEA had for Herlinda Gomez.

"As I said, this area isn't known for drug activity. It's a middle-income neighborhood. Lots of kids, nice yards, decent, hardworking people. The neighbor who called it in did so within days of the traffic starting, which was a month after the new renters moved in. This house is new, as in within the last few weeks."

"Then it's not one of Jimmy's," Tucker confirmed what I suspected. "Jimmy doesn't set up in nice quiet neighborhoods. He doesn't like nosy neighbors. He uses chaos and filth as his cover. If all the houses around him are shit, having late night parties, lots of coming and going, no one's paying attention to what's happening at his place."

Tucker would know. He spent a long ass time under-cover working with the Lonesome crew.

"Something else I don't think I have to tell you but I'm going to anyway. If Jimmy's scoping out the place that means he's aware it's there. Which means he'll make one approach and tell the dealer to fold up shop. They don't heed that one warning there will be hell to pay. His preferred method is to set explosives and burn the house down."

No, Tucker didn't need to tell me that.

"Haven't forgotten."

"Good. Then after Jimmy makes his approach you'll follow up and get whoever's running that house to agree to pack up and get the fuck gone. A low-level dealer might not know who he is and want to play tough guy. If it's someone who has some firepower, they might not want to give up the territory. Both would be trouble but one would start a war."

I'd lived through one Lonesome war; I had no desire to live through another while the streets of Hollow Point turned into a battle zone.

"Did you know he was back in town?" I asked.

"Nope. I've already sent a few texts."

Read: Tucker was pissed he hadn't been kept up to speed.

"Are we following him?" Evan asked from the driver's seat.

"No."

"When will you be back at the station?" Tucker inquired.

I barely contained my growl of frustration when I answered, "Two hours."

"Meet you at the station."

With that Tucker disconnected and I turned to Evan.

"Conversation is dropped."

"For now," he agreed.

That was too fucking easy and I knew why a moment later.

"I want to meet her."

Christ.

"Tonight," he went on.

There was no use fighting Evan. He'd find a way to meet Jaclyn even if that meant going to TC to speak to Logan. Agreeing meant I got to control the situation.

"This weekend—"

"Tonight. Balls Deep. I owe Matt twenty bucks. Two birds and all that."

"Why the hell do you owe Matt twenty bucks?"

And since when were Matt and Evan buds?

"Don't worry about it."

What the hell?

"I wasn't worried but now I am."

Before Evan could respond my phone beeped with a text.

Thanks for making coffee.

I read and reread the message. Four words that gave nothing away.

Fuck.

Another one came as I was still trying to find the hidden meaning behind the last.

Are you busy tonight?

Four more words that were more confusing than the last four she'd sent.

I was on the verge of breaking down and asking Evan his opinion on her short texts when another one came through.

I'm sorry I pushed you last night. My impatience hurt you and made you tell me something you weren't ready to tell.

I blinked at the text, read it three more times, and was still having issues comprehending what I was reading. I'd been a supreme asshole, told her I was responsible for a man's death, ran out on her—and it bears the repeat was a total asshole—and she was apologizing to me?

What in the actual fuck?

Your note said you were on a stakeout this morning so no need to respond. I know you're busy. Be safe!

For the first time since I'd been a dick, I felt my lips twitch. I absolutely didn't tell her I was on a "stakeout." I told her I was doing surveillance this morning with Evan.

I think you've watched too many episodes of Law & Order. I texted back.

At this point I think Law & Order is as American as apple pie.

She wasn't wrong. Between that show and *CSI* every citizen thought they knew my job better than I did.

Before I could change my mind I sent her another message.

Evan would like to meet us at Balls Deep tonight. Cool? After that you're at my place again.

Yes to Balls Deep. No to your place. We're at mine tonight.

I wanted Jaclyn in my bed but I wasn't stupid enough to squabble.

Copy that.

I think I just shivered, Officer Kent.

Maybe it was from the overwhelming relief I felt or maybe it was because she was being her normal cute self but I couldn't stop my burst of laughter.

My Tuesday was no better than my Monday had been. I had a quick meet up with Tucker at the station—which was nothing more than him dropping off more files and a promise to stop by Balls Deep that night for a drink. It was a dual-purpose plan of getting Matt and Tucker together and to have him there to run interference with Evan and Jaclyn. I trusted my partner but I also knew he spoke his mind. And if his mind wandered to him wanting to play Mr. Fix-It he'd have no issue talking to Jaclyn about shit I didn't want him talking to her about. With Tucker there, he'd never bring up my past or my issues or his opinions about self-forgiveness, which was his new kick and had been for the last year. Evan was of the mind that if I was preaching to my siblings about letting go of the past, I should be doing the same.

Something about leading by example or some such shit I had zero interest in hearing about. I was more of a do-as-I say kind of guy when it came to moving on from the legacy my parents had left us. But then I was the one who'd fucked everything up, so I didn't get the luxury of self-forgiveness. My best hope was to bury the guilt deep enough I could make a go of things with Jaclyn and not fuck them up.

After checking the addresses Tucker left with us, our plan to do a drive-by of the warehouse Dick gave us went to shit. The address was on the list of known or suspected locations Herlinda Gomez was running her drugs through. Which pissed me off for more than one reason. The first and most important one was there was probably a shit ton of cocaine in that warehouse. The second irritation was the DEA had this information and had not shared it. And if they had it, that meant they'd been through the area recently—something the higher-ups in the department likely knew but didn't share.

That didn't piss me off; it infuriated me.

We were all cops, we all took the same oath, we all wore the same uniform, yet depending on how many stripes marred the sleeve or gold stars on the collar some officers seemed to forget we all played on the same team. That was not to say all, but there were certainly some who were higher up on the food chain than I was who were willing to play the game of politics. My direct chain of command didn't, which meant the decision to keep the DEA in Hollow Point on a need-to-know went to the state level.

That was only to make Tucker's job more difficult since he was the agent who'd been sent in and there would be some who weren't going to be happy learning the DEA had been running an operation without their knowledge.

"You taking this to the captain, or am I?" Evan asked.

"You."

"Coin toss?"

That was a fuck no. I wasn't taking a chance of losing.

"Nope. It's your day to drive. Your day to report to Cap."

"I'm not trackin' that logic," Evan grumbled but still pushed his chair back from the table.

My logic might've been bullshit but we both knew Evan's disposition was better suited to deal with the shit hemorrhage our captain was going to have.

"I'll just wait here while you work your magic."

Evan swiped a stack of papers off the table, flipped me the middle finger, and wordlessly strolled out the door.

A better man would've hidden his smile.

I continued to go through the file Tucker had left on Herlinda's recent activity while I waited for the eruption from my captain's office. A lot had changed since Jimmy's arrest. Herlinda had cemented her alliance with a Colombian cartel and had new routes through Guatemala and new smuggling operations in Mexico. The woman had certainly made a name for herself and her family. Back in the day she was known to be ruthless, now she was downright feared. That was a lot of firepower at Jimmy's back.

My phone beeped with an incoming text just as I heard my captain boom, "Where's Kent?"

Fucking hell. So much for Evan working his magic.

I checked the message on my way out of the briefing room, smiling at the picture of Jaclyn with her face pressed against a black horse's jaw, a huge smile on her pretty lips with the caption, "we made friends" while I thumbed a reply.

Good, baby, now be careful.

She sent back a rollie eye emoji and a question.

What time am I meeting you at Balls Deep?

7 work for you?

Perfect.

I refrained from sending another apology or asking her the real question that was weighing heavy—how in the fuck was she being so cool with me after I'd hurt her after I'd told her the truth?

That should've been enough to make her run away. Make her open her eyes and see me for the man I was and not the hero she made me out to be.

I wasn't Logan Haines.

Not even close.

18

JACLYN

I WAS EARLY BUT I'D PLANNED IT THAT WAY. I WANTED to talk to Chelsea before Echo and his partner Evan got to the bar. It was time I made the effort to get to know the people who had welcomed me into their tightknit group without question or reservation. Sure, a lot of it had to do with me being Logan's little sister but everyone had also made it clear they just plain liked me.

Beyond that I was dying to ask about Hadley's babies. The day the twins were born my brother had given me the details like he was filling out one of those SITREPs he was always complaining about writing up, or at least he'd given the information the way I assumed how one of those reports would read—boring and to the point.

Everyone's fine. C-section. Two boys. Fraternal. Benjamin Jasper. Caleb Jason.

No other information. Not how big the boys were, not the drama that I knew had to have taken place since this was Hadley Walker giving birth. Just the boring stuff. Not that Hadley and the boys being fine was boring but...I wanted the juice.

Chelsea beamed a smile as soon as she saw me and waved me over to the bar.

"Hey, what brings you here?" she asked.

"I'm meeting Echo. But I came early to find out how Hadley and the babies are doing."

Her pretty smile widened.

"You mean get the deets? Girl, you missed the chaos."

"Chaos?"

"*Kay. Os.*" Chelsea broke the word apart and nodded. "Let me get you a drink and check on a few customers then I'll be back. What'll it be? Fake beer?"

For a moment I was confused and thought she was offering me a non-alcoholic beer. Then it hit me—Echo called my Angry Orchard "fake beer." The fact that Chelsea remembered hit me square in the chest. Maybe it was because she and Matt owned a bar and she was a bartender so she remembered people's drink orders. But something told me remembering mine wasn't a hazard of the job and more because she was my friend.

I nodded but didn't verbalize my answer before she flitted away.

There was something about Chelsea I really liked. She was friendly but it was more than that. There was something about her fun, free-spirit attitude that drew me to her. She also had an underlying toughness that I admired. Not a don't-get-close-or-I'll-cut-a-bitch toughness but a she's-been-through-a-lot-and-came-out-the-other-side-stronger personality. Which was something I not only admired but respected.

I swiveled on the bar stool and took in the bar. It wasn't as busy as I'd seen it but it was surprisingly full for six-thirty on a Tuesday. All the pool tables were taken and one of the two dart boards had people throwing darts. There were still seats available at the bar and not all the booths and high round bar tables were occupied but there was still a crush of smiling, happy people with drinks in their hands.

"So," Chelsea started and placed my beer on the bar. I turned back just in time to watch her roll her eyes. "Jasper Walker is a menace and I mean that in the best way possible."

I wasn't sure how being a menace could be considered the best anything but I didn't ask. Not that I would've had a chance before Chelsea launched into her story.

"Okay, so as you know, Hadley's water broke so we get to the hospital, she's rushed up to labor and delivery. I guess with twins they don't fuck around because she was rushed upstairs quick. The rest of us barely get into the waiting room when Jasper and Emily come in. Emily, cool as can be. The woman is the picture of happiness she's getting two more grandbabies. Jasper? The man looks like he's been hit by a truck, backed over, then got into a heavyweight boxing match and lost." She paused to finally suck in a breath. "Not that Jasper Walker would lose a boxing match—or anything for that matter—but you get what I'm saying."

I didn't get what she was saying. Jasper had always seemed very reserved and in control every time I'd been around him.

"This is Hadley, *his* girl. I mean, he loves all his kids, but Hadley's his Mini-Me. There's something a little different with her. So he comes in looking haggard as in scared. Like his girl's the first to ever birth two babies at once even though his wife had already done it thirty-some-odd years ago. Then Jasper's eyes land on Adalyn, his baby, and everything calms. He has his touchstone. So everything's fine until Brady comes in to tell us Hadley's going in for a C-section."

Jeez, Chelsea could talk fast.

I put my hand up to interrupt.

"How many hours did she labor?"

"No hours. The doctor saw her and one of them had turned. I don't see how the little munchkin managed that with his brother squished up against him but he did it. So with one breech they took her and prepped her for surgery. Anyway, Brady makes his announcement, locks eyes with Jasper, and that beastly man walks right to his son-in-law, hooks him around the back of the neck, rests his forehead on his and for the whole room to hear says, and I quote, 'there is no man on this planet who deserves this more than you, Brady. Go. Be with your wife and welcome your boys home.' There wasn't a dry eye in that room. I'll never forget the way Jasper's voice cracked. That was all Brady needed —just that from his father-in-law."

That was beautiful and moving and as much as I would've loved to have witnessed that moment I disagreed with Jasper. Not that Brady didn't deserve all the love and happiness he had in his life but I could think of another man on this planet who deserved to welcome his children into the world. Welcome them and love them and teach them how to be good, strong, honest people like he'd done for his siblings.

Echo deserved his own family, but more than that he

needed it. He needed his own children to love him unconditionally. He needed to love them back and give them everything he never had.

"Then," Chelsea continued, drawing out the word. "The boys and Hadley were finally moved to a regular room and pandemonium ensued. We weren't all allowed in her room for obvious reasons but it was also a good thing the hospital had the foresight to have a two at a time rule since there were two babies or I fear a knockdown, drag-out fistfight would've happened. Delaney and Addy played rock paper scissors to decide who was going in first. While they were doing that Jason snuck out of the room with Mercy and got in right after Jasper and Emily were done."

I loved that Hadley and Brady and now Ben and Caleb had so many people who loved them. Loved them enough to fight over who got to meet the boys first. Though I'd bet Jasper went straight to his daughter to check on her before he met his grandsons.

"Well, do you have pictures?" I asked.

"Um, hello, of course I do." She reached into her back pocket and pulled out her phone.

After a few taps on the screen, she handed it to me.

"There's about fifty. If you see a picture of Rebel you swiped the wrong way." Rebel was her horse and the name fit the stubborn girl. "I have to check on some customers."

Chelsea left me with her phone and on the screen was a picture of the cutest, chubby-cheeked, black-haired little boys.

Wow.

I smiled at the thought of them getting their mother's dark hair and green eyes. The combination was striking on

Hadley and Addy. On little boys who shared genes with Brady Walker the mix of two beautiful parents meant Hadley better buy pepper spray and condoms. She was going to need the former to keep the trollops away and the latter to pass out during the boys' teenage years when the' pepper spray stopped working.

I was lost in picture after picture of baby goodness so I missed the man sitting down on the stool next to me until Chelsea came back and I heard her ask, "What can I get 'cha?"

"Coors draft please," the man ordered in a gravelly voice.

My eyes tipped up from the phone to find the man looking over at me. No, not just looking over—looking me over. As in checking me out with blatant interest. Way too much interest if you asked me. Actually he was checking me out with more interest than any man, including Echo, had ever looked at me with. The hunger in his eyes made the hairs on the back of my neck stand on end. The stranger's gaze dipped to my boobs before he licked his lips.

Gross.

"Can I buy you a drink?"

"No thanks, I have one."

I needed to move away from this man for a variety of reasons. The first being he freaked me out and I always listened to my gut. The second reason was if Echo walked in and saw this guy staring at me like he was ready for action and didn't care if my answer was no, he would lose his mind.

"Here." I offered Chelsea back her phone even though I wasn't done. "I'll look at the rest later."

Proving that Chelsea paid attention both as my friend and also as a bartender who had probably had her fair share of run-ins with assholes, she jerked her head to the side and covered my ass. "Are you ready to go back to the office?"

"Why are you going back to the office?" Echo asked from behind me.

I turned my neck and watched as Echo scanned the crowd. I knew the moment his gaze landed on the man sitting next to me.

Everything about Echo changed yet nothing did. Outwardly his features stayed blank; he hadn't moved a single muscle, not even a twitch. But there was something ugly rolling off of him—violently so. Waves of hostility and fury.

What in the world?

"Chels was going to show me something but now that you're here we can go get a table," I lied in hopes of getting Echo away from the stranger as quickly as I could. I pushed off the stool which unfortunately meant I had to face the man next to me to get by him. I needn't have worried. The stranger had his gaze fixated on Echo's arm which reached out to guide me. And by fixated I meant eyes glued to Echo's tattoo, jaw clenched, hunger gone.

Holy shit. I wonder if the stranger knows Shiloh. There was no missing the name scrolling on Echo's forearm. All the Kent brothers had the same tattoo. A sweet homage to their baby sister.

Once Echo had me pinned to his body he looked over at Chels.

"Matt in?"

"Yeah, he's finishing up payroll. I'll go get him."

Oh, yeah, Chelsea could read a room.

"That'd be good."

Echo shifted and guided me through the small crowd. His fingers curled around my upper arm, the tips pressing in deep like he was worried someone was going to attempt to snatch me from his hold.

Sure, the weird guy had given me bad vibes but I thought this was a little over the top since no one in their right mind would continue to be a creep to a woman when her six-foot-five boyfriend saddled up next to her.

"How much of a problem was that?" I heard a man ask.

"Not sure but I'd guess huge," Echo returned.

"Fuck."

Fuck?

Fuck what?

And what was a problem?

"Echo, honey, he was creepy but—"

"Creepy?" he grunted.

Well, shit, maybe I should just stay quiet. Which was exactly what I did until Echo stopped next to a booth and gave me a gentle push to slide in. He scooted in next to me and across from us sat a very good-looking man who looked to be nearing fifty—doing that with all the makings of a silver fox.

Um, Echo's partner was hot.

"Jaclyn, I'm Evan," he unnecessarily introduced himself.

"Hi, Evan. Please call me Jackie."

Evan jutted his chin, using the same nonverbal language Echo and my brother often used.

"Creepy?" Echo growled a repeat of his question.

"He was just looking at me weird so I was getting ready to go into the office and wait for you."

"What'd he say to you? How long was he there? Did he touch—"

"Jesus, brother," Evan cut in. "Take a breath."

I didn't think that was the right thing to say and a moment later when that same hostility and fury came back I knew I was right.

"You can tell me to take a breath when that piece of shit is sitting next to your woman giving off creepy vibes."

So this had to be one of Shiloh's ex-boyfriends. I couldn't imagine Echo using that tone about anyone else except a man who'd done his sister wrong.

I quickly attempted damage control.

"He had just sat down. The only thing he said was to ask me if he could buy me a drink."

Echo glanced back across the bar. My eyes followed and I scanned the room. I didn't see the guy sitting at the bar, and I breathed a sigh of relief when he was nowhere in sight.

Crisis averted.

"I need to text Tucker and tell him he can't come...*fuck*."

Holy hell, what now? And who's Tucker?

I was still looking around the room trying to figure out what the new issue was but the only thing that caught my attention was Matt shaking hands with a man who I'd never seen before. Not that that meant much; I hardly knew many people in Hollow Point. But Matt seemed to know him.

"Baby, stay here with Evan a minute."

Before I could question him, he slid out of the booth and was on his way to Matt and the new guy.

"Good. I didn't think I'd get the opportunity to do this," Evan said and my attention went to him. "I hope you don't take any offense but I don't have time to sugarcoat this."

"Sugarcoat what?"

I must've looked super confused because when Evan started speaking again, he did so with his face soft and concern in his eyes.

"I need to know you're strong enough to take Echo on."

Okay, so now I was more confused. As mentioned, not many men were strong enough to take Echo on, let alone little ol' me...

"Emotionally," Evan finished.

Realization dawned. Evan was worried about his friend and I wasn't sure if that indeed offended me that he'd ask me such a question, or if I was thrilled Echo had a good friend to look out for him.

"I hope you won't take any offense when I tell you that what's between me and Echo is—"

"I'm not asking about what's going on. I'm asking you if you're strong enough to take on Echo."

I felt my temper flare to life.

"It's rude to cut people off," I noted.

Evan's lips twitched. My eyes narrowed. His lip twitch turned into a full-fledged smile.

"You're right. It is. My apologies."

Shit. Sometimes I hated that mother taught me manners, which meant I couldn't be bitchy now that Evan had apologized.

"Did you know before Sunny met Luke her nickname was Killer Frost?"

"I'm sorry, what?"

"Sunny's nickname fit. She'd ratchet up the bitch and freeze out anyone who got minutely close. River's always intense but out of all of them he'd give a person the benefit of the doubt. You get one chance with him, but he at least gives people a chance. Phoenix, he's always made people work hard to get close to him. That was, until he met Griff. That kid had Phoenix in knots from the jump, and with Griff came Wren. Never thought I'd see the day Phoenix opened his life to anyone. But it makes sense since it started with Griff.

"Now Echo, he gives no chances. He's closed off and gives zero fucks what that says about him. But then for a few months I saw my friend happy. I had no clue who was making him happy, didn't ask. Then he went from happy to miserable. Not his normal gruff, closed off, grunting self. Miserable. Now he's back with you and miserable in a new way so I have to ask—Jaclyn, are you strong enough to withstand the emotional mess that is Echo Kent?"

I thought that was sweet that it had been Griffin who'd softened Phoenix. I also knew it to be true. Phoenix adored that kid and showed it.

What I didn't think was sweet was that Evan thought Echo was miserable.

"Let me get this straight," I began and leaned into my forearms resting on the edge of the table. "You think Echo's miserable now that he's back together with me?"

"Darlin', that man is tied up so tight he can't breathe. He's searching for a way to escape and hold on at the same time. Loving you means he has to face all his demons." Evan paused. His face went from soft and gentle to painfilled and full of anguish. "He's gonna run, Jaclyn. He's gonna push you away. He's gonna tell you every bad thing he thinks about himself. He's gonna punish himself and make you watch while he does it."

That sounded awfully familiar.

Not only that but it hit too close to home.

"He's already started," I whispered.

Evan nodded. "You got someone?"

"Got someone?"

"To take your back," he explained and glanced over to Echo and Matt.

"Yeah. My brother."

His gaze came back to mine. The look he gave me told me he knew my brother and about our past. It wasn't the same pitiful looks I'd get in Bad Axe. Evan's gaze held knowledge and pride.

"I take it you know Logan?" I asked. Evan jutted his chin. "So you know I'm strong enough to take on Echo. And if this will help you, he doesn't scare me. He tried that last night and I stayed. I figure he's gonna do it again and I'll stay. I'll keep staying until he believes I'm not going anywhere."

"You're not a doormat—"

I lifted my hand and held it up.

"No, Evan, I'm not. I can give as good as I get. He pushes too far, I'll push back. I have no problem calling him on his bullshit. What I mean is I won't abandon him."

"Good," he softly murmured.

"Good," I repeated. "Are we done with that?"

"Yeah, Jackie, we're done with that."

The smile he gave me was damn near criminal. I glanced over at Echo still huddled with Matt and the new guy.

"Who's Echo talking to?"

"Tucker Mitchell. He and Echo go way back. They met while Tucker was undercover. He's DEA."

Undercover.

I had a flashback from last night and quickly shoved it away.

"Is he undercover now?"

"No, Jackie. If he was, I wouldn't have told you he was DEA."

Oh, yeah, right. *Duh*. That made sense.

"So what's up with the guy earlier? Why'd Echo get so pissed?"

I saw the muscle in Evan's cheek jump and his hazel eyes studied me before he shook his head.

"Echo should tell you about him."

"So let me get this straight. You'll grill me about my relationship and tell me about a DEA guy who used to be undercover but you won't tell me about some creep who offered to buy me a beer while staring at my..." I trailed off when Evan's gaze became heated.

Well, I guess Evan was made of the same stuff my brother and Echo were made out of. That stuff being over-protective and overbearing.

Great.

"What was he staring at?"

"My...hair."

Evan's eyes flicked to the messy bun on top of my head.

When they dropped down to mine he noted, "You're a bad liar."

I shrugged off his insult, not sure if it was actually an insult since no one wanted to be a good liar.

"Since you won't tell me about the creep, are you married?"

"Nope. You got any single friends?"

My mind immediately went to my sister.

"No, but I have a twin sister."

Evan's smile was slow. It was also devilish.

"There's nothing I can say to that, that wouldn't get my ass in trouble with Echo."

"Say to what?" Echo asked as he slid into the booth. I looked around for Tucker but he hadn't joined Echo.

"I was telling him about Jillian."

"Not a chance," Echo growled.

"What? Why not? Jill's awesome. Plus she totally has her life together."

Echo put his arm around me and pulled me to his side. As soon as I was there, I burrowed closer and breathed in. I waited and just like always, I felt something inside of me settle. It was like the moment Echo was near, my soul relaxed. The residual fear I carried from my childhood melted away. I knew it'd come back tomorrow when I went to work but as soon as Echo was close it'd be gone again.

"Baby, think it through. She's your identical twin."

It took a second then I got it.

"Oh, please. Would that really bother you?"

"Bother me? No. It'd make me murderous to hear this idiot go on about how hot your sister is."

I feigned shock.

"You think my sister's hot?"

Echo rolled his eyes to the ceiling and shook his head.

I, however, looked at Evan and smiled.

"Just so you know, my sister's totally hot but she has a mouth on her."

Through his laughter Evan mumbled, "No comment."

But he did add a wink.

It was too bad Jill was still in Bad Axe and she had no plans of ever moving.

19

ECHO

Jaclyn tossed her purse on the couch then turned and threw her arms wide.

"Cool, isn't it?"

I glanced around the Vrbo taking in the open floorplan of the downstairs. For a duplex it was a cool design. Nice, inviting furniture, big screen TV mounted on the wall, brightly colored area rug placed under the coffee table of the living room space.

Nice. Neat. Sterile.

This was not Jaclyn beyond the obvious reason—that being, the duplex wasn't hers—there wasn't a lick of personality to it.

When I didn't answer, her laughter filled the room.

"What's funny?"

"Your face."

"My face is funny?"

"Yeah. Your face. You're standing there trying to come up with a lie or alternately trying to stop yourself from telling me what you really think."

She nailed that.

"I'm trying *not* to tell you that while it's nice, clean, in a good neighborhood, I fucking hate that you're living in a Vrbo. No, I don't hate it; that's not a strong enough word. I *despise* that you're living in a place that's not yours."

If the way her body relaxed and the sweet smile she shot my way was anything to go by she'd taken no offense to me telling her the truth.

"I'll find a place soon. I just wasn't sure where I wanted to live so instead of signing a lease then finding out I didn't like the area I thought I'd jump around. As soon as Miss Louise gets back from her vacation, I'll be looking for a new place."

I didn't know who Miss Louise was and I didn't much care. What I cared about was Jaclyn looking for a new place. I cared about her signing a lease and being locked into a place for six months or a year.

"That'd be a waste of time and money," I told her.

"An apartment. Not another Vrbo," she clarified.

"Still a waste of time and money."

Jaclyn's eyes widened and I wondered if she had any clue that she did that when understanding struck. It was as if her eyes were literally and figuratively opened simultaneously.

"I don't want to wait six months before you move in with me."

"Echo—"

I knew she'd eventually ream my ass for cutting her off yet I did it anyway.

"What do I have to do to convince you to move in with me?"

After the shit I'd pulled last night, this was probably—okay, definitely—not the right time to ask her to move in with me.

Her answering silence told me I was more of a jackass than I thought.

"Jac—"

"Hold that thought," she interrupted me. "If we're having this conversation, I don't want to have it standing ten feet apart in the living room."

Without any further explanation she headed for the stairs. She was halfway up when I went to the front door and bolted the lock then followed.

By the time I made it upstairs she was already undressed and in the bathroom, leaning her hip against the basin, eyes on me as I entered, brushing her teeth. When she saw me, she held up a toothbrush still in the package with her free hand. I instantly hated the bedroom as much as I hated the downstairs. There was nothing wrong with the room; it was just as nice and devoid of personality as the living room. A big master bedroom, with a king-sized bed—thank fuck—nightstands, a dresser, and an attached bathroom you could see into from the doorway. So the layout of the room sucked but that wasn't why I hated it. The cream walls and beige bedspread were bland and boring. Jaclyn was neither of those. She was vivid and vibrant. She was full of personality, outspoken, smart, beautiful, sexy, powerful. There wasn't a single object in the room that would depict the woman sleeping in that bed.

I toed off my shoes, pulled off my shirt, dropped it before unbuckling my pants, pulled them off along with socks, and left my clothes in a pile before I made my way across the uninviting room, detesting every step.

When I stepped into the small bathroom Jaclyn gave me a white foam smile.

"You really don't like this place, do you?" she said around a mouthful of toothpaste.

"I hate it."

She finished brushing her teeth while I loaded my brush up with paste, trying to come up with a plan to get her to leave this place tonight and move in with me. That was a whole lot ambitious but if I could manage it, I'd be happy.

I was angrily shoving the brush in my mouth when I felt her wrap her arms around me, press her chest to my back, and rest her cheek on my lat.

"I need you to explain to me what happened last night." Jaclyn tightened her arms around me. "Not what you said, what I did to make you leave. That's the part I need to understand so I know how to navigate us as we go on."

The severity of what I'd done slammed into me.

I'd been the asshole while she thought she'd done something wrong.

I told her I'd killed a man and she hadn't questioned me. She hadn't looked at me in fear or disgust. She'd climbed into my bed and waited for me to come home. Not only that she'd allowed me to hold her. She was right then wrapped around me holding me like I wasn't a worthless piece of shit.

She was holding onto me.

I dropped the toothbrush in the sink, rinsed, spit out the foam, and she held on.

I reached for the towel, wiped my mouth, tossed it on the counter, and she held on.

Holding on.

Wrapped around me.

Not running.

"You did absolutely nothing wrong."

"Echo—"

I turned, breaking the hold, and looked down into a pair of trusting eyes.

"You did nothing wrong."

"I pushed you to talk about something you didn't want to talk about."

"So? That doesn't give me the right to drop a bomb then run out on you."

Not wanting to have the rest of this conversation in the bathroom I found her hand, maneuvered her to the side, and with a sharp tug I led her to the bed. When we got there, I flipped the covers back. Jaclyn climbed in and I followed, intending to instigate damage control. But before I could finish what I'd started to say in the bathroom, Jaclyn twisted, swung her leg over my lap, and straddled me.

"I need to tell you something," she started but didn't share what that something was.

"So tell me," I invited.

"I want to hear everything. The good, the bad, all the ugliness you lived through, and I want to share the same with you. But I want you to tell me when *you're* ready, not because I pushed you into telling me something you weren't ready to share. Not with that. Other stuff, I need you to be open and honest with me. But I won't ever push you about your childhood and that's a promise."

My hands went to the top of her thighs and I stared up at the beauty that was Jaclyn, feeling my stomach clutch and the guilt starting to crush my heart.

"You need to know," I rasped out, feeling my throat constrict. "You have to know who I am and what I've done before you..."

Christ, I couldn't even say the words.

"Fall in love with you?" she supplied. "Too late, Echo. I fell a long time ago."

I drew in a breath but instead of it being calming it burned my lungs as they filled.

No woman other than my sister had ever loved me. Not even the woman who'd pushed me out of her own body cared enough to stick around. No woman had ever come close to earning that from me—save Sunny. There hadn't been a single woman in my life with whom I'd entertained the thought of a future. Now I couldn't imagine one without Jaclyn in it.

And that scared the fuck out of me.

When my mother left, all I felt was dread—the weight of more responsibility. She hadn't done much around the house or for her kids but at least she was there to pick up some of the slack.

Then she was gone.

The bitch took off uncaring what would become of her children—what would become of *me*. She left us in filth to save herself. It had taken Sunny the longest to get over our mother taking off; the rest of us dealt with it and moved on within months.

Months.

Not years.

That was how little the bitch did for us. But she was still our mother and we all felt the sting of rejection when she never came back.

Then there was Jaclyn. It would not take me months or years to recover if she left me. There would be no sting of rejection. Simply put, there would be no getting over her.

A man does not recover from that kind of loss.

"You can't—"

Her palms landed flat against my chest with a loud slap.

"Don't you dare tell me I can't love you," she seethed, leaning forward and putting pressure on my chest, which did nothing to help the inferno charring my lungs, making it harder to breathe. "I know what I feel, and I'll be damned if you tell me otherwise."

Love you.

Those two words repeated in my mind.

Words that no one other than my siblings had ever said to me. Maybe my mother had when I was a kid but if she did, I'd been too young to remember.

How in the fuck could two words hurt so fucking bad yet feel so fucking good at the same time? How was it I wanted her to tell me again and again, yet never wanted her to say them again?

This beautiful, strong woman deserved so much better than me. Someone who wasn't fucked up, who was whole and could take care of her. Someone who wasn't damaged, who wasn't flawed, whose imperfections wouldn't tarnish her future. Someone who wasn't tainted with a family legacy that was so fucked up there was no way to erase the history. Someone who was strong enough to conquer the demons that lived within. Someone who hadn't shattered the lives of everyone he loved. Someone whose soul wasn't fractured.

She deserved better but I wasn't letting go.

Before I could stop the words, they poured out of me in one painful breath.

"Please don't leave me."

My voice sounded ragged and raw and I didn't give the first fuck she heard it. I tightened my grip on her legs, securing her to me even though she was balancing her weight on one hand while the other slid up my chest, over my throat, and came to rest on my jaw.

"I'm not leaving you."

"You will."

"No, Echo, I won't."

Fuck.

"I need you to ask me."

Her brows pulled together and her head tipped to the side.

"What do you need me to ask?"

"Everything. I can't...I don't know how to tell you. I need you to ask."

"Okay," she whispered.

There was a long beat of silence but that didn't mean she wasn't communicating with her eyes locked on mine. The trepidation was clear. Hesitancy a close second. But there, casting a light over her anxiety was love. I couldn't see it as much as I could feel it. Not from her palm on my chest, or her hand cupping my face, or her legs pressing into my sides, or from her sitting on my lap. It was more than that—the emotion was filling the room, choking out the fear threatening to overtake me.

"Tell me about Officer Smith."

"Jac—"

Her hand on my jaw slid up until her palm covered the side of my face as she leaned closer.

"I know you didn't kill him, honey. What I want to know is why you *think* you did."

"I did kill—"

"No, Echo, Lester pulled that trigger."

I didn't bother fighting my body going to stone, which was good since I needed the energy I was no longer using to breathe to stop myself from tossing Jaclyn off of me.

"Jac—"

"I gotta know, Echo. Just this. The rest I'll wait for. But, honey, I know you didn't kill that man. I know you believe you did and that's what I've got to understand. I can't help you work that poison out of you if I don't know what I'm mining."

Good *Christ*.

I tried my best to keep the poison, the toxic sludge that sloshed in my gut, the guilt from rising to the surface.

I tried and failed to keep the demons at bay.

They pushed to the surface and came out of my mouth before I was ready. Not that there was a way to cushion the truth but I didn't stand a chance against the past.

I never did.

The demons always won.

"I called the cops," I admitted.

"You called the cops?"

I nodded, taking her hand with the movement.

"I don't understand."

"I was pissed off and impatient. CPS wasn't helping. Lester wouldn't let me move out and take Phoenix and Sunny with me. River wouldn't move out because I wouldn't leave. And Lester knew there was no way I was leaving my kids behind. So he had me trapped. Me *and* River. We only had a few more years until Sunny was eighteen then we all could've left together but Lester's temper was flaring more than normal and I was afraid it was only a matter of time before he popped off and hit River or worse, Sunny. I needed to get my family away from him. We'd been arguing about it but he wouldn't budge."

Not to mention Lester had been turning on Phoenix. That was the driving factor behind me calling the cops that day. For some reason Phoenix had always been Lester's favorite. My father hated me, he was indifferent when it came to River, he had no use for Sunny, but Phoenix, he'd bonded with. There were times when I thought there was a smidgen of goodness in Lester. A tiny sliver of decency when I watched him with his youngest son, teaching him how to change a tire or showing him how to take apart an engine. But I'd learned that there was nothing good about our father. There was no shred of humanity in him. Lester used Phoenix as a way to control us. He was nothing to Lester but a way to manipulate me and River. But the older Phoenix got the more he saw through Lester's bullshit. And that was when shit went really bad.

"So you called the police for help?"

"No, I called the police to rat Lester out. I came home early from work and found a shit ton of stolen property in the living room. It was perfect; River was in class and

Phoenix and Sunny were at school. None of them would be there to see him get arrested for the five hundredth time. I called the cops thinking that this time while he was in custody, I could file the paperwork to get guardianship and we'd be free."

Jaclyn's gaze didn't leave mine while she listened intently. I didn't know if it was the connection that gave me the strength to finish or if now that everything was coming out I couldn't stem the flow. But for whatever reason words kept spewing out of me.

"Lester came in from the garage and caught me calling it in. I should've known he was up to something when instead of packing up the stolen goods and leaving before the cops got there, he sat on the couch and started laughing at me. It took less than five minutes for a patrol car to roll up in front of the house. Which wasn't surprising seeing as the cops had been to our house so many times there was probably a dedicated unit for our address waiting down the street. There was a knock on the door. I moved to answer it but Lester got up and beat me there."

I stopped to swallow down the bile as the ringing in my ears started.

"I saw it happen," I croaked. "I saw him pull the gun out of the back of his pants. It happened so fast it was done in a flash yet I can see it in my mind play out in slow motion. Lester opened the door and shot. That was it. Officer Smith went down; I tackled Lester before he could fire a second round but it was too late. Smith was dead, GSW to the head."

Jaclyn's eyes closed and I was grateful for the reprieve.

"Before Smith's partner cuffed Lester, he told me I'd have to live the rest of my life knowing I killed that cop."

Jaclyn's lids popped open and her fingertips pressed into my cheek.

"He wasn't wrong, Jaclyn. I live with that every day, knowing I killed Smith."

"You did *not* kill anyone."

I heard the conviction in her tone. The need for her to believe that to be true no matter how wrong she was.

"Jac—"

"You didn't kill anyone, Echo. He did. And fuck him for saying that to you. Fuck him for being a piece of shit. Fuck him, Echo."

Her voice rose with every 'fuck' until the last one was nearly a shout.

"I called them there—"

"Yeah, so? You called the police for *help*. You did nothing wrong. God, Echo, do you hear yourself? You wouldn't leave *your kids* behind. He'd trapped you in that house because he knew if he lost you, he'd lose everything. You were the only person keeping that house afloat. He was going to be arrested, you were going to take *your kids* and go and when he got out, he'd have nothing."

I didn't know what to say to that so I said nothing. I just looked up at Jaclyn's deep scowl and thought she never looked more beautiful. I also thought her love for me was coloring her perception of reality. I held the blame just as much as Lester did.

"I see you don't believe me," she mumbled. "What do River, Phoenix, and Shiloh say about it?"

"They don't know."

There it was.

The secret I'd kept from my siblings for almost two decades. The one thing I was afraid they'd never forgive me for.

"What do you mean they don't know?"

"They don't know I was the one who called the cops."

I lost Jaclyn's hand on my face when she reared back and asked, "Why not?"

She must've seen my unease, sensed I'd had all I could take for one night and lowered herself to my chest, giving me all of her weight.

"That's enough for one night," she whispered.

My hands traveled up and around her hips to her back and I held her to me.

After a few moments she tried to roll off me and my arms tightened.

"I want you here."

"Need to turn off the light."

I reached over, fumbled to find the small lamp on her nightstand, and plunged the room into darkness. When I was done, I grabbed the comforter and yanked it up to cover her back. After that, Jaclyn snuggled closer and gave me what I needed.

I had no idea if this was what unconditional love felt like but whatever it was, it felt damn fucking good.

So good I fell asleep with my woman blanketing me. And I did that with the knowledge that for the first time in my life I was the one being protected.

20

JACLYN

I woke up in the same position I'd fallen asleep— on top of Echo's big body with his arms wrapped tight. I'd never slept on top of anyone before, never thought it would be comfortable, yet when my eyes came open and the clash of emotions set in immediately, I was grateful neither of us had moved. That when the joy and sorrow warred in my heart Echo's arms were still holding me. When the pain of last night rushed back I had him under me to snuggle into.

At first glance I'd been drawn to Echo. He was enigmatic, unattainable in a way that would take a good deal of effort to get through all the layers. Untouchable in a way that would be near impossible to breach his walls. Yet I'd taken one look at him and welcomed the challenge. Actually, that wasn't the whole truth—I'd taken one look at him and knew he was the man for me and being that I was the woman who'd been made for him. I knew it with such certainty it had crushed me when he'd let me go and, in an effort to protect myself from any more pain I'd allowed him to walk away.

Up until last night I'd regretted that decision. But now I understood. It wasn't that Echo had to lose me to realize what he had. The man wasn't stupid, he was punishing himself. He was denying himself the happiness he didn't think he deserved. Pushing me away meant he was denying me what I wanted, what I needed, the happiness I deserved. And that was what losing me had shown him. So, no, I no longer regretted allowing him to walk away if that meant when he came back his eyes and heart were open to me.

Knowing all of that, I had a decision to make. I knew Echo wouldn't let my living situation slide. Before he left my house this morning, he was going to bring up me moving in with him. On the one hand it was too soon. But too soon or not I wanted to move in with him. And unlike my twin I was not a planner. I was a fly-by-the-seat-of-my-pants type of person and let the chips fall where they may and if I screwed up, I picked myself up and started over. My mother knew this about me and as much as it drove her around the bend, she didn't try to change me. Lucy was a little like me, just with more caution so I wouldn't get any flak from her. Ian was a wildcard and so was Logan. Normally my antics would send my brother from zero to sixty and if this were any man other than Echo I could see Logan kidnapping me and locking me in his basement. It wouldn't matter that his house didn't have one; he'd dig one by hand in the name of protection.

But this was Echo, so I could see Logan being a little apprehensive. Watchful definitely but murderous, no.

Jillian might attempt to stage an intervention, which would work in my favor if that meant she'd have to come to

Georgia. I could introduce her to Evan and hope they hit it off so she'd move here. I'd never gone this long without seeing my twin. That was the only downside to moving. FaceTime and texts weren't the same as hanging out.

"You're thinking awfully hard up there."

All of my earlier thoughts flitted away as Echo's voice, still rough with sleep, rumbled under my cheek.

I lifted my head, pressed my lips to his chest, and replied quietly, "Morning."

Echo's reply was to shift me higher and kiss me.

His kiss was better and it got hotter when he swiped his tongue over my bottom lip.

Yes, much better than my kiss.

I could wake up like this every morning and be happy, especially when Echo's hands started wandering—gently at first up and down my back until he deepened our kiss and grabbed two handfuls of my ass.

Oh, yeah, I could totally wake up just like this every morning. Though I'd already known I could. There was a reason why when I'd stayed at his place during our thing, I'd stayed in bed even after I was awake. I knew this was what I was going to get, or some version of this, but the ending was always the same—me panting my orgasm.

Echo flipped me to my back, went up on his knees, hooked my panties, tore them down over my ass to my thighs. I bent my knees to assist and he shook his head. He lifted both legs—held together by my undies—and rested my heels on his chest. He walked his knees closer, pushing my legs up as he went. His left arm wrapped around my legs, keeping them tight against him while his right hand dipped between us. I felt the head of his cock slide over my sensitive clit as he glided lower, found my entrance, and slowly pushed in. My gaze swept over his handsome face straining with need, down to his shoulders, then to his arm holding my legs with my panties still around my thighs. The sight before me so fucking hot I jerked my hips and he slid in deeper, taking his time when I wanted him to slam home and fuck me.

"Hurry," I demanded and grabbed ahold of the sheets.

When he didn't immediately comply with my demand, I rocked my hips again.

Echo's hand came out from between my legs. His palm went to my stomach to hold me still.

"More."

This time I didn't have a chance to rock into him before his hand slid between my legs again and he pinched my clit.

My eyes shot to his blazing blue eyes and I froze.

I'd seen those eyes full of pain, anger, desire, need, hunger but I had never seen them burning with so much intensity. So hot they looked like blue flames sparking as he slowly continued to sink deeper until finally, we were connected.

"Do you love me?"

I blinked at his deceptively calm tone more than his strangely timed question.

"Yes."

Echo made a sound, not a grunt or a groan, a mewling rumble from his chest as his finger rolled my clit and he pulled out and pushed back in.

"Echo," I whined.

Another slow withdrawal and a glide in.

"Do you love me?"

His tone was no longer calm, he sounded almost feral, angry even.

"Yes."

I was expecting another slow glide but instead his hips pulled back and he thrusted in hard.

"You sure?"

"Yes."

With that, Echo came undone, went totally and completely wild. From the way his eyes shifted over my body, to the way he fucked me, to his finger circling and pressing on my clit.

"*Echo.*"

It was a plea.

A plea for more, to slow down, to never stop, to never let me go, to let me love him, to love me.

"Christ," he bit out and closed his eyes. "I need you to love me, Jaclyn."

"I do."

My reply came out as a whoosh of a breath as my body jolted with each hard drive.

"You can't stop, baby."

"I won't."

Echo hugged my legs tighter. His finger on my clit stopped rubbing and started rolling, his cock drove in deeper and harder. My climax building fast—too fast—so fast I tensed to hold it back.

"Let go, Jaclyn," he growled.

I shook my head even though he couldn't see me.

"Let go, baby."

"Echo, *honey...*"

My head tipped back, my back bowed off the bed, my scream filled the room as my orgasm tore and burned through me.

With one last brutal thrust he groaned my name and spilled into me.

I didn't wait. I couldn't. I needed to touch him, to hold him close to me, to feel his body pressed against mine.

I jerked my legs out of his grasp, bent my knees, reached up, and fumbled with my underwear. As soon as my legs were freed, I wrapped them around his back. Echo dropped forward, keeping some of his weight on his elbow but gave me what I needed. My arms curled around his back, pulling him closer. I felt his lips on my forehead, then my temple. His hand brushed my hair aside and his mouth went to my neck.

"I hope you know I love you, too."

Whisper soft.

So quiet I barely heard.

But I had and at those words my body convulsed.

"I've never said those words to anyone but my siblings. Never thought I would. Never felt anything close. And, baby, I'll never say them to anyone else. Just you."

Just me.

I felt wet hit my eyes.

"You sure?" I repeated his question to me. Only mine was broken and raw.

"Positive."

Firm and resolute and I wondered if my confirmation had sounded like the vow his did.

I hoped so.

We laid there in the silence, my mind racing with a

thousand thoughts, a million questions, none of them important except for one.

"Are you okay?"

"No."

Unfortunately, at that moment nature had taken course and he slipped out of me. Echo rolled us until we were on our sides facing each other.

"No?"

"Scared as shit."

"Scared?"

His eyes shifted to someplace over my shoulder, his hand on my hip twitched, his fingertips dug in, and his brows pulled together.

"Of you leaving me," he started. "I learned young that love was a choice."

He was right but he was also wrong.

"Not always." Echo's gaze came back to mine and I continued. "Sometimes there's just a connection so strong you feel it so deep in your soul you don't have a choice. It just happens."

"My mom chose not to love us enough to stay."

Sadly, I couldn't argue that.

"And in doing so she missed out on all the beauty that is you. She missed out on knowing the man you became. She missed out on knowing River and Phoenix and Shiloh and who you raised them to be. She missed their weddings and River becoming a dad. And she'll continue to miss everything because you're right—she chose to leave."

"Right and if you leave, I won't recover."

I felt my lip curl in revulsion.

"I'm not your mom."

"No, Jaclyn, you're nothing like her. You're the woman who has all the power. You hold all the cards. My future is in your hands. At the time, her leaving hurt. You leaving would kill me."

I wasn't sure if I hated or loved he felt that way.

My hand went to his neck and I squeezed.

"Echo—"

"There's nothing to say to that, baby. It's the straight up truth. You asked so there it is, I love you so much it scares the fuck out me."

I knew that fear. I also knew the pain I felt when I lost him. Though I didn't think now was the best time to remind him of that.

So instead, I asked, "What can I do to ease your worry?"

"Don't leave."

Well, that was easy.

"Okay."

Echo's gaze roamed my face, the pessimist in him searching for the worst. He could look all he wanted; I was telling the truth. I wasn't leaving.

But I needed him to know something else.

"I choose you," I whispered.

Echo's big body jolted right before he turned to stone.

"Every day, honey, I'll choose you."

With a mighty roar he rolled over me, crushed his lips to mine, and stole my lips in a soul-mending kiss.

"YOU DON'T HAVE COFFEE."

We were in my kitchen. This was after he finished kissing the ever-loving daylights out of me, we'd taken a shower, Echo had dressed in the clothes he'd worn yesterday, and I was dressed for work.

I glanced over at Echo and pinched my lips.

Oops.

I didn't remind him I'd switched to tea.

"Reason seven thousand for you to move in with me."

"What are the six-thousand-nine-hundred and ninety-nine other reasons?" I asked and reached into the fridge for orange juice.

"I'll tell you tonight when you move in."

I couldn't move in tonight. I needed to keep an eye on Miss Louise's place until she got back. I straightened and asked, "How about you tell me five of those six-thousand-nine-hundred and ninety-nine right now."

"I love you. You love me. I love you. You love me. I love you."

Well, those were the best reasons I'd ever heard in my life.

"I'll move in next week."

Echo leaned against the counter, his big arms crossing in front of him and his eyes narrowed.

"Next week?"

"I told you I'm watching my neighbor's place."

"And you have to live here to do that?"

He had a good point. I guess I didn't have to live here but I did need to check her mail and do a daily walkthrough of her house like I'd promised. And it wasn't like Echo lived all that far away. I could stop by after work on my way home.

Home.

With Echo.

My heart jumped in my chest.

"Okay."

"You're gonna move in with me?"

"Yes."

"Today?"

"Tonight, after work," I clarified.

Echo pushed off the counter and started stalking my way. I held up my hand and warned, "You can't kiss me again. I'm already running late."

"You're gonna be later," he told me.

"Echo—"

His body collided with mine and his hand went under my chin to tip my head back. But he didn't slam his mouth on mine; he slowly lowered it, stopping just shy of our lips touching to whisper, "I love you, Jaclyn."

Then he took my mouth in a slow, gentle kiss that was no less soul repairing but also breathtakingly beautiful.

He broke the kiss and wrapped his arm around me, keeping me close.

"Before you leave, we need to talk about Jimmy."

"Who?"

"The creepy motherfucker who offered to buy you a drink last night."

Oh, shit.

"Do you remember what he looks like?"

"I guess."

"You guess or you do? This is important, baby. Do you remember him?"

I thought about the creepy guy. Brown hair with gray

sprinkled throughout, brown eyes, decent looking but that was only at a push and if he wasn't giving off a creepy vibe.

"Yeah, I remember what he looks like but he was sitting so I couldn't tell you how tall he is."

"He's five foot eleven, a hundred and seventy pounds, or at least he was when he was arrested."

"Arrested?"

"Jimmy Lone is why Tucker's in town. He just got out on parole and is already making moves to set up his old crew."

That sounded bad.

Really bad.

"If you see him you call me."

See him.

"Why would I see him?" I asked. "Wait, did you arrest him? Does he know who you are?"

"I was on the take down team but he doesn't know who was on the team."

How was that possible?

Echo must've read my confusion because he explained, "We go in covered. Long sleeves, gloves, masked, hats. We cover everything we can."

Something from last night hit me.

"He was looking at your tattoo."

"Yeah," he grunted.

"You think he knows you?"

Echo gave me a soft shake.

"I don't know. I also don't want you scared, I want you smart. If you see him, you call me. I don't answer, you call 911."

I didn't want to be scared either but I kind of was.

"I'll call you if I see him."

Five minutes ago, I was thrilled I was moving in with Echo. Happy beyond belief. But now I was relieved I wouldn't be coming home to a Vrbo but instead to Echo.

"Good. I gotta go home and change and you gotta roll out. What time are we packing?"

"I have three suitcases. I can—"

"What time?"

I felt my eyes get squinty.

"You know there are times I let your rude interruptions go, but it's still rude to interrupt me when I'm trying to speak."

"Says the queen of interrupt—"

"The queen of interruptions?"

Echo's head tipped to the side, his lips curved up into a smile, and he belted out a laugh.

At that juncture since I'd proven him correct I thought my best course of action would be telling him what time to meet me.

"I'll be home by five-thirty."

"Right."

"You're really lucky I love you because you're a serious pain in my ass."

"Right."

My first call was to my mom. She asked all the normal mom questions before she admitted she was happy for me. Then she told me she and Ian were finalizing the details of the move and would be down in Georgia next week. And with them would come the rest of my stuff. Not that I had much left after I'd sold everything but I did have some boxes of keepsakes and knickknacks they were bringing. I needed to remember to talk to Echo about that just in case he thought all he was getting was me and my clothes in his house.

I rang off with my mom and was almost to work when I called Logan.

"You good?"

I rolled my eyes at my brother's greeting wondering if there would ever be a time when he stopped asking me that. Already knowing the answer to that was no, I wondered why I bothered wondering in the first place.

"I'm perfect. How are you?"

"Perfect?"

I didn't miss the skepticism in my brother's tone.

As promised, I had texted him a few times since the other night when I'd called him. He knew Echo and I were smoothing things out but obviously he didn't know what had transpired last night.

"I'm moving in with Echo."

"Say again?"

"I. Am. Moving. In. With. Echo," I repeated slowly.

"Less attitude, more explaining."

On a normal day it was easy to annoy my brother, but couple that with the news his baby sister was moving in with a man and he was extra-duper testy.

I told him just enough about my conversation with Echo to put his mind at ease and focused on the part that he needed to know—that being that Echo loved me.

"He told you that?"

"Told me what, that he loved me?"

"Yes. That. Echo told you he loved you?"

What the hell?

"Yes."

"Straight out, the man said he loved you?"

I was getting irritated.

"Yes, Logan. Would you like to ask the same question a different way for the third time so I can give you the same answer, for the *third* time? He told me he loved me. Actually, he told me more than once he loved me."

Logan whistled a breath before he said, "Never thought..."

When he didn't finish his thought I asked, "Never thought, what?"

"Nothing."

"Logan, I'm pulling into work. I don't have time to annoy the answer out of you. What did you never think?"

"Never thought I'd see the day would come when I'd be happy my baby sister found herself a man. Never thought I'd trust a man to care and look after my sister. Pick one, they're both true."

I knew my brother loved me. There was never a day I doubted it. He'd told me often over the years but more the way he took care of me proved it. Yet still, every time he said or did something sweet it still filled me with warmth.

"I'm at work," I announced. "I love you, Lo-Jack. Talk soon."

"I hate that—"

I disconnected before he could finish telling me he hated that stupid nickname as much as I hated Jack Nuts.

21

ECHO

A HIGH-PITCHED SQUAWK FOLLOWED BY A LONG TONE woke me from a dead sleep. Jaclyn stirred, nuzzled my chest, but other than that made no move. That was, until my phone on the nightstand rang.

"Why?" she groaned and shifted her legs higher.

Without disengaging Jaclyn's body mostly sprawled over mine I reached for my phone, saw a name I wasn't expecting, and quickly took the call.

"Yeah?"

"Sorry to wake you but I figure you're gonna get a callout any minute and I wanted to brief you," Tucker said, sounding wide awake for...I glanced at the alarm...three-oh-nine in the morning.

The callout already came, I just hadn't responded yet.

"Give me a second."

I pulled my phone away from my ear and muted the call.

"Roll off me, baby." Jaclyn started to roll. I tightened my arm around her back and dipped my chin. "Kiss first."

She tipped her head back. I found her lips in the dark and gave her a too-short kiss before I let her go.

I tagged my shorts off the floor on my way out the door, waiting until I was in the hallway to pull them on, and went back to my call.

"Back. What's up?"

Tucker launched right in.

"Two of your undercovers hit paydirt tonight. Thirty grams of coke. Three nine mils. Two fully auto KRISS Vectors."

I ignored the drugs and the handguns.

"Vectors?"

"Yep."

Fuck.

For reasons only known to Jimmy, the KRISS Vector was the rifle he kitted his crew out with. The weapon was expensive to buy legally. Illegally they were astronomical; they were also hard to come by. Which was probably part of the reason the Lonesomes carried the Vector. Posturing. It went beyond street cred and straight to perception. The crew carried what was considered the Lambo of rifles.

Jimmy was also stupid enough to engrave those rifles.

"Do they have the mark?" I asked.

"Yep. Deal went down as planned, your undercovers took their shit, dealers went their way. Cover team followed the dealers who idiotically went straight home."

Wait.

A tingle went up my spine.

I hadn't heard about any undercover buys set up for tonight. That didn't mean it wasn't a last-minute operation or a buy of convenience, but something felt off.

"You keep saying *my* undercovers, was this a narco buy?"

"Gun unit."

Christ, that meant Phoenix's team was likely involved.

"What's the state of play?"

"SWAT's en route now. Barricade situation."

Fucking terrific.

The possibility of Phoenix *and* Sunny.

"You waiting around?"

"I'm in the command van now. Just wanted you prepped."

"Preciate it. See you soon."

"Later."

I disconnected, fighting the urge to call my siblings. If they weren't both on the scene I didn't want to wake them like a crazy idiot needing to make sure they were safely tucked into their beds.

Shit was so much easier when they were kids. When I knew where they were going, who they were going with, and what time they'd be home.

Parenting adult children sucked.

Parenting adult children who were all police officers was terrifying.

I went back into my room and made quick work of getting dressed, stepping over Jaclyn's shoes that now littered the closet floor. I did this fighting my neat-freak tendencies, I also did it smiling. Her shoes in my closet meant she was in my bed. The explosion of cosmetics and hair shit all over the bathroom meant she got ready in that bathroom. Her bent of leaving her mug in the sink instead of the dishwasher meant she drank her morning tea in our kitchen. So, yeah, I could look the other way and do it happily.

I stopped by the side of the bed and stared down at Jaclyn's naked body in the muted light coming from the hall. Fuck, she was gorgeous lying in my bed, hugging my pillow, hair wild and falling down her back, knee cocked up, and perfect ass on display. I wanted to crawl back into bed with her and have a do-over of last night's activities.

With very little coaxing—and this was going way back to the beginning—Jaclyn lost all inhibitions. She had zero hang-ups when it came to sex. The woman was sexy as fuck and she knew it. If I wanted to eat her pussy while she was riding my face, she complied. If I wanted her to suck me off while she straddled my chest with her ass and pussy on display, she complied. Not only that but she got off on giving me a show, rocking her ass back while I finger fucked her. She'd swallow my come, take it up her cunt, on her tits, wherever I wanted to give it to her. Just as long as I gave it, she was happy. And the same for her—around my cock, my fingers, my tongue—she never held back. She screamed her pleasure, panted it, moaned it, however it came out, no reservations. From the first time to last night she'd never had any reservations showing me or telling me what she wanted.

She was the perfect woman—beautiful, smart, funny, and fucking phenomenal in bed. I had long since stopped worrying about our age difference. I was nearing forty, not seventy. The excuse I'd used to end us was nothing but bullshit. The twelve years between us meant nothing when Jaclyn was world-wise beyond her twenty-seven years. The age gap was meaningless when the person who was younger was actually the one with more emotional intelligence than the older one.

I was lucky as fuck she'd forgiven me. Luckier she loved me through all the roadblocks and bullshit I'd put in our way.

Knowing if I didn't leave right then I wouldn't leave at all, I opted not to tempt my dick and brushed her hair off her shoulder, leaned down to press a kiss there. Not that the feel of her soft kiss under my mouth didn't get a stir but it was safer than going near her lips.

"Gotta go, baby," I whispered when she lifted her head.

"Um...okay. Be safe," she returned sleepily.

Fuck, I did not want to leave. A problem I'd never had before, seeing as I'd never rolled out of bed while the woman I was in love with was wrapped around me. Hell, I'd never rolled out of a bed when any woman had been beside me. A problem I hadn't had in the last week she'd been living with me since this was my first callout. Something we'd talked about since it was my life and happened regularly so she knew what was happening without me having to explain.

"Always. Be home soon."

When she didn't immediately drop her head back to the pillow I slid my hand up to cradle her face.

"Go back to sleep, Jackie."

"Be safe, Echo," she repeated.

Christ, that felt good.

"I will, promise."

With that she lowered her head.

I needed to get on the road and call Evan but I needed to kiss my woman more. So that was what I did—thoroughly making sure she knew how much I loved her before I broke the kiss and left.

THE FIRST THING I noticed when I pulled up to the staging area was the BEAR ACP was gone. In an attempt to relieve some of the tension, I exhaled. If it was Sunny's team they were already in play. I scanned the parking lot looking for Evan's SUV but instead caught sight of Phoenix talking to Tucker next to my brother's truck. I swung into a spot not too far from Phoenix and Tucker. Within minutes I had my gear out of my trunk and was on my way over to the duo.

"Yo," my brother called out like we were meeting for a drink and to shoot the shit. But I didn't miss the worry lines around his eyes.

My brothers liked to give me shit but they all worried about our baby sister as much as I did. There was a silent understanding she was to be protected at all costs. Since she was a baby, Shiloh's safety had been our purpose. She was the glue that had held our family together. For her eighteenth birthday River, Phoenix, and I got matching tattoos. Her name scrolled on our forearms. Not a gift to her, but a reminder to all of us that even though she was technically an adult nothing had changed nor would it ever.

Shiloh was ours.

She was everything.

"Evan's talking to your cap in the CP," Tucker informed me.

I didn't bother hiding my need to know my sister's

whereabouts nor the urgency in which I needed this information.

"Sunny?"

"Already rolled out with the entry team."

Fuck.

Yeah, Phoenix put on a good game face and if you didn't know him his answer might've sounded blasé but I heard the strain in his tone.

"Full team?"

Phoenix understood my question. We trusted Sunny's team; they were good men, they had her back. Not that the men on Bravo team weren't just as skilled but her team, those men, they understood her in a way that not many people did.

"Yeah. Talked to Valentine and Gordy before they rolled. Bravo's pulling cover duty tonight. They're not taking any chances."

That was good news. It was also bad.

"What's the brief?" I asked, not caring who answered, just needing to know what we were walking into and what Phoenix's role would be.

It was Phoenix who answered. "We had a buy scheduled for tonight. Our UCs saw the coke and renegotiated the deal. Units followed the suspects, called in the address which happened to be one Tucker had flagged as part of one of your investigations. Our warrants were ready, just needing the details filled in, got those done, signed, and here we are."

I glanced around the parking lot and saw Evan coming our way. We were in a shit part of town, totally Jimmy's style. He prayed on the weak, the destitute, the down on their luck. The man had exploited the poor and had made a mint doing so.

"Anyone got eyes on Jimmy?" I inquired.

"Nope. No one's seen him since the night at the bar," Tucker told me something I very well knew. "We still need to talk about something. I don't like the way you said he was looking at your tattoo."

Goddammit.

Tucker and his big fucking mouth.

"What's this?" Phoenix grunted.

I hadn't told my brother about Jimmy. It was a long shot he'd seen my tattoo during his takedown. I was careful about keeping my arms covered. Just like now I was in a long-sleeved shirt—summer, spring, dead of winter it didn't matter; I covered my tattoos.

"It's nothing. I gave Luke the heads up—"

"You told Luke but not me?" Phoenix interrupted.

Maybe Jaclyn was rubbing off on me but the interruption irritated the fuck out of me.

"Like I said, it's probably nothing. I saw Jimmy at Balls Deep. The asshole was sitting right next to Jaclyn hitting on her. I strolled up not seeing him on her other side. When I got there his eyes went to my arm and lingered. I'm being safe, that's all."

"That's not probably nothing, brother," my brother growled. "That's what's called an ID."

I understood his displeasure. If the roles had been reversed I would have had a shit hemorrhage he'd kept this information from me. But he wasn't me. I was the oldest. It was my job to protect him.

Before I could respond Evan stepped into our huddle right as his radio crackled to life.

"Six-thirty, this is six-ten." Sunny's voice came over the radio. "I've got movement in window three A-side."

"Copy, six-ten," Mereno returned. "We see him."

"What's the status?" I asked Evan, who'd obviously been listening to the SWAT comms.

Which was something I learned never to do. My need to rush into a scene to back up Sunny was borderline irrational. It was best I stayed off her channel and waited for the call to come in that she and her team had cleared the house and they were ready for me to come in.

It wasn't lost on me that my baby sister was securing a house for me to enter. It also wasn't lost on me that she was a badass and very good at her job. I just wished it was the other way around.

"Three males, one woman confirmed in the house. The call was given to enter, SWAT's moving into place to prepare—"

A call came in, cutting off Evan. "Alpha, take it. Bravo, hold your position."

"Copy," Sunny returned.

My jaw clenched.

Fear hit my chest.

Being my partner for many years, Evan knew it was time to cut his radio. Which he did, then jerked his chin at me.

"Gear up, brother. Your sister will have that shit locked down in no time."

He was right. She would. And until I got to the scene to

see for myself that she was okay, my chest would burn with terror.

I looked at Phoenix and found him already staring at me.

My baby brother who was no longer a baby. Hell, he wasn't even a young man. He was a husband and a father. It was time. I just didn't know how I was going to make the transition; I just knew I had to. He needed to know how much I respected him and the best way to do that was to stop treating him like he wasn't my equal.

"You're right, Phoenix. I should've told you."

I watched my brother's torso swing back before he righted himself and scowled.

"Is this a trick?"

I sighed out a frustrated breath. That frustration was aimed at myself.

"It was a dick thing to do," I admitted. "Won't happen again."

My brother's deep frown slowly morphed into a lopsided smile, one I rarely saw anymore but witnessed all the time when he was growing up. Now his grins were cocky, or back before he'd met Wren, they were wicked when he aimed them at a woman he was trying to bed. Rarely lopsided or goofy, the boyish smile he saved mostly for Sunny when he was teasing her.

"Glad you finally found it, brother."

He was talking about me finding my happy.

I was, too.

However, I wasn't talking about it while our sister was kicking in a door and my heart was torn between the woman I'd left in my bed worried if she'd gone back to sleep and my sister who was right then in grave danger.

I also couldn't tell my brother to go fuck himself. The Kents had one rule that was carved in granite never to be broken. No angry words or arguments before an operation.

With the jobs we had, every time we strapped on our vests there was a real possibility that would be the last time we did it. The danger was such that each time we left the house we knew we might not return.

"You coming to the scene or are you here with the sole purpose to give me shit?" I asked by way of noting my brother needed to kit up.

"Fuck yeah, I'm coming. Can't let the two of you have all the fun."

Right.

He wanted eyes on Sunny just as badly as I did.

I WAS RIDING SHOTGUN, Evan in the back seat, leaving Tucker to drive the short distance from the staging site to the house, Phoenix with his partner following us.

"How's surveillance coming on the warehouse?" I asked Tucker.

The DEA had more resources than we did when it came to equipment and install so they were thankfully taking the lead on that. It would give us eyes on the property considerably faster than what we could do.

"Finished up yesterday," he answered. "Also I did a personal drive-by of the house on Maple earlier just to confirm the occupants had moved out. House is clear.

Neighbor next door said they hadn't heard a peep or seen a car out of place in the last few days."

"Do they teach you that shit in DEA school?" Evan joked from behind me. "You knew Echo and I stopped by two days ago and reported back the house was cleared out. We even went in with the owner. Not even a sock was left behind and the whole place reeked of Mr. Clean."

"What can I say? I'm thorough."

"No, you're an untrusting DEA agent," Evan continued to rib Tucker.

I personally didn't give a shit if every detective on my team did a walkthrough of that house, I was just pleased that they'd heeded Jimmy's warning to get out of the neighborhood. Of course, we didn't have any solid evidence to prove that it had been Jimmy who made the approach but it was his MO and the occupants didn't pack up their stash house and move out because eighty-year-old Mr. Fleming from next door went over and asked nicely. Bottom line—I was pleased they'd moved before Jimmy could deploy his normal intimidation tactics.

Tucker parked behind the police barricade. I pulled my balaclava down over my face, put on my gloves, and double-checked my sleeves were down to my wrist. Presumably Evan was doing the same in the back seat.

The three of us got out of the car, I adjusted my vest, tapped my thigh rig, double-checking my weapon was holstered before I moved to my chest and fingered all my mags.

"Good to go?" Tucker asked.

"Yep."

We made our way through the crush of police officers.

Some SWAT, mostly uniformed units on the scene to keep the perimeter secure. My eyes scanned for my sister.

"There." Evan pointed.

Off to the side of the house with Valentine and Gordy —two of her teammates—Sunny stood still fully kitted out in her tac gear. Her rifle cradled in front of her, barrel down, stock tucked under her armpit. A vision I'd seen too many times.

Sunny's head slowly turned, examining her surroundings until her eyes stopped on me. Then they looked over my shoulder and she smiled.

"Don't know if it's the uniform," Tucker muttered under his breath. "Don't know if it's the way she holds that rifle like it's her baby. Don't know if it's because I know she can kick my ass but goddamn, your sister's fine."

"You know I can kick your ass, too, right?" I grunted.

"Just paying her a compliment."

"How about you never pay her another one," Phoenix suggested.

Evan chuckled and joined in. "Don't know if you know this or not but Echo's woman has an identical twin. Seeing as Echo's woman takes fine to a whole new level, her sister does, too. I'd suggest you not comment on that either. The Kents are half a step up from caveman when it comes to their women."

Evan was clearly referring to the comment he'd made the other night about Jaclyn's looks and my reaction.

"How about you keep your advice to yourself," I told him as together we made our way to the house.

Sunny's captain was stepping out as we hit the porch.

"Thompson," I greeted.

The man's eyes flashed with recognition, though with my height he didn't need to hear my voice to know who I was.

"Messy as fuck in there."

My heart stalled at the information and I fought the urge to check over my sister again.

She was safe.

Whatever had happened, she was safe.

The reminders did nothing to quell my constant worry.

"Suspects down?" Evan asked.

"Two. Three in custody. One male DOA from an apparent OD. They'd dragged him to a back room and dumped him. Can't say until the ME gets here but by the smell it's been a few days. Dual operation out of here. One room storage, one room packaging. Not the narco expert but I'd guess you're looking at thirty, forty kilos of cocaine in there. There's a third room." Thompson's gaze went to Phoenix. "Looks like they robbed a gun store and not a small one, a Walmart sized one. I counted fifteen long guns and ten handguns out on display. Not our job to search so I reckon you'll find more."

Thirty kilos of cocaine?

Christ.

I glanced at Tucker. His jaw was clenched and the muscle in his cheek was jumping.

I'd bet when those bricks were tested we'd find they'd come from Honduras and by the way Tucker was grinding his teeth I knew he agreed.

"Appreciate the intel," I said, hoping Thompson didn't think I was dismissing him, but I wanted to get this over and get home to Jaclyn.

"See you when you're done."

Thompson moved to the side, allowing us entry.

I did my best to take in the bullet-riddled couch with a professional lens instead of wondering if those holes were from Sunny's weapon.

By the time we hit the back of the house the smell of body decomp was overwhelming.

"Jesus," Evan muttered and glanced into the open door of the room the OD victim must've been in.

I nearly slammed into his back, he stopped so suddenly.

"Jesus fuck," he grunted and stepped inside.

There was nothing that was going to get me to go into that room.

But whatever Evan was looking at had his body stiff and his head bowed.

"What is it?" I asked from the hall.

"Dick."

"Come again?"

"Dick Burns."

Oh, fuck.

"Evan—"

"Fuck," he growled. "Fuck. *Fuck.* Fuck."

Apparently, there *was* something that would make me step into a room that reeked of decomp. I got to Evan, wrapped my hand around his arm, and guided him back out into the hall.

"Don't," he muttered.

"Wasn't going to."

I gave Evan a shove to get him moving and refrained from offering him any words of wisdom. Logically Evan knew he couldn't save every junkie, the same as he knew cutting Dick loose as an informant didn't cause Dick's OD. However, the man still felt every loss like a personal failure.

"I need a new fucking job," Tucker grumbled from behind me.

Unfortunately dead bodies were part of the job. It never got easier but you got used to it. But considering Tucker's job and the undercover work he did going months on end living with the dredges of humanity, I didn't disagree with him.

"I heard TC's hiring," I joked.

"I'll send them my CV seeing if I qualify."

Tucker was overqualified for any job Triple Canopy could offer him and he knew it. Which made me wonder if he was joking or if he was ready to make a career change.

22

JACLYN

I FELT THE BED DEPRESS BEHIND ME, BUT BEFORE I could turn, Echo fitted his chest to my back and hauled me tight against his big body. I cracked my eyes open to see the early morning sunlight making its debut through the slatted blinds.

Echo was home.

"Everything go okay?" I asked and wiggled closer.

"Yeah, baby, go back to sleep."

Even though I had tossed and turned for hours after Echo had left, meaning I had just fallen back asleep, I was wide awake but he sounded beat. So I laid there in silence enjoying the feel of him wrapped around me.

I did this for a long time until I'd obviously fallen back asleep. When I woke the second time I knew it was in a way that I'd start to get restless if I laid there any longer. I carefully lifted Echo's arm in an effort to extract myself from the bed.

"Where are you going?" he mumbled.

His sexy, gruff morning voice worked wonders on my lady parts.

"Getting up. Sleep, honey."

He moved his arm and let me roll away, a true testament to how tired he was. Echo rarely, if ever, allowed me to exit the bed without at least one orgasm if not two. Which only complemented the way he put me to sleep.

A girl could get used to three or four orgasms a day.

Who the hell was I kidding? This girl was already addicted to my daily dose of climatic brilliance.

I tiptoed to the bathroom, did my business, went to the closet, found some clothes in the mess I'd made, added cleaning up said mess to my mental to-do list, then quietly left the bedroom. I did all of this without waking up Echo.

I was in the kitchen setting a kettle on to heat, staying close so I could catch it before the kettle whistled, scrolling through my social media when I came to a picture my sister had posted last night.

I pulled up my text app, found Jill's name near the top, and opened the thread.

Bitch, you didn't tell me you were going to dinner at Mavericks.

She sent me back a shrugging emoji.

I narrowed my eyes on the screen, wishing Jill was standing in front of me so I could spear her with a dirty look.

You broke our deal!

Her reply was immediate.

I did not.

You did.

I heard the kettle start to jump on the stove and set

down my phone. I made quick work of making my tea and quicker work of unarming the alarm so I could go out into the backyard. It took effort not to spill my mug full of hot water (blah) while holding my phone and opening the slider. Once I managed that I settled into one of Echo's comfy patio chairs and engaged FaceTime.

The call was denied.

Denied.

My sister denied my call.

What in the hell?

I went back to the text and tapped out a message.

Answer.

I'm not alone.

My shoulders jerked in a way that I was seriously happy I wasn't holding my brewing tea or I would've dumped it all over my lap and sustained third-degree burns —wait, were those the bad burns that required medical attention or the burns you just needed to put under cold running water while cussing your face off because they hurt? I never could remember but I figured boiling water spilled over my legs would cause the burns that required medical attention.

Besides, that was a whole different level of 'spill the tea' I wasn't in the market for.

I was not recovered from my sister's groundbreaking news when I responded.

WHJAT?

I saw my typo and sent another.

WHAT?

Shh. I'll call you later.

My sister was shushing me. Seriously, what a cow.

I will not shh. Tell me who you're with.

Later.

Don't make me text our brother.

COW! Zach Wild.

Zach Wild?

Who the hell is he?

I will call you when I'm alone.

I could feel my sister's frustration through the phone and felt a tiny bit bad.

Sorry I threatened to call L.

No, you're not.

Okay, so I wasn't sorry-sorry like I wouldn't do it again if I needed to. And besides, it wasn't like she hadn't threatened to call Logan on me to get me to spill something she wanted to know. So, I let that go and picked up my tea. I forced myself to drink the hot liquid while pretending it was delicious and I loved it more than I missed coffee.

Newsflash: I didn't.

I missed coffee—a lot. I missed it so much I wondered why I'd hopped on some crazy healthy living bandwagon when I was the queen of junk food. I had yet to finish my deep contemplation of this while the warm Georgia sun warmed my bare legs when the phone in my lap rang.

I nabbed it and flipped it over, not expecting to see Hadley's name displayed.

"Hey, how are you?" I asked her.

"Tired. Sore. And more tired."

I smiled at Hadley's phony complaints.

"I might believe that if you didn't sound blissfully happy about being a momma. Sorry I haven't called to congratulate you and Brady but...twins. I didn't want to bug you."

"Yeah, twins. Did you know that means there are two of them?"

Again she sounded unbelievably happy about having two healthy baby boys.

"Really, two? Damn," I played along.

"Um, *yeah*. That's times two everything."

"Twice as many snuggles, friend," I noted.

"Yeah," she whispered. "They're so beautiful you wouldn't believe."

Oh, I believed it. Hadley was gorgeous and Brady was a good-looking guy. Their genes mixed together equaled perfection.

"I can't wait to meet them."

"Glad you said that," Hadley chirped. "My house, today at three."

It was only a little after ten. That gave me plenty of time to clean up my mess and let Echo sleep.

"Sounds perfect. What can I bring?"

"Nothing. Just you and Echo. I mean that, and this next part doesn't change the answer. I'm throwing Addy a surprise baby party. I'm tired of her telling me she doesn't want a shower, so fine, we're having a party with no gifts. And I mean that. Addy's already going to be pissy. If all of our friends bring something she'll birth kittens in my living room. Us Walkers have birthed babies on kitchen floors before so a litter of kittens in my living room isn't beyond the realm of reality."

I hadn't been in attendance for any such birth. But I had heard about them. Though Hadley's sister Delaney hadn't given birth to Ford on the kitchen floor but that was only because her husband Carter had learned from his brother's trauma and had been prepared.

"Okay, I'll wait to give her her present until after she has the baby, but I am bringing yours. I'll sneak it in and leave it in the babies' room for later."

"Thanks, Jackie."

"And for the record, Addy won't be pissy. She'll pretend she is but she won't be and you know it."

"I don't know. Addy comes off all sweet and innocent and I'm the one nicknamed Hurricane Hadley but really, Adalyn's temper is scary."

"It's a twin thing," I told her. "Jill blamed me for everything growing up so I was labeled the troublemaker but really she's cray-cray with a side helping of vindictive if you piss her off."

"Yeah, it's a twin thing," she agreed.

I could hear the pride in her voice. She was a twin who now had a set of twins. So she knew.

"Thanks for inviting us."

"Of course. But I have to run, I have five hundred more calls to make to invite everyone. The downside to having a loud-mouthed family—I can't invite anyone to a surprise anything until the day of or someone will blab."

Seeing as most of her family was former military or DEA or FBI or current police and fire and rescue, that was surprisingly accurate.

"See you at three."

I rang off but before I set my phone down I sent another text to my sister.

Going to Hadley's today to meet the twins. She's having

a surprise shower for Addy. But that's a secret. Don't tell Logan or Mom or anyone.

A moment later my phone beeped.

Jelly. Send lots of pictures.

I refrained from telling Jill if she lived here with me she wouldn't be jealous. I'd beaten that particular horse to death and had run it over three times. As soon as that thought flitted through my mind my lip curled.

Ew.

Where in the hell had that saying come from and why was I thinking it?

Poor horsey.

———

It was coming up on noon. I was still outside soaking in some rays, recharging my batteries reading a book on my Kindle app. That was after I'd talked to Mom to make sure she and Ian were settling in and making plans to go over to their new place next weekend.

I'd already been by the house to see her several times since she'd arrived and Echo had gone with me one of the times. My mom and Ian liked Echo so thankfully there hadn't been any weird meet-the-parents vibes going on, nor had they treated him any differently now that he was my boyfriend and not just Logan's friend. But we hadn't gone over there for dinner or had them at our place. This was only because my mother was more of an Echo-variety of person—a neat freak. She was going nonstop getting the house unpacked and set up the way she wanted. Ian being madly in love with my mother gave zero input about the house and where things should go. He simply followed orders. However, when it came to the garage my mom returned the favor and stayed out of there.

So next weekend it was.

Our first official dinner with the parents.

My plan was to finish the current chapter I was on then go in to start the dreaded chores now that I wasn't worried about waking Echo. Read: done procrastinating like a boss. When I got a text.

From Echo...

Weird.

Bedroom. Now. Clothes off before you come in.

He didn't have to tell me twice.

No, seriously he didn't; I was up out of the chair and opening the door when his second message came through.

I'm hungry, baby, so hurry your sexy ass up.

I had my clothes off before I hit the bedroom. And Echo wasn't lying, he was hungry—starving, actually. He'd pulled two orgasms out of me with his mouth before he bent me over the bed and fucked another out of me.

It wasn't even lunchtime and I'd had three phenomenal orgasms already and I knew I'd get more of that later.

Brilliant.

I WAS HOLDING the cutest newborn I'd ever seen, thinking Hadley had been right—their babies were beautiful—when Echo sat down beside me.

"Which one do you have?"

"Caleb," I told him without looking at him.

"Are you sure?"

That made me look at him.

"Positive."

He eyed the baby who was mostly swaddled, save his cute little face and one arm he'd fought to get free.

"How do you know?"

"They're not identical. Caleb's got a little more hair than Ben and he also has baby acne on his right cheek that Ben doesn't have."

"But if they were identical, how would you know?"

His question was bizarre but the look on his face said dead serious.

"My mom painted our toenails different colors to tell us apart," I told him. "But parents of identical twins do lots of different things to keep the identities straight. Why are you asking?"

He didn't answer. Instead, he dropped a bomb.

"I want kids."

I blinked, or at least I thought I did, or my eyes closing rapidly could've been the mini seizure I felt like I was having.

"Okay."

"Do you want kids?"

"Yes."

There was a beat of silence, after which he unnecessarily told me, "I'm almost forty."

"Are you telling me that because you're afraid your penis will—"

"Jaclyn," he snapped.

"Well? What does forty have to do with your ability to have children?"

Little Caleb started grunting and rooting around, looking for something I didn't have.

"I'd like to be able to throw a ball in the backyard with my kids before I'm using a walker," he hilariously shared.

"Right. I can see how a walker would get in the way of the tackling and stuff. But why are you asking about how to keep twins separate?"

"You're a twin."

Ah.

I smiled and shook my head.

"Only fraternal twins are hereditary. Identical twins aren't genetic."

"Yet Hadley's an identical twin and had twins."

"Right, but that was an anomaly. Totally random."

Echo narrowed his eyes and asked, "Are you telling me you think Brady's sperm are better than mine?"

At that comment my mouth dropped open.

Literally.

But it snapped shut when Brady said, "Of course, my sperm are superior. Have you seen the children they produce?"

"I think your wife actually produced them," I returned.

"No. She grew them. I did all of the fertilization."

"Did you and Hadley put in a garden?" Jasper asked from behind his son-in-law.

For such a big, tough badass, Brady paled.

Actually. Paled.

I glanced at Echo to see him looking anywhere but at Jasper.

"What are you talking about?" Hadley asked. "You

know I can't keep a house plant alive. Who said we had a garden?"

"Brady said he did all of the fertilization..." Jasper trailed off, his eyes narrowing on the back of Brady's head.

I tried, I really, really did.

But I lost the battle and belted out a laugh that woke up poor Caleb. Instead of handing him off to Hadley I stood and offered him to Brady.

"Here, congrats on your proper fertilization." Brady took his son from me with a frown. "Sorry I forgot to get you a blue ribbon. Maybe next time."

"Jesus, you're a Haines," Jasper grunted and strode off.

"Not for long," Echo muttered under his breath.

Kids and marriage with Echo?

Yes, please.

23

JACLYN

I was in the drink aisle at the grocery store, my eyes dancing between the bag of my favorite coffee blend and the boxes of chamomile tea, trying to decide if I'd tortured myself enough, when the back of my neck started tingling.

I looked up and down the row but other than a woman with a toddler sitting in her shopping cart there was no one there.

Weird.

I grabbed both the coffee and tea with the lie I was telling myself the coffee was for Echo when I knew I was going to break down and drink it myself. Two weeks of living with Echo smelling the delicious aroma every morning had been torture. Echo had offered to stop making coffee at home and pick his up from a drive-thru on his way to the station but I'd never ask him to do that.

I was in the produce area when my phone beeped with a text from Echo.

Callout. I won't be home for dinner. Love you.

Shit. I hated callouts.

Okay. Be safe. Love you.

Promise.

I liked that answer much better than "always". I didn't want him to tell me he was always safe. I wanted the promise he would be.

The blood oath he would be safe and come home to me.

Well, shit. Now that Echo wouldn't be home for dinner, I contemplated who to bum a meal off of—my mom and Ian, or Logan and Lauren?

My mom.

With any luck I could talk her into making sausage-stuffed peppers.

Before I had a chance to call her and ask, that feeling was back.

The spine tingle.

I glanced around. This time I noticed a man in a baseball cap who had very obviously been looking in my direction before he turned around.

What the heck was wrong with me?

Maybe all the stories Echo had been telling me about his job were starting to freak me out more than I thought they were. I mean, I *knew* they freaked me out but I thought it was because the stories he told me were things that he saw every day and none of the things he saw were rainbows, unicorns, or fairy dust. Every day he encountered a situation that was dangerous and tragic.

I hated that for him but he loved being a cop. He told me he couldn't imagine ever doing anything else. Which meant I thought that statement this the perfect segue to talk about undercover work again and implore him to take an assignment. He had been unmovable. However, his reasons for not wanting to go under had more to do with not wanting to be away from me and also Griffin, who he texted daily and saw whenever he could. So I dropped it. I knew Echo held that regret, but didn't we all have regrets? Things that we wished we would've done or things we wished we hadn't done.

I stopped in front of the bell peppers and called my mom.

She picked up on the fourth ring, sounding out of breath.

Gross.

"Bad time, Mom?"

"What? It's never a bad time to hear from one of my girls."

Except when you're out of breath and panting.

"You sound... weird."

"Oh, I had to run to the phone. It was in the study and I'm starting dinner."

Damn.

"How far into dinner are you?"

"Why?"

I picked up a bell pepper.

"Because I was hoping I could talk you into making stuffed peppers?"

"I don't have—"

"I'm at the grocery store. I'll bring over everything."

"Jaclyn Ann, you know better than to interrupt someone when they're speaking. It's rude."

Damn Echo for being right.

"Sorry, Momma."

My mom sighed. "I'll turn off the water. What time will you be over? And if Echo's coming you need to double the recipe."

"He's working late."

"Ah, there it is, the reason why my girl's coming over... so she doesn't have to cook."

Well...

"No, I love you and you're the best cook ever and I want to see Ian."

I bagged six big bell peppers and twisted the bag before I knotted it and tossed them in the cart.

"You saw us last night."

That was true.

Last night was the first official dinner with the parents and it went exceptionally well. Ian and Echo hit it off and had set a time to golf together with Tucker and Evan. I loved that Echo was making it a point to get to know Ian better.

"Okay, fine. I want to see my mom because I just want to see you and I don't want to cook but I'm still doubling the recipe so I can bring Echo home dinner. And to answer your question, I'll be at your house in about thirty minutes. I still have to grab a few things."

"See you soon, doll. Drive safe."

My mom disconnected and I went back to shopping.

It happened again, this time when I was picking out the sausage I needed. It was not the tingle up my spine that alerted me that something wasn't right. It was the hairs on the back of my neck that stood on end, alerting me to danger.

I glanced to my right and saw him.

Creepy guy.

Jimmy whatever his last name was.

Shit.

I grabbed the first package of sausage that looked remotely close to the kind my mom normally used and moved down the aisle going in the opposite direction. I was headed to the checkout area hoping my mom had bread-crumbs because there was no way I was staying in the grocery store with a man who made Echo's face harden and his body tense the way this guy Jimmy did.

I got to the self-checkout, pulled out my phone to call Echo like I'd been instructed to do, but remembered he'd been called out to a dangerous situation. One that needed his full attention so he could come home safely to me. I pocketed my phone and scanned my items, keeping my eyes moving around the area.

No creepy guy.

Thank God.

I made it to my car, tossed the groceries in the trunk, kept looking around the parking lot just like Logan had taught me to do. I even glanced in my back seat to check it was empty and no one was hiding back there only to pop up from behind and strangle me as I drove down the road. Yes, my brother was a little overprotective and had told me this was a possibility and he told me that story at fifteen.

He was a little nuts.

Thankfully traffic was light as I made my way to my mom's. It was funny how when you got freaked out all thoughts turned to your mom and wanting to see her as if she could fight off all the bad guys and keep you safe. I was almost desperate to get to her house and impatiently tapping my thumbs on my steering wheel while stopped at a red light when I checked my rearview mirror. I couldn't see the face clearly but it was the same hat Jimmy had been wearing. At least I was almost positive.

Or was I positive?

Shit. I was almost to my mom's and if Jimmy was behind me I was not leading him there. I knew Logan would tell me to head to the nearest police station but a nagging feeling in my belly started to churn. I checked to make sure my doors were locked before I pressed the phone button on my steering wheel.

"Call Logan," I said.

"Calling Logan," my car returned in a very proper British accent I had programmed because it never failed to make me smile.

Only it failed that time. I wasn't smiling. I was freaked out and a little pissed I was going to freak my brother out which meant he was going to act crazier than normal for the next month.

If creepy guy wasn't behind me and this was a false alarm I was going to be seriously mad.

"You good?"

Fuck.

"Um...I think so."

The light changed and I inched forward, wishing the car in front of me would hurry up and move.

"Where are you?"

Damn, he sounded freaked.

"On Oglethorpe. I'm on my way to Mom's. I just left Kroger."

"Where's Echo?"

I could've guessed that would've been his next question.

"Work. He had a callout."

"What's—"

I didn't have time for twenty questions so I interrupted my brother even though I'd just been scolded by my mom about that very thing a few minutes ago.

"Did Echo tell you about that creepy guy Jimmy?"

"Yes," he grunted. "Had a talk with Matt about him. Also watched the security footage of that fucker staring at you before I gave it to Echo."

Eek.

I didn't know Echo had gotten the security footage from Matt, but that made sense.

"Okay, good. I think he's following me."

"You think?" he roared and I quickly lowered the volume on the call. I didn't need Logan yelling at me and I certainly didn't need to hear it coming out of my premium JBL speakers in full surround sound.

I glanced in my rearview mirror and sure enough the same car was behind me. Though I was on a highway so that wasn't unusual.

"I saw him while I was at the grocery store," I started then rushed out. "He didn't say anything to me but I saw him. Echo said if I ever see him to call him. I didn't but only because he's on a callout but I did leave immediately and I watched while I was walking through the parking lot and yes I parked under one of the lights and yes I had my keys ready and I checked my back seat. I did all the things, Logan. And yes I planned on telling Echo when he got home tonight. I didn't see him so I started driving to Mom's.

I'm going there for dinner. I was just stopped at a red light and I think he's behind me but I'm not a hundred percent because it's dark but he was wearing a hat and I think it's him."

When I was done I was breathing heavily and freaked out more than I was before I called my brother.

"Okay, Jackie. I'm already driving in your direction." I squinted at the road at my brother's very calm, very rational tone. "I want you to stay on Oglethorpe. You're gonna pass the turn-off to Mom's and keep going straight. There's a police station off MLK. Do you know where that's at? There's a Quick Stop on one corner and a McDonald's on the opposite."

I was pretty sure I knew where that was at.

"Yeah, Rodeo's there, too?"

"Yep."

"Logan, I'm gonna be really embarrassed if this is for nothing and I'm overreacting," I admitted.

"And I'd rather this be nothing than you be in danger and not call me. Not to mention I'd be pissed. And, sister, hate to tell you this but your man would be even angrier than I would be."

I knew he was right but damn.

"Okay. I'm driving to the police station and you're meeting me there."

"You're staying on the phone with me and I'm gonna try and intercept you before you get there to escort you the rest of the way."

Oh, goodie, my big brother's going to give me an escort. Somehow I'd made it to twenty-seven without my brother having to come to my rescue. I really wished I could've made it the rest of my life. I was never going to hear the end of this.

"If you give me shit..." I trailed off when I saw the flashing lights ahead of me. "Damn, there's an accident or something up ahead."

"Where are you?"

Since I was on the phone and didn't have my GPS up on the screen in my dash, I had to go old school and look around for a street sign. I was a strictly hands-free, no messing with technology kind of girl. I made zero exceptions. I wasn't going to drive distractedly even if creepy guy was behind me.

"Um..." I mumbled and finally found a sign up ahead. "Ryon Avenue."

"That's residential," he grumbled.

"Well, if you want me to take it, tell me now."

"Take a left."

Thankfully I was in the left lane. I flipped on my blinker, got into the turn lane, and made the turn.

My stomach dropped when the car behind me made the turn, too.

"Um...Logan?"

"He turned with you," he guessed.

"Yes."

Now I was officially scared.

"What's the traffic like?"

"There's no one in front of me."

"Gun it."

I took in the residential area, the small two-lane road, and listened to my brother.

I gunned it.

My car shot forward and I pressed down on the accelerator harder.

"Speed limit's thirty," I noted.

"Fuck the speed limit. Ryon's going to curve to the right and turn into South Main. The curve isn't sharp but you're going to need to slow your speed to take it."

Now that he mentioned speed, I checked my dash. Sixty-two in a thirty. That would be one hell of a ticket. Though right now I would happily pay it if it meant a cop would show up to pull me over.

"What's he doing?" Logan asked.

"Still behind me." I glanced in my side mirror. "Actually..."

What the hell was he doing? He'd switched lanes and was driving on the wrong side of the road.

"He's coming up beside me," I rushed out.

"Hit the brakes. Hard. Let him fly by you."

I took my foot off the gas but it never made it to the brake.

Jimmy hit the left back side of my car. There was no warning before I was spinning out of control.

"Logan!"

My scream filled the car before everything went dark.

24

ECHO

I CHECKED MY GEAR FOR THE THIRD TIME. Everything was in place yet something still felt off.

"You missing something?" Evan asked.

"Nope."

"Then is there a reason you're feeling yourself up?"

Fucking smartass.

"Something's not..."

I paused, not wanting to put any bad vibes out there in the universe right before we were going into an unknown situation.

"Where's Tucker?" I asked instead of finishing my sentence.

"Talking to the cap in the van."

I slid my gaze across the parking lot to the van. My unit didn't have any fancy ACP vehicles like SWAT. We still used circa 1980s A-Team vans when we rolled in.

"Did you get everything done you needed to today?" I asked.

Evan almost looked ashamed when he nodded. Richard

Burns' body had been released today. Evan had seen to it that Richard was cremated. Not in the county crematorium where the unclaimed bodies were sent to. Evan had paid to have Richard sent to a funeral home.

"Good. Let me know when and where and I'll go with you to spread his ashes."

This wasn't the first time my partner had paid for a cremation or a funeral for that matter. But as far as I knew this was the first time he'd have no one to give the ashes to. Something we learned when I was helping him find next of kin. Richard had a sister but she lived in California and wanted nothing to do with her brother's remains seeing as she'd wanted nothing to do with him while he was alive. That hit Evan hard. He understood where the sister was coming from; addiction was an ugly, torturous evil that affected everyone who loved the addict. And that was something Evan knew very well.

"Tucker told me the report came back on the coke." Evan changed the subject.

Indeed, the report was in and it confirmed the cocaine we'd found last week had been smuggled in from Honduras. It also turned out to be fifty bricks. That was a large stash to recover in one bust along with the guns that were seized. Jimmy's crew took a hit. Which we now had confirmation on thanks to one of the men arrested. Though the man hadn't personally seen Jimmy but had ID'd known associates. Further from that, during interrogation he said he'd heard conversations about Jimmy being back in town.

This was to be expected. It was how Jimmy had been able to stay in power for as long as he had. He was tight with a select, trusted few in his crew. He didn't socialize with anyone but his inner circle and he never gave a direct order outside of those men he trusted who then carried out and passed along the directive.

So, no one seeing Jimmy didn't surprise me. But it did make me uneasy.

Jesus, my chest hurts.

"You sure you're okay?" Evan tried again.

"Yeah. I just want this done."

A shipment had been delivered to the warehouse yesterday. Before it could be sorted and sent out on the street, I wanted it in police custody. According to the surveillance footage two U-Hauls had been driven into the cargo area, the unknown contents unloaded, and the trucks were pulling away ten minutes later.

Evan checked his watch.

"We have ten minutes until sunset."

Ten minutes until our ten-man team rolled out.

Ten more minutes and we could get this shit started. Not that that was where my night was going to end. We'd have hours of paperwork and processing to do, putting me home well after midnight.

I watched Tucker jump out of the van, then glance around at the rest of the team until his eyes landed on me and Evan standing off to the side. With a jerk of his head he summoned us over.

"I'm gonna ask you one more time, Echo. What the fuck's up with you?"

Fuck.

"I just have this feeling."

"What kind of feeling?"

"Obviously it's nothing or you would've already called

it." And that was the truth; Evan had an innate ability to *feel* things.

It wasn't some psychic voodoo feeling. It was just that he was able to sense things before the rest of us. He chalked it up to his childhood, having two volatile parents who could and often did have violent outbursts at random, so he learned to feel a room, a situation, the people around him. He was attuned to everything.

"You know that doesn't mean shit. Is it the operation?"

That was the fuck of it. I didn't know. If Sunny's team was here and they were kicking in the door for us, I'd say that was it. If Phoenix was here, and his team was coming in with us, I'd say that was it. But neither was here.

"I don't think so. I can't place it. I'm just antsy. I need this to end so I can get home."

A look passed over Evan's features, a look I didn't like.

"Call your woman before we brief and roll. I'll cover for you with the team. You'll feel better after you hear her voice."

Christ, now Evan was making me sound like a codependent pansy ass who needed to be attached at the hip to his woman. He wasn't far off the mark but...I wasn't *that* fucking bad.

"I'll wait—"

"Trust me, Echo. Call her. You need your attention on the takedown. It won't be if your mind's on other things."

Without another word Evan walked away.

He hadn't made it three feet when my phone vibrated in my pocket. I pulled it out expecting it to be River returning my call. Instead, it was Logan.

Shit.

I tapped the screen to answer the call.

"Yo, brother, not a good time. I'm at a—"

"Jackie's been in an accident," Logan heaved out.

His words hit my chest and ricocheted around, slicing my organs as they bounced around until they slammed into my heart.

"Where is she?"

Evan spun around and was jogging back. Tucker had broken away from the rest of the team huddled near the van waiting to be briefed and he, too, was jogging my way.

"Gone. Jimmy followed her..."

I heard nothing else.

My head turned over every possible scenario. All the ways Jimmy could hurt her.

That motherfucker.

Piece of shit motherfucker.

My phone was taken out of my hand. Evan pinned me with a look that dared me to argue as Tucker skidded to a stop in front of me.

"Logan, you got Evan. Where do you need us?"

"Call just came in. Jimmy rolled up to a house we're watching, with a woman—"

"Evan!" I yelled. "Give me my phone." Then back to Tucker. "What's the address?"

"Echo—"

"He has Jaclyn, Tucker. What is the fucking address?"

Before Tucker could give me the location all hell broke loose. There was an explosion in the distance that lit the darkening sky. All eyes went in that direction just as gunshots rang out.

Fuck.

I was reaching for Tucker as he was already dropping to the ground. It was a bad fucking day when your only option was to hit the pavement during a drive-by.

"I need my fucking phone," I barked.

"Maybe can you wait until the goddamn shootout's over?" Evan shouted over the continued gunfire.

Ten seconds of a continuous barrage of bullets felt like an eternity. Any other time, when my woman wasn't in the hands of a felon who was out for revenge, I would've been returning fire, or at least attempting to get descriptions and plates. Now, I was pissed I had no choice but to lay face first on the asphalt until the assholes ran out of ammo.

"In two fucking seconds I'm leaving," I announced.

Tucker's hand reached over and wrapped around the back of my neck.

"You move, I'm shooting you."

I counted to three, started to roll, and the gunshots stopped. I faintly heard the squealing of tires which would've been much louder if my ears hadn't been ringing.

"Phone," I growled as I rolled up on my hip. I gave Evan a once-over as he handed me my phone. "I got an address," I told Logan.

"Jesus fucking hell," Logan seethed. "Was that—"

"A warehouse exploding followed by a drive-by? Yeah. I'd say our operation's blown, literally." I got to my feet, then turned to check all the men by the van were up and moving. When my body count was complete my attention went to Tucker. "Location?"

He rattled off an address. I relayed it, then added, "My car's full of bullets. I'm not sure if there's a vehicle here that's operable."

Which I was certain had been Jimmy's plan. Take me out in an explosion, or a drive-by, or at the very least leave me stranded ten miles from where he had my woman, giving him time to kill me another way.

"I'll send a car," Logan told me.

"Tell them I'm hoofing it so they can pick me up on the way."

"That's—"

"Like I give the first fuck if it's a hundred miles. You get to her now. I'm hoofing it. I'll be there as soon as I can."

"Right."

I took a breath and started, "Logan—"

"No need, brother. I got this until you get here. She did good…" His voice broke at the end and he cleared it and tried again. "She knew you were busy, so she called me. She did everything right."

I didn't give a shit if she did everything wrong but it was good to know Logan was on his way to her.

"See you when I get there."

I disconnected and called Phoenix.

"Yo, bro." My brother's cheerful voice came over the line.

"I need you," I croaked.

"Where?"

I gave him a quick rundown and the location. My brother hung up on me with the promise he was on his way to Jaclyn. The next call was harder.

"How's my favorite—"

I cut off my sister's greeting and repeated my earlier plea.

"I need you, Sunny."

No hesitation. Just like Phoenix. The same would come from River if he was close.

"Where are you?"

I gave her the same information I'd given Phoenix, including the address.

My stomach bottomed out and hollowed when she said, "Luke and I are on our way. Love you, big brother. See you there."

See you there, like we were going to a family gathering.

Not going in to rescue my woman.

Fucking hell.

I turned to Tucker. "I need you to tell the cap—"

"Fuck that, I'm going with you."

I didn't bother asking Evan, I knew he was going to follow me. And when I took off in a full sprint I was proven correct.

"Goddamn long-legged bastard," Evan called out from behind me.

I had no response.

I had no further thoughts except the ten miles that separated me and Jaclyn and how fast I could get there.

"Take this left and cut through the park," Evan huffed.

"Main roads," I called back. "For pick-up."

"Fuck," Evan grouched.

If we were hoofing it on foot the whole way, cutting through the park would've shaved off at least half a mile. But I needed whoever Logan sent to pick us up to see us and not be driving around side streets wasting time.

I rounded another block when a black SUV came to a screeching halt in the middle of the street. My hand went to my thigh, I drew my sidearm, and brought it up.

The high beams flashed and I kept my gun level until the window rolled down and Matt's head appeared.

I shoved my gun back into my holster and darted across the street.

Nothing was said while we piled in.

Matt made a U-turn, bouncing up on the curb instead of executing a three-point turn, and sped off.

"Update?" I asked, out of breath.

"Shiloh called it in and SWATs there. Not her team, Bravo. She's suited up and with them. Last call I got, the entry team wasn't waiting for the negotiator. Thompson's used Luke before, he's perched up and ready. Brady and Trey are on the scene. Trey reported it looks like all of Hollow Point's police department's present."

Thank fuck.

"Where's Logan?"

Matt went silent.

"Matt?"

"Locked down."

My head lolled forward and my eyes closed.

All of this was my fault.

My fuck-up.

"Get your head right," Matt grunted. "Logan went willingly. He knows he's too close. He knows he can fuck the operation. And if you're smart, you'll join him in the CP and let us do our jobs without having to worry about you or Logan going ape shit and going down for murder."

I was my father's son.

I would happily join Lester if it meant Jaclyn was safe.

25

ECHO

Trey wasn't exaggerating when he'd reported to Matt.

In all the years I'd been a cop I'd never seen a police presence of this magnitude. Seeing it, however, didn't stop me from running past the line of uniformed officers blocking the street. None of them said a word, but all of them did dip their chins.

Motherfucker.

I came up on the old two-story Victorian house that at one time would've been beautiful but now looked like it needed to be condemned just in time to witness something I'd seen dozens of times, and each of those times my heart stopped for a split second. A sight I hated with every fiber of my being. That didn't mean I wasn't proud of my sister but goddamn, seeing her enter a house put the fear of God in me.

And this time, she was going in to rescue my woman.

The two women I loved more than anything in this world being in danger was a new form of torture.

"She's got this," Evan rumbled from beside me. "She always does. But tonight, she's going in there for you. She'll take extra care, Echo; she knows what this means to you."

I stayed well away from the perimeter SWAT had set up and searched the crowd. I knew I wouldn't see him but I looked anyway.

Luke was out there somewhere watching his wife kick in a door.

For me.

My sister was putting her life on the line to save mine and Luke was being forced to watch.

Jesus.

"I need to—"

"Hang tight and not fuck this up," Tucker wrongly finished my sentence.

I heard glass shattering. My attention went back to the house, this time to witness men running out.

"Bomb!" one of them yelled.

Officers started scrambling, members of Bravo Team getting behind the BEAR that would offer protection if a bomb were to go off.

The two people I needed to see didn't come out.

The two women who meant the difference between life and death for me were nowhere to be seen.

I felt Tucker grab at me as I took off across the grass.

"Echo!"

I ignored Evan's shout and jumped up the flimsy stairs that led to an equally flimsy excuse for a porch and reached for my weapon.

All the lights were on in the house when I entered. Wallpaper peeled down the wall in large sheets, folded over halfway down, strips of it missing altogether in some spots revealing the old plaster. Chunks of the ceiling were nothing more than exposed rafters. It was a miracle the damn house was still standing. The mildew stench was a telltale sign it had sat vacant for a long time. But the strong odor of ether explained why the power was still on. No one might've been living here but someone had been cooking meth in the place.

Then I saw them and when I did I had to blink away the flashes of fury sparking like a halo around Jaclyn tied to a chair strapped with explosives.

My sister kneeling at her feet.

"Sunny, can you move?"

"Yes," she cried.

"Then I need you to get up and get outside."

"Echo—"

"Now, sweetheart. I need you to get out of the house."

"He's right," Jaclyn sobbed.

I didn't look at her again. I couldn't until my sister was out of the house. I needed to stay strong or Shiloh would never leave me to die in this house with Jaclyn.

"Echo—"

"I *need* you to do this for me."

My sister slowly stood and turned. The creaking around us would've been worrisome if there wasn't a bomb in the room.

Christ, this place was going to crumble around us before Jimmy got his fucked-up revenge and blew the place to shit—with us in it.

"Where's Phoenix?"

"Right here."

My heart cracked at the sound of my brother's voice.

"Go with Phoenix, Shiloh."

Her tear-filled eyes held mine.

My sister, my girl, so fucking strong.

"Always knew you'd grow up to do great things, sweetheart."

Phoenix's hand hit my shoulder. I lifted mine to cover his and pressed down.

My kid brother, my boy, who never did learn patience, but he did learn how to be a fine man.

"Get your sister, Phoenix."

With a squeeze on my shoulder, he let go and moved to Sunny, wrapping his arm around her waist, forcing her to walk. Phoenix's gaze lifted to mine and I finally saw all that I'd missed, all of the things I'd refused to see because I was so caught up my own shit. My guilt, my loneliness, my issues. He hadn't grown up to be a fine man; he'd become the foundation of this family. Shiloh had always been our reason to band together. But Phoenix, he was my touch-stone. He was my reminder that Lester gave us one thing that was beautiful—our family.

And now there they stood in front of me, ready to give me something that neither wanted to give.

"We'll see you both outside." Phoenix's firm tone was almost believable.

"You will," I lied.

Time was ticking.

Literally.

I needed them both to leave.

It was Phoenix who broke the stare with a dip of his chin.

"You know, right?" he asked.

"Down to my soul, brother. I love you both."

Sunny let out a gut-wrenching sob, which meant it was time to get her clear of the house. I watched as Phoenix guided her through the living room and out the front door.

Only then did I take a breath and turn back to Jaclyn.

The sight brought me to my knees. I landed with a thud a foot away from where she was strapped to the chair.

"I need you to leave with them, Echo," she whispered.

I scooted closer, taking in the floor around her, checking for pressure sensors, seeing how I could cut her ankles free.

"What are you doing?"

"Cutting you free, baby."

"No, Echo. No. You need to leave."

I purposely avoided looking her in the eyes, knowing if I saw her fear, I'd crumble completely and there wasn't time for that.

"Did he set a timer?"

"He said... he...has a remote."

Fuck.

I crawled around the chair and sawed through the ropes securing her hands to the back of the chair.

"It's going to hurt when you move your arms," I warned.

One arm fell free to her side. I heard her suck in a breath, but when the second arm came down, she gasped out a groan.

"The tingling will go away in a minute. Did he have you sit on anything?"

"No."

"Okay. Sit tight another second."

The vest packed with explosives wasn't connected to the chair and I couldn't see anything that would detonate the vest if she moved. But not seeing anything didn't mean much. I knew enough to get by but I was in no way an ordnance expert.

I moved around to the front of the chair, got up on my knees, and finally locked eyes with her.

The fear was so stark it leaked out of her pores and crowded the space between us. The terror filled the room, surrounded us, pressed in, filled the house.

"Please leave," she whispered.

"No."

"Please, Echo. Please. I don't want you to die in here with me."

I raised my hands, cupped her face, pulled her forward, and gently brushed my lips over hers.

"I choose you, Jaclyn. Understand? No matter what, I choose you. If this bomb goes off it takes both of us."

"I'm scared."

Her cried admission tore at my insides. Anger and violence flooded my veins—flowed and pulsed through me with no outlet. The need to rip something or someone apart nearly snapped my control.

I needed to be strong—for Jaclyn. I would not add to her fear.

I watched the tears roll down her cheeks, catching them with my thumbs as they fell.

"So am I, baby. So fucking scared."

Suddenly she sobered and narrowed her eyes.

"I need you to give me this, Echo. They need you. You have to leave."

"As you and everyone else has pointed out, they are adults. I gave them everything I could. Now I'm giving myself something. I'm taking my happiness over them."

"Dying here with me is your happy?" She huffed out a hysterical laugh.

"You're my happy. Full stop."

Jaclyn was shaking. We were wasting time. I needed to get this vest off of her.

"How about we work on this vest now?"

"I don't want you to die in here with me," she whispered.

"No one's dying, baby." I hoped I wasn't lying but had a feeling I was. "Did you watch him tape this on you?"

I examined the silver duct tape wrapped around her torso to keep the vest secured tightly. I couldn't see a single wire and only a few slivers of a plastic bag I assumed—but it'd be a pretty damn good assumption—was holding the brick of C4.

"Yes."

Thank fuck her voice was a little stronger.

"Did you see wires?"

"Yeah, over here." She pointed to the left side of the vest where the rectangular block was concealed.

"What about on the other side?"

"No. The bomb is here." She pointed again. "He said he was going to blow my heart out of my chest."

Motherfucker.

Stupid *motherfucking* idiot.

"You're positive, baby? You didn't see him wrap the

wires completely around your waist, your chest? All the components are on the left side?"

I heard a creak coming from above me and was seriously starting to get nervous that the ceiling was going to cave in. I had no doubt the SWAT team hadn't been careful as they cleared the old house. I could see them running through the second floor without care or concern for the structural integrity when they opened doors and closets and tossed any furnishings to make sure no one was up there hiding. And this old heap sounded like she was ready to be put out of her misery.

It was now or never.

I pulled my knife back out and used my thumb to flip open the blade.

"What are you doing?"

"Cutting you out of this."

"No. Wait. You can't. He said it would go off if I tried to take it off."

"He lied, baby."

Jaclyn reached out and touched me for the first time since I'd cut her free. Her hands on my jaw tipping my head back was almost too much to bear. Her soft, sweet hands on me while she was wearing a vest meant to kill her, put on her by a man who wanted me dead.

Yeah, it was too much.

But I didn't move away.

"Trust me," I pleaded.

Her response was instant and full of conviction.

"I trust you."

I leaned forward, kissed the corner of her mouth, and waited for her hands to fall away.

When they did I moved to her right side and lifted my knife.

If I was wrong, we were dead.

Not just dead but my last breath would be taken knowing I killed Jaclyn.

"Do it, Echo. I trust you."

I pulled the vest material at her armpit away with my left hand and with my right I sunk the tip of my blade through the layers of tape, careful not to stab her. I made one long slice down the length, only cutting through half the tape.

We were alive.

I went back up to the top and tipped my eyes up to meet Jaclyn's downcast ones.

"I love you, Jackie."

That earned me a radiant, beautiful smile that I hoped wasn't the last one I ever saw. But if it was, I was going to die with that fresh in my mind.

"Love you, too, Echo."

I made my second pass, felt the Velcro strap of the vest under my blade, and cautiously sawed through the belt. I tugged apart the remaining fibers of tape and opened the vest.

Adrenaline surged through me as hope began to tinge my thoughts.

Almost there.

"I'm gonna pull this up over your head. Lift your left arm."

Jaclyn complied as I slowly lifted the vest.

It cleared her head, then her arm, then her hand.

When she was free, I wasted no time throwing the vest across the room. I scooped up Jaclyn and ran for my life.

I was out the front door, jumping off the porch, when a gunshot rang out.

Jesus *fucking* hell.

I went to my knees, dropped Jaclyn to the grass, and folded myself over her to shield her.

I sensed movement around me.

I didn't move.

I heard yelling, pounding feet rushing by us, total pandemonium.

I didn't move.

"Echo?"

"Yeah, baby?"

"Thank you."

My eyes closed but other than that, I. Did. Not. Move.

26

JACLYN

I wasn't sure how long we laid there on the ground. Echo folded over me, shielding me from the mayhem. What I did know was I'd never felt more protected.

We needed to get up, and not just because my legs were going numb from being curled into a ball with a big, huge, beast of a man giving me some of his weight. We also needed to get up because I could hear someone crying and my guess would be it was Shiloh.

"Honey, your sister needs you."

I thought for sure that would get him to his feet. There wasn't anything he wouldn't do for his family, but Shiloh was the baby—*his* baby. He spoiled her the way Logan did us girls.

But he didn't jump up. He shook his head instead.

I tried a different tactic. "We're safe."

He shook his head again.

I was going to try a third time but thought better of it. If this was what Echo needed, he was going to have it and he was going to have it for as long as he wanted.

"I love you, Echo," I whispered and settled in.

THE NEXT FEW hours were a blur. A total, insane blur. I'd never been hugged so much in my life.

First it was Shiloh. She didn't want her brother, she wanted me. And as soon as Echo came up on his knees next to me and I started to sit up, Shiloh tackled me back down and sobbed in my arms. When she was done—or more accurately, after Echo lifted her off of me—my brother was there to scoop me up off the ground and look me over. Once he'd ascertained I was okay, he didn't hug me; he walked ten feet away, dropped his head, balled his fists, and let out an almighty roar that could wake the dead. Once that was done he stalked back over and then he hugged me. From there I was passed around to too many people to count. People I didn't even know were hugging me. Some Echo introduced to me as men and women he worked with, others just gave me a squeeze, clapped Echo on the shoulder, and motored away.

When that was done, a detective came over to introduce herself. She asked if she could get some basic questions answered while they were fresh in my mind but she would wait a few days, and not only that she would come to the house. I thought that was cool of her and wondered if I was getting special treatment since I was Echo's girlfriend. Then I realized I didn't care if I was getting special treatment, I'd almost died. Echo had almost died. I was going to take special treatment and be grateful. Throughout the questioning, Echo was on one side of me, Logan on the other. I was safe and protected and that allowed me to tell my story.

The tense part was when Echo's captain finally came over to talk to him. At the time I didn't understand why his shoulders had gone stiff and he looked like he was bracing to get kicked in the balls. Even as the man asked how I was doing Echo was getting more and more tense and I couldn't figure out why. The man was totally cool with me. Then he dropped the bomb—pardon the pun—and I learned that while I was being tied to a chair a warehouse that Echo had been scheduled to raid blew up. Then right after that he'd been involved in a shootout. And if that wasn't enough, Echo had run miles to get to me before Matt had picked him, Tucker, and Evan up.

Miles.

After being shot at, Echo had run miles to get to me.

I could take no more.

That was my breaking point.

In the front yard of the house I'd almost died in. The house where Echo had risked his life to save mine. The house where Echo had very literally said what he thought were his last goodbyes to his siblings because he was all-in to die with me, I had a full-blown come apart.

This was where it got blurry. I didn't remember getting home, I just knew Echo never let me go. I didn't fully remember taking a shower, I just knew Echo undressed me, washed me, and redressed me. I kind of remembered Echo taking me to the couch, sitting me down next to my brother, and wrapping a big fluffy blanket around me. However, until Lauren walked into the living room, I hadn't realized she was there.

"It's coffee," she told me, snapping me out of my haze. "I know you drink tea now. But this is not tea time, this is a coffee moment."

Damn, she was right about that.

I took the mug and did my best to muster a smile. I was pretty sure it came out wonky and ridiculous-looking but she loved me enough not to say anything.

"Thanks."

"Oh, and I spiked it with Jack. Or maybe it's half Jack, half coffee."

"Have I ever told you, you're my favorite sister-in-law?"

"Don't let Dotty hear you say that."

"Dotty's never fixed me spiked coffee after I almost got blown to pieces."

Two extremely disgruntled males growled.

I tipped my eyes back up to Lauren.

"Too soon?"

"Does it matter? I think right now you get to say, do, behave however the hell you want and the rest of us roll with it. You want to joke about it, I'm here for that. You want to scream and cry, I'm here for that. You want to punch, kick, and bite, your brother's got you."

Before I could respond the front door opened and more chaos ensued. And you guessed it, through it all Echo was by my side. The only time he didn't grunt when someone took me from his side to hug me was when my mom crashed into the house and yelled my name. Wisely, he took me straight to her and all but shoved me into her awaiting arms.

I had no idea what my mother said to me, partly because she was crying as she said it and partly because I wasn't listening. All of my attention was taken by the feel of my momma's arms around me, the smell of her shampoo, the feel of her hands rubbing up and down my back. When she finally settled down I pulled my face out of her neck and looked around. Echo to my right, Logan to my left, and Ian standing behind my mom.

Thank God for Ian. After the shit my mom had gone through—the abuse, the trauma, the pain, the hardship—she now had a good, gentle man who loved her.

"Wren stopped and got some food," I told my mom. "Are you hungry?"

I had yet to see what she brought but Lauren told me the kitchen counters were full of containers.

"I can't eat now." My mom placed her hand on her stomach.

"Momma, I'm fine."

"Yes, Jaclyn, I can see that."

My mom was cute when she was being snappy and scowling. It was her version of sarcasm but she'd never been very good at it.

"No, Mom, I'm fine."

"Yes, *Jackie*—"

I slid out of her arms to grab her hands and give them a squeeze.

"You're not listening to me." I paused and wondered if now was the best time to say this when it was fresh but I needed her to understand. "When I say I'm fine, what I mean to say is I'm better than fine. I'm better than great. I have everything. A great mom, great sisters, the best brother ever, I have Ian, I have Echo's family. I can either use what happened tonight, dwell on it, let it screw with my head, or I can remember I'm alive. And I'm alive because I have a man who loves me so much, he refused to leave me even after I begged him to. I'm alive because he was willing to die. That's not love, Mom. I don't know what it is, but it goes so far beyond love I don't think there's a word for it. So please hear me—I'm *fine*."

My mom's hands in mine tightened to the point of pain, her eyes flicked to Echo, then came back to mine, but at no point did her hands loosen.

"If I've told you and your sisters once, I've told you all a million times. It's rude..."

My mother got no more out. This time it was Logan who interrupted and he did it by barking out a sharp laugh before he totally lost it and roared with it. With one more tight squeeze my mom dropped my hands.

But before she walked away, she leaned in deep and whispered, "That's called devotion, honey. What he has for you. Faithful until the end."

As soon as my mom stepped away Echo claimed me.

I glanced around the living room, shocked that so many could fit in the not-so-big space. I couldn't find who I was looking for. But more than that, I couldn't remember seeing her.

"Where's Shiloh?"

Echo went still beside me.

"Echo?" I prompted.

"She's with Luke."

Okay, that didn't explain why his body had turned to stone.

"And where's Luke?" I slowly asked.

Echo's eyelids slowly lowered and when they came open he blew out a long breath that scared me.

"He had to go back to the station to fill out some paperwork."

What in the world did that mean? Surely Shiloh would want to be with her brother after he almost died and Luke was just as...*devoted*—yeah, that was the perfect word for it —to Shiloh as Echo was to me. He'd make sure Shiloh had what she needed.

"I don't get it."

I could feel, actually feel, Echo trying to relax his body and that scared me, too.

"He took out Jimmy Lone."

Took out?

What did that mean?

"I don't understand."

"Luke's a sniper," he told me something I knew.

"I know."

"Tonight he was overwatch. Shiloh's team has used him before. Without knowing who was in that house with you or what Bravo Team would find when they hit the house, they used him tonight. And it's a damn good thing they did. No one else caught it because no one else was watching the second-floor windows."

I still wasn't understanding so I asked, "Are you saying Jimmy was in the house with us?"

"Yeah. He was upstairs the whole time."

My gaze slid away and down to the floor. Jimmy was in the house the whole time? How did I not know that? And I saw two or three guys run past me...but I couldn't see the stairs from where I'd been sitting. Did they not check the second floor? Did they just see the bomb and run out? I tried to remember how much time had elapsed but it happened so fast it was all a haze.

"But I heard people running around upstairs," I told the floor. "I was sitting there thinking the ceiling was going to come crashing down with all the noise that was coming from up there."

"Did you see Jimmy leave?" he softly asked.

"Obviously not if he was upstairs."

"Here's the theory but only you know the facts." My eyes tipped back up to Echo. "Jimmy thought he'd have more time. He didn't expect the neighbor across the street to call 911 and report a man pulling a screaming woman into the house. A house that's been on the DEA's watch list for years. It's one of the places Jimmy used before he went to prison so when the call came in Tucker was notified immediately. I was on the phone with Logan so the connection was made immediately where Jimmy had taken you. Response time to that house was unusually fast. Shiloh called her captain and he had Bravo en route within minutes. We don't think he had time to leave so he hid in the attic to wait it out."

So he was never going to detonate the vest. Not with him still in the house. That whole time I thought I was going to die, I was safe.

I didn't know what to do with this.

Was I supposed to be relieved? Because I wasn't. I was pissed. I was so fucking angry we'd spent all that time thinking we were going to die when that asshole was still in the house.

"I heard the SWAT team upstairs," I semi repeated, unable to get past that.

They checked. I know they did.

"When SWAT went back in, the access stairs to the attic were down. He was in the attic hiding."

"The attic? I thought you said Luke saw him on the second floor?"

I felt another panic attack coming on and unlike the first one, I didn't understand the cause.

"For whatever reason Jimmy came out and went to the window. Maybe to check on the state of play, see how many cops were out there. Maybe to listen to what was happening with you. Maybe he was going to try and sneak out the back. Who knows? But the bottom line is Jimmy's dead, Luke saw to that."

Jimmy was dead.

Creepy guy who'd run me off the road, and when I'd come to he was yanking me out of my car by my hair, dragging me kicking and screaming to his car. Then handcuffed me, drove me to a drug house, dragged me in there, proceeded to point a gun at me, forcing me to put on the vest which I stupidly did because I didn't know what it was, then tied me to a chair, and wrapped me with duct tape.

That guy was dead.

I couldn't muster up any emotions, not even relief.

"He wasn't... he was never...we were never...you said goodbye..." I stuttered out a few choppy sentences that made no sense and I couldn't keep a thought long enough to form a coherent statement.

"Jaclyn—"

"You said goodbye to your family!" I screamed. "You looked at your baby sister and said goodbye, Echo!"

"Jac—"

"I saw you looking at them. I watched you saying goodbye, choosing me over them. And they let you. Fuck him. Fuck him for making you do that. Fuck him for putting them through that. *They let you go.*"

He said nothing and I knew why when my gaze followed his as it shifted around the room.

"Shit," I hissed.

All eyes were on us. But above all I felt Phoenix's heavy stare.

Damn.

"Phoenix," I whispered.

At the same time Echo said, though his voice was stronger and louder than mine, "Brother."

Then at the worst possible time the front door opened and in walked Shiloh followed by Luke. A few feet into the house Shiloh stumbled to a halt and glanced around.

"What's going on?" she asked, her eyes bouncing between her brothers.

Luke stopped beside his wife, put his arm around her shoulder, and pulled her tight against his side.

When no one answered, she asked again, "What's going on?"

"I'm sorry," I blurted out.

"Sorry? What's happening?"

What *was* happening? Why was I so angry? Why now after everything was over and we were all safe back at home did I feel like I wanted to scream or lash out and punch something?

"Nothing's happening," I snapped. "That's just it. All of that for *nothing*."

"All of what?" Shiloh asked slowly.

"That! Him saying goodbye to you. Phoenix being forced to leave his brother behind to die. He made you cry. But we were never going to die with Jimmy in that house."

Shiloh patted Luke's chest. His arm fell away and she unfortunately made her way to stand in front of me.

"I wasn't crying for the reasons you think I was, Jackie," she said softly. "I was crying at the unfairness. I was crying because after a lifetime of my brother giving everything to me and my brothers, he finally found her, found his happiness, and he didn't get to fully enjoy it. I was crying because I love my brother and losing him was going to leave a hole in my heart. But mostly I was crying for you."

"Me?"

"Jackie, you're the last piece. You make our family whole."

Holy shit. Some of the anger slipped away but not much.

"I hate him."

Obviously, I was talking about Jimmy, not Echo.

Which Shiloh seemed to understand when she said, "Me, too."

"I'm sorry," I repeated.

"Why are you sorry?" Phoenix joined the conversation.

Anger morphed into guilt.

Ugly guilt. Even though minutes ago it was what had fueled my speech to my mother, now I was thinking it was wrong.

"He stayed with me."

Shiloh jerked back and scowled.

But it was Phoenix's reaction that kept me enraptured. The pain that sliced through his features and filled his eyes. The youngest brother who Echo had always had the hardest time seeing as a grown man. Not because Phoenix wasn't a good, respectable man but if I had to guess, Echo saw Phoenix as the baby of the family even though Shiloh was. She was the little sister who all the brothers doted on; she'd always be their Sunny.

But Phoenix, he was Echo's heart.

"I would've stayed with Wren. River would've stayed with Letty. Shiloh would've stayed with Luke. Know why?" I didn't get a chance to answer. "Because that's what he taught us." Phoenix jabbed a finger toward Echo and with his finger went his gaze. "When I walked out of that house, I did so knowing my brother was the man I knew him to be and I did it proudly."

I wasn't sure what to say to that or if I should say anything, though when I caught sight of my brother staring at Echo, a small smile on his lips, I couldn't think about anything other than that grin and what it meant.

Logan's gaze transferred to me along with his smile, and I didn't have to wait to learn.

"I told you," he mouthed.

I tipped my head to the side, not understanding what that meant.

"You're everything," he mouthed again.

A moment later I got it—the conversation we had in the backyard of the Vrbo before his wedding.

No, Jaclyn, not enough. You're everything. Everything he

needs to open his eyes and do the hard work so he can keep you.

Luckily for me, Echo had certainly opened his eyes. He'd done the work to keep me. But he still needed to heal one last thing with his family.

But now was not the time for that.

Now I needed to apologize for something else.

"I'm a little...freaked out. It's not every day I get run off the road and kidnapped. I'm sorry I had a..." What did I have? "A meltdown."

"Brother, if that's what she considers a meltdown you're in for smooth sailing," Luke said from across the room.

Shiloh whipped around to face her husband. Phoenix's eyes went wide but he was smiling. And Echo, he pulled me close and plastered my front to his side.

"Are you insinuating I have—"

"Nope." Luke's hands wisely came up in surrender. "I'm just sayin'."

"I don't believe you."

I watched a smile form on Luke's mouth. It went from playful to downright sexy in less than a second.

I couldn't see Shiloh's face, and maybe she was used to her husband's devilish grins, but I doubted a woman got used to seeing that kind of smile.

"You're lucky you shot someone tonight to save my family or I'd argue you were totally suggesting I have epic-sized meltdowns."

"Those are your words, Sunshine, not mine."

When their exchange was done—or mostly done

because Shiloh was still mumbling under her breath—Echo leaned down and asked, "You good?"

I rolled my eyes to the ceiling.

Great, now I had two men asking me if I was good.

By the time they rolled back I realized that only meant I was twice as blessed.

At least I'd tell myself that for the next month. After that I'd put a stop to it.

"Yeah, honey, I'm perfect."

"That you are."

27

ECHO

"No nightmares?" River's question came at me through the speakers in my car.

My hand came off the steering wheel to rub the ever-present ache in my chest. It had only been a week but I was beginning to wonder if the pain of that day would always stab my heart.

"None."

"Good. And Sunny? She doing okay?"

Our sister had moved on from the day the way she did everything else in her life—by being a pain in the ass.

"For now."

"What does that mean?"

"It means if she doesn't stop calling me every day to ask how I'm doing I'm going to stop answering my phone and move so she can't find me."

I turned into the parking lot of Triple Canopy and scanned the packed area looking for a parking spot. Being the last one to arrive at a TC barbeque sucked. Soon they were going to need to provide a shuttle service or start carpooling. The parking lot wasn't big enough for their ever-growing family.

"Um, brother, she called you every day before you almost died seeing as that's what you've demanded she do since she got her driver's license and was able to be somewhere you weren't."

I found a spot on the grass and parked.

"Right. She's supposed to call me to check in, not ask me if I'm alright."

"You know you sound crazy, right?"

That wasn't the first time or even the fifteenth time I'd been asked that in the last week.

Though Jaclyn didn't tell me I sounded crazy. She told me I was acting crazy. But fuck, the woman who was my whole life almost died. What did everyone expect me to do? Go on like it was business as usual and Jimmy Fucking Lone hadn't taken her because he was pissed at me.

That fucking tattoo.

I was half tempted to get it lasered off but it was Sunny's mark and the thought of it not being there was unthinkable. I was damn near obsessive now, making sure that no part of my arms showed during an arrest, and at the station I was just as careful wearing long sleeves. That was one of the many things Jaclyn told me I was being crazy about.

But what was the saying...

Better crazy than sorry.

"Speaking of crazy, how's Letty?"

River chuckled before he said, "Finishing up the baby's room."

"Know that, brother, she FaceTimed us last night. How's *she* doing?"

"Nervous. Excited. Happy."

"Won't be long before little Ziggy's here," I joked as I stepped out of my car, the thick Georgia humidity covering me.

Christ, maybe River had the right idea moving to Idaho.

No, I'd miss the sunshine.

"Don't start," River grunted.

"What, no Ziggy? What about Birch or Cedar or Bridge or—"

"I'm hanging up."

And that was what he did.

I pocketed my phone and made my way to the party. There was a time not too long ago when a Triple Canopy barbeque was contained to the small grassy area behind the building. Now picnic tables were brought in and the side yard was used as well. Soon they'd have to take over part of the shooting range the way this family grew.

It didn't take me long to spot Jaclyn talking to Chelsea and Sunny.

Our family was growing as well. River and Letty were giving us the first Kent baby. Phoenix had already given us our first nephew and it wouldn't be long before Sunny and Luke started making babies—at least I hoped they did that soon.

I watched Jaclyn smile at something my sister said, transforming her normal beauty to stunning. There wasn't a day that had gone by since the day I'd met her when I didn't know she was it for me. My sister had been right when she told Jaclyn she was the missing piece. She was who we'd been waiting for, who *I'd* been waiting for to complete our family.

Jaclyn

I COULD FEEL his eyes on me even though he was across the lawn talking to Evan, Phoenix, Logan, and Ethan.

And it wasn't my brother's eyes I could feel, though in the last hour I'd caught Logan staring at me. This time it was Echo. While my brother's look was full of concern, Echo's was full of love.

"I like the way he looks at you," Lauren said.

I stopped pushing the last of my potato salad around on my plate and tipped my eyes to her across the table from me.

"I do, too."

My sister-in-law smiled and shook her head.

"I bet you do."

"You'd know all about the *look*, girl, Logan gives you the same one," Liberty Hayes teased.

My gaze went to Liberty's unusual eyes, the brown, green, and blue swirling together, reminding me of a cat's eyes and nodded. I didn't know her as well as I knew Chelsea but only because she was still in the Army. Actually, the woman was as badass as Shiloh and had followed in her father and uncles' footsteps and gone into Special Forces.

Since I wanted to change the subject from how my

brother looked at his wife which might lead into a conversation about their shock collar kink, I moved the conversation in a new direction.

"I heard Wren say you're getting out of the Army."

"Yeah. I have six months until I go terminal."

I had no idea what that meant.

"Terminal?"

With a wave of her hand, she explained. "The end of my contract. The last month is basically me doing admin to separate from the Army. I won't be sent out for training or workups. And I only have another month until I'm marked non-deployable. I know Drake's excited about that. No more last-minute callouts."

I bet her husband was excited about that. When Echo got a middle of the night callout, he was home by dinner. I couldn't imagine him being gone days or weeks or months.

"Hey, did you hear about Tucker?" Chelsea asked, leaning into the table.

"No? What about him?"

"Matt told me he quit the DEA."

I scanned the party, trying to find the man in question and when I did he was with Jason, his father Jasper, Carter, his father Lenox, Drake, his father-in-law Levi, Brady, whose father-in-law was Jasper and Trey, whose father-in-law was also Jasper. The men were all huddled together in what looked like a serious conversation.

"You think he's coming to work at Triple Canopy?" I asked.

"Yep," Liberty answered, obviously having the inside scoop as her father was one of the TC originals, as was her mother Blake, and now she was married to one of the new generation of men who'd taken over the business when her dad and uncles had retired.

"Really?" Chelsea smiled.

"Yep. Drake told me Tucker's only reservation was Matt. I guess they talked and Matt gave his blessing so he took the job Jason offered him."

"Really?" Chels drew out the word. "I see my husband's keeping secrets from me."

"It happened five minutes ago, Chels."

"Yet *you* know."

"I know because I went into the office to hit the head and saw them talking. I asked Drake on my way back to the table. I asked, he told me."

Our conversation stalled when Hadley, Quinn, and a very pregnant Addy hit our table.

"Hey, ladies," Liberty greeted. "Are you okay out in this heat?"

The question was obviously meant for Addy. She didn't miss a beat and rolled her eyes.

"I'd be better if everyone stopped asking."

"Well, you know, it's a valid question. Popping a kid out at Aunt Reagan's house is one thing. We all know she keeps her floor so clean you could perform surgery on it. But here? In the grass? Girl, that's just nasty. So, if you could please refrain from—"

Quinn got no more out before Addy's hands went to her belly, she pitched forward, and let out a low groan.

"Oh, shit," Quinn gasped. "I'll get Brice."

Brice was her husband; he was also a firefighter EMT. I looked around for Echo, wondering if he knew how to assist in childbirth.

Addy groaned again, not letting go of her belly.

"Adalyn, you need to sit down," Quinn commanded. "No. We need a blanket. You should be—"

Addy suddenly straightened, dropped her hands, and smiled.

"Faker." Hadley laughed.

"What?" Quinn looked between her sisters.

"How'd you know?" Addy complained.

"Um, are we having a baby in the grass or..." I let that trail off, not exactly sure what was going on.

One second Addy was moaning and groaning the next she was smiling.

"It's only been a little over a month," Hadley started. "I know people say you forget how painful childbirth is but believe me, that memory doesn't go away for a long-ass time."

Quinn narrowed her eyes on her sister.

"You're an idiot."

Addy shrugged off the insult and sat next to me.

When she did, she bumped me on the shoulder. "All good?"

I glanced around the party again, took in all the smiling happy faces, and let the happiness of the day wash over me before I answered.

"I'm alive. I have Echo. My brother is deliriously happy, my mom is married to a man who loves her so completely which means she's deliriously happy, so yeah I'm good."

The only thing—or person—who was missing was Jill.

I wish she was here.

"I'm scheduled to be induced tomorrow morning," Addy announced.

"Thank God. One normal birthing experience," Liberty put in.

I listened to the women chatter, thinking, yeah I was good.

I was better than good.

I was a woman who had it all.

Everything I could ever hope for and then some.

Echo

MY BROTHER and sister approaching at the same time gave me heartburn. Not the same kind it did when they were children and they were racing to me to tattle on one another but heartburn nonetheless.

Unsurprisingly, it was Sunny who started.

"When are you asking Jackie to marry you?"

Christ.

Ambush.

"When I'm ready."

"Ready? Why aren't you ready now?" she pushed.

"Because her ring isn't finished and I'd like to have it to give to her when I propose."

"Oh. Okay, then."

Now that my sister's argument was deflated, I looked at Phoenix and waited for him.

When he said nothing I prompted, "Brother?"

"I got nothing, I was just here for backup."

Right.

Phoenix taking his sister's back, not unusual.

Since we had relative privacy and I'd put it off too long I needed to come clean about a few things.

Namely, Officer Smith.

"There's something you both need to know."

Fuck, now that I'd started, I wasn't sure I could do this. I waited for the poison in my gut to start churning, I waited a little longer, then I searched for it. The toxicity of Lester Kent. The poison that gathered in my stomach before it infused the rest of my body. Yet, I couldn't find it.

"What's up?"

Phoenix's nonchalance made me question if now was the right time. We were enjoying the company of good people, extended family, something we never had growing up. People who Sunny had brought into our lives when she got together with Luke. They'd welcomed her, then River, Phoenix, and me, and from the first get-together we'd attended they'd pulled us in. They offered their friendship and opened their lives to us. They'd given us something we never had—a good, clean, happy family.

No, now was not the right time.

"We'll talk later," I suggested.

"We'll talk now," Phoenix demanded.

My eyes locked with my baby brother.

"That dad-voice work on Griff?" I teased.

My brother didn't feel like joking if his scowl was anything to go by.

"It's about Dad," I told them.

"Did the asshole finally bite it?" Sunny snickered.

"No clue."

After Lester had sent Phoenix a letter telling him he was sick and dying and wanted to see his children one last time—which compelled Sunny to make a trip to the prison to visit our piece of shit father—I'd made some calls and had stopped all communication from Lester. Something I should've done after we'd received his first letter. Yet I hadn't in hopes the asshole would change while rotting in his cell and finally give River, Phoenix, and Sunny an apology. That never happened nor would it. So I made it so his letters went into the trash—where they belonged. Though if he was dead I reckon someone would notify me. Sadly no one had.

"What about Dad?" Phoenix asked.

Impatient as always.

"We should wait—"

"Just tell us," Phoenix interrupted.

"You know now that Jaclyn has pointed it out it is incredibly—"

"Rude. Yeah, I know, I was taught manners," Phoenix barged into my admonishment. "Seeing as you taught them, I figure you know I have them though not when it comes to Lester. There's never a good time to talk about the dick, so just tell us now and get it over with."

He had a point; there never was a good time to bring up the asshole.

I glanced around the party making sure no one was listening, which they weren't. Everyone including Jaclyn was enjoying the beautiful day.

I looked back at my siblings. Both were looking at me expectantly.

Now or never.

"The day that Dad shot Officer Smith," I began, then paused, not knowing how to tell them.

"Yeah?" Sunny encouraged.

"I came home early from work; Dad hadn't stashed his shit yet so I called the cops to report it. I didn't know he was home. He was, and when he heard me on the phone he just went to the couch and sat down."

"What a dick," Phoenix grumbled.

"Phoenix, I called the cops. Officer Smith was there because he was answering a complaint."

"Yeah, Echo. He was doing his job."

I clenched my jaw, relaxing it just enough to ground out, "Dad shot him because I called in—"

"Fuck no," Phoenix seethed. "Dad shot him because he's a motherfucking asshole. That's not on you."

Phoenix was wrong; it was my fault.

"Seriously," Sunny spat. "Is that why?"

I glanced at my sister and had the urge to take a step back. I perused my memories trying to remember a time she looked this pissed. I found none. Not even when she'd stand on a chair to be eye level with one of us while throwing a holy hell fit about something one of us had done had she looked this angry.

"Why what?" I cautiously asked.

"Why you've refused to allow yourself to be happy? You think that Officer Smith's death is on you?"

I said nothing because that was precisely what I thought.

"I could kick you right now," she bitched. "And if I didn't want nieces and nephews from Jackie, I'd kick you straight in your balls, you idiot."

Well, it was good to know my balls were safe though I wasn't a fan of my sister calling me an idiot.

"I'm calling River, we need to stage another intervention—"

I cut into Sunny's rant, "Do not call River."

"Why not?" Phoenix fumed. "Because you know he'd be just as pissed as we are that you've been holding something back from us for two decades? Sitting on guilt that's eaten away at you, not giving us the opportunity to help you work it out or, I don't know, maybe help you see that your guilt is misplaced."

There was that but also, "It's my fault the Kent name was dragged through the mud. Our legacy is completely fucked—"

"You did not just say that!" Sunny shouted.

Fucking hell.

I looked around, checking she hadn't garnered attention, and sure enough she had. Luke was on his way over followed by Logan and Jaclyn.

"Sunny," I snapped. "Quiet."

"Fuck quiet, brother. I don't care if every damn person here hears me. Maybe you'll listen to one of them."

Without asking what was going on Luke came to a stop behind Sunny. His hand went to her hip and he tugged her close.

As a man, I respected that. As a brother who wanted my sister not to air our dirty laundry in front of others, I wanted Luke to leave. But he was family and he had every right to be involved in the conversation.

"Shiloh." I tried to calm her down. Unfortunately Phoenix picked now to rejoin.

"All my life I've looked up to you. All my life you were the person I could trust with anything. Any problem, any fuckup, I knew you'd help me. When I struggled after Lester went down, it was you who told me it was okay to love parts of him. You told me to hold onto the good memories, the good he gave me even if it was a single moment. You got me through it all, everything. So it really fucking hurts you didn't turn to me when you were struggling and let me help you."

Fucking Christ.

I hadn't yet recovered from that blow when Phoenix landed another.

"You want to talk about our family's legacy? This is what the Kent family's about." Phoenix lifted his hand and swept the entirety of the party. "This is what Echo Kent taught us. This is what he made us. This is the legacy I get to give to Griff and any other children I have and I do it proudly."

Jaclyn made it to my side, and much like Luke she said not a word as she joined our huddle. But instead of standing behind me, she tucked herself under my arm, plastered herself to my side, and wrapped an arm around my stomach.

I waited for Sunny or Phoenix to say more. When they didn't, I struggled to find something to say to defend myself. But the realization had hit me; there was nothing I could say in defense of keeping a secret from my family.

Though the secret I thought I was keeping was far different from the one I'd actually kept.

"You're right, Phoenix, I should've told you all."

My brother jerked back and frowned.

"Told us what?" he asked suspiciously, the way you'd ask a child what they were apologizing for to make sure they understood the message you were trying to teach.

The role reversal wasn't lost on me. Phoenix had the lesson to dole out and he wasn't wrong in delivering it.

Jaclyn's arm around me went tight and she pressed closer, and that was all I needed to admit the truth.

"That I was feeling guilty. That I blamed myself for Dad killing Smith. That I didn't want to burden any of you with my shit so I carried it alone."

Phoenix nodded then took a step closer, his eyes bouncing from me to Jaclyn.

"What would you say to me if I just told you I blamed myself for anything Dad did?"

Jesus.

When the hell did my brother get so fucking smart?

"It's easier being the fixer," Logan joined the conversation and I braced. "It's easier to hide when you're on the receiving end of everyone else's problems. You don't have to face what's eating at you."

My attention went to him, his knowing eyes locked onto mine. I immediately regretted my decision. He saw me. For all the ways we were different, we were the same.

The fixers.

The protectors.

"So now the question is." He dipped his chin and skewered me with a look that told me there was only one right answer. "What are you afraid of? Facing that guilt or being freed of it?"

With that he strode away, but the damage he'd inflicted remained.

"Freed," I told his back.

"Yeah, I get that." He stopped and looked over his shoulder. "But, brother, you missed it—you already are."

Jaclyn gave me another squeeze, tipped her head back, and smiled, confirming her brother was correct.

All that was left to do was let the last of it go.

I leaned down, gave Jaclyn a quick lip brush, then straightened and looked back at the Dastardly Duo.

"I shouldn't have kept any of that from you. Both of you are rightly pissed at me and I'll repeat, I'm sorry."

"Good. That's done and I didn't have to resort to physical violence. Also, who knew Logan was so wise?"

"I did," Jaclyn piped up.

"I would argue with you about whose big brother is the smartest but I'm thinking now's not the best time to challenge you when mine's been acting like a dumbass."

When Sunny was done breaking my balls Phoenix shook his head.

"You know you have more than one brother."

"Yep."

"And, so, maybe you want to argue that one of us is smarter than—"

"Nope."

"You could, to be nice to the rest of us," Phoenix complained.

Instead of stepping in to referee the two adults who were going to continue to bicker I guided Jaclyn away from my siblings.

"If you want someone to be nice to you, go find your wife."

"Should you stop them?" Jaclyn asked.

"Nope. They're adults. And besides that, I think when I walked Sunny down the aisle, I gave her to Luke."

On that thought I smiled.

"Speaking of, who's going to walk you down the aisle, Ian or Logan?"

"Both," she answered immediately. "Logan because he's Logan. Ian because if he hadn't come into our lives and fallen in love with my mom, we wouldn't have come here as a family to make sure Logan behaved and I never would've met you."

I stopped walking and turned Jaclyn to face me.

"I would've met you."

"Maybe."

"No maybes. I would've met you. Somehow, someway we would've crossed paths." I paused to cup her cheeks then repeated my very smart sister's words. "You're the last piece. Now the Kent family is whole. Now all we need to do is watch it grow and add to it when we're ready."

"Is that the part where you fertilize the—"

I cut off the rest of what she was going to say and I did it in a way she wouldn't chastise. I knew because when my lips met hers she opened, and when my tongue glided against hers, she moaned. Shortly after that her arms went around me and she slanted her head to deepen the kiss.

I lied to Jaclyn when I said love was a choice.

I didn't know it then, but I knew it now.

Her love was unconditional, unwavering, unrelenting. I had no choice but to love her. But if I'd had the choice, I'd choose her. Every day for the rest of my life, I'd choose Jaclyn.

Dalton

THE MUSIC WAS loud but not so loud I couldn't hear the balls slapping together at the pool tables behind me. The bar was also packed. I wasn't sure who outnumbered who—strangers who were there to drink and play pool, or my partner Phoenix's friends. He'd made so many introductions I couldn't keep all the names straight so I'd stayed sitting at the bar with Echo shooting the shit about work. But I knew it was only a matter of time before I lost his company and he went in search of his woman.

Jesus, Echo Kent had a woman.

I'd say hell had frozen over but the day had topped out over a hundred with a hundred percent humidity so I knew that wasn't the case.

"Need another?" Chelsea asked.

I was about to decline when Vanessa walked in the door.

Now, one would ask how I saw the beautiful woman slip in the door through the throngs of people—that was easy. The woman was magnetic. Pale blonde hair, deep brown eyes, creamy skin that begged to be caressed. Or more to the point, a body that would have me begging to touch her. She'd also become a friend. If by friend I meant I'd met Wren and Phoenix for dinner and Vanessa had been there. If by friend I meant I'd seen her at the gym twice and we'd chatted. So friend was a slight exaggeration but one I was going to rectify as soon as I could.

"Please," I answered Chelsea.

"Wren's her boss," Echo murmured from the stool next to me.

There was only one response to that, "Yep."

Whatever Echo was going to say next was cut off when Chelsea dropped off my beer, her husband, Matt, coming up beside her.

"I have a question," Matt announced.

"You don't have a question," Chelsea contradicted. "Go play pool with Luke. He needs some competition."

Matt ignored her and looked at me.

"I have this idea."

"No, you don't," Chelsea groaned.

"How does Banging Behind Bars sound?" Matt continued.

"Like a strip club that caters to ex-cons," Vanessa said, coming to stand between me and Echo.

"See?" Chelsea chirped and pranced away. Or maybe she'd meant to huff away but she missed the mark by a mile.

"Not that there's anything wrong with a strip club," Vanessa continued.

Matt chuckled and shook his head. "I was actually thinking of buying a music studio."

When no one said anything, he went on, "You know, banging on instruments, laying down bars..." he trailed off, looking among the three of us.

"Dammit, now I have to admit she's right."

As soon as Matt stalked off Echo slid off his stool.

"I'm gonna go find Jaclyn before she makes another bet and loses."

My gaze followed Echo's to the pool table.

Sure enough, Jaclyn was throwing some bills down on the table.

"Good luck. Looks like she's already placed her bet."

"Vanessa," Echo greeted.

"Hey, Echo."

"Was it something I said?" she asked and slipped onto the stool Echo vacated.

"No. Matt had to go eat crow and since I've been here Jaclyn's lost three rounds and keeps placing wagers," I explained.

But even if it had been something she'd said I would've been grateful for a few minutes alone with her.

There were a few beats of silence before she swiveled to face me. Instinctively, my knees opened to bracket in her legs. Her gaze dropped to take in our intimate position—too intimate for sort-of-friends, yet I couldn't bring myself to give a fuck. When those chocolaty eyes came back up and locked with mine a hundred inappropriate thoughts ran through my mind and I had the sudden need to know what they'd look like desire-filled, dancing on the edge of ecstasy.

"Listen, I...um know we don't know each other all that well but I was wondering if I could ask you a favor."

The woman could ask me anything.

Unfortunately, the fear in her pretty eyes was a damn good indication the favor she'd be asking wouldn't be for countless orgasms and a sore throat from screaming my name.

THE END

Just kidding...Triple Canopy will continue in the spin off

series **Hollow Point** starting with Book 1 **Playing with Lies**, Dalton and Vanessa

Make sure you sign up for my newsletter to be notified when the book becomes available for pre-order.

xoxo, Riley

Rebels Newsletter

ALSO BY RILEY EDWARDS

Riley Edwards

www.RileyEdwardsRomance.com

Takeback

Dangerous Love

Dangerous Rescue

Dangerous Games

Dangerous Encounter

Dangerous Mind

Dangerous Hearts

Gemini Group

Nixon's Promise

Jameson's Salvation

Weston's Treasure

Alec's Dream

Chasin's Surrender

Holden's Resurrection

Jonny's Redemption

Red Team - Susan Stoker Universe

Nightstalker

Protecting Olivia

Finding Mercy

Claiming Tuesday

Adoring Delaney

Keeping Quinn

Taking Liberty

Triple Canopy

Damaged

Flawed

Imperfect

Tarnished

Tainted

Conquered

Shattered

Fractured

The Collective

Unbroken

Trust

Standalones

Romancing Rayne

Falling for the Delta Co-written with Susan Stoker

AUDIO

Are you an Audio Fan?

Check out Riley's titles in Audio on Audible and iTunes

Gemini Group

Narrated by: Joe Arden and Erin Mallon

Red Team

Narrated by: Jason Clarke and Carly Robins

Gold Team

Narrated by: Lee Samuels and Maxine Mitchell

The 707 Series

Narrated by: Troy Duran and C. J. Bloom

The Next Generation

Narrated by: Troy Duran and Devon Grace

Triple Canopy

Narrated by: Mackenzie Cartwright and Connor Crais

More audio coming soon!

BE A REBEL

Riley Edwards is a USA Today and WSJ bestselling author, wife, and military mom. Riley was born and raised in Los Angeles but now resides on the east coast with her fantastic husband and children.

Riley writes heart-stopping romance with sexy alpha heroes and even stronger heroines. Riley's favorite genres to write are romantic suspense and military romance.

Don't forget to sign up for Riley's newsletter and never miss another release, sale, or exclusive bonus material.

Rebels Newsletter

Facebook Fan Group

www.rileyedwardsromance.com

facebook.com/Novelist.Riley.Edwards

instagram.com/rileyedwardsromance

bookbub.com/authors/riley-edwards

amazon.com/author/rileyedwards

Made in United States
Orlando, FL
19 May 2023

33288395R00196